AN UPSIDE-DOWN SKY

AN UPSIDE-DOWN SKY

A NOVEL

Linda Dahl

SHE WRITES PRESS

Published 2022

Printed in the United States of America

Print ISBN: 978-1-64742-329-2

E-ISBN: 978-1-64742-330-8

Library of Congress Control Number: 2021921005

For information, address:

She Writes Press

1569 Solano Ave #546

Berkeley, CA 94707

She Writes Press is a division of SparkPoint Studio, LLC.

ETIQUETTE for travelers to NAMYAN*

1. Do not attempt to wear any footwear or socks (including foot liners) into a Buddhist temple, pagoda, stupa, dharma hall, or *na-san* (animist spirit house). Note that footwear may also include bandages and casts, at the discretion of the authorities.

2. Do not point your feet at any person.

3. Do not touch your feet to anyone else's, including a shrine or statue of the Buddha.

4. *Never* point your feet at a shrine or statue of the Buddha

5. Do not post anything about the Buddha that could be construed as disrespectful on social media, including jokes, cartoons, etc.

Trent & Koss Adventure Tours *Guide to Magical Namyan,* page 6.

*Ignoring these rules may result in fines or, in rare cases, incarceration.

The Tour Group

Eighteen people have signed on for Trent & Koss Adventure Tours' high-end trip to Namyan, one of the first after fifty years of quarantine by the West:

Clint and Betsy Hodges. Both are tall, mid-seventies. A retired oilman, Clint is suitably lantern-jawed and steely-eyed. Betsy describes herself as a "homemaker." They reside in Oklahoma City. Reason for the trip: They won two all-expense-paid tickets at a silent auction at their church. Betsy plans to visit congregations while there. Clint likes that they have some mountains. Clint has been diagnosed with melanoma, Stage IV. Nickname: The Poisons.

Tim and Tammy Steinman. Short, mid-seventies, possibly older. Not particularly fit, but dress as if they are. He's a retired engineer (mechanical), she's a retired legal clerk; she has a serious collection of badges, buttons, and pins of travel destinations. One son, troubled (booze), one grandchild with a serious physical handicap. Reason for the trip: They go somewhere new every year. Nickname: Buttons.

Ward and Trudy Wong. Short, trim, and energetic, early eighties. He's a semi-retired architect (school buildings), she's a retired school administrator. Reason for trip: To reconnect with members of her extended family who have lived for generations in Namyan for the Chinese New Year. No nickname.

Barton Liu. Single, forties, on the "spectrum" of Asperger's, forties. A videographer, he is Ward Wong's nephew, adopted as a child by the Wongs. Reason for trip: Paid for by his uncle and a chance to add to his vlog, "The Undetected." And, of course, to meet the relatives. No nickname.

Colonel (Ret.) Ken and Sally Lattimore. Well-preserved, seventies. Ken was in the military in the Vietnam War and in some murky military capacity afterwards in Thailand. Sally is rather witty, a shopaholic and likes her cocktails—a lot. Reason for trip: Old Asia hands, curious about the one country they don't know there. No nickname.

Ed and Ann Boren. Medium height, seventies. Ed refers to himself as a "bug man," is an entomologist of some standing. Ann is a talker. Reason for trip: Ed's quest to add exotic insects to his collection, especially killer wasps and Lepidoptera, a.k.a. butterflies, of which Namyan has a rich supply. Nickname: The Bores.

Ted and Franklin Leibitz-Kai. Very good shape, hard to tell their ages, but Ken looks older. Ted is a retired firefighter and EMS, Franklin runs a boutique. Reason for trip: Franklin wants to shop. Nickname: The Boys.

Lars and Catherine Vonderville. Lars is in his late seventies, Catherine (Catty) in her early seventies. He is a retired investment banker and she a retired documentary film producer. Reason for trip: Curiosity about the world. Nickname: The Vonderpoops.

Lidia DeCampos. Early sixties. She is a visual artist undergoing a difficult, if unspecified, time in her life. Reason for trip: Her friends Lars and Catty convince her it would be good to get away. No nickname.

Klaus Haynes. Tall and energetic, seventyish. Born in Germany to a white mother and a Black American serviceman, he has dual citizenship. He moved to New York in his twenties. After working in appliance sales, he studied photography and now focuses on an adventure blog specializing in remote, politically fraught places. Reason for trip: To lay the groundwork for a trip to visit one of Namyan's many minority groups embroiled in civil war. No nickname.

Mrs. Hills. Carolyn Hills, late eighties, determined but frail, never married officially but partnered from the 1950s to the '80s with a fellow female teacher, now deceased. Carolyn was a school administrator in Hong Kong for many years before she moved back to the States. Reason for trip: One last hurrah in Asia. No nickname.

Thila. Tall and well educated, early thirties, Namyanese. Tour guide for Trent & Koss Adventure Tours. Family obligations impede fulfillment of her desires. Reason for trip: This is the best job she can hope to find in Namyan. No nickname.

1

DESPITE A TOTAL OF sixteen hours of flight time plus several more waiting in airports, Lars Vonderville convinced Catty, his wife, and Lidia DeCampos, their old friend, to visit the old part of Gonyang, the capital of Namyan, once they'd showered and changed.

"But just an hour. *One* hour," Catty agreed reluctantly, giving in only because, as she told Lidia, she knew that if they slept now, they'd be wide awake at two in the morning. Plus, visiting the old, shabby part of Gonyang was not on the itinerary, so this was probably their only chance to see it. Most of it had been destroyed in the Japanese invasion in World War II, but some notable architectural blends of the native and Victorian styles had survived.

Lidia came too, figuring she should cram in as much as possible during this trip, which she was thinking of as her reentry into the world.

The traffic on the way to the old part of the city was as terrible as in any big city in the world, even though Namyan, long a pariah state, had only recently rejoined the world economy. Arriving, they found the crumbling streets teeming with the homeless, just like in their own city, New York. Down-on-their-luck drug addicts and/or crazy souls who squatted in the rubble and dank hallways of neglected buildings. Yes, like New York, above all the New York of their youth, the 1970s and '80s. With the difference that, while Lars and Catty had had to walk past the squalor, they'd lived in tony Upper East Side apartments, while Lidia, in classic young artist fashion, had arrived from the Midwest without money or connections and lived in the middle of the chaos.

Her dirt-cheap apartment on 102nd and 2nd Avenue had a claw-foot bathtub in the kitchen, the toilet in a closet, a permanently broken lock on the front door of the building, and a super who drank in his basement lair. But her fifth-floor walkup had great light—a timeless artist's garret. Lidia accumulated furniture from the street, pots and pans from Salvation Army, and New York stories: a rat she first thought was a stray cat came in the kitchen, a guy in a wife-beater scaled the walls and tried to pry open her window but, on hearing her scream, fell and broke his leg—best possible ending. Old Gonyang reminded all three, but especially Lidia, of that funky time.

And just as there is a rose in Spanish Harlem, so too did old Gonyang have its special funky charms. It was Southeast Asia, after all. A charming little girl with raisin eyes held up tiny bananas for sale. Lidia watched as Lars, who was clearly not yet sure about the exchange rate, forked over some *takys* for a bunch. The girl's eyes widened and an instant crowd gathered around the rich white man.

"Isn't this fantastic?" Lars said after schmoozing with them, if you can schmooze with gestures. He strode on in his naturally exhilarated way with his bananas.

They passed old women sitting easily on their haunches behind piles of oddly shaped, unidentifiable vegetables and silver-black, leathery dried fish. Men minded tables piled with foliage and cones of spices and herbs. "*Yoongi, yoongi!*" they called shrilly to the foreigners.

"Must be betel nut," said Lars, who handily knew so many outré things. "Going to give it a try."

"Lars, no." Catty's pale olive skin was pinched with jet lag. "Please don't, let's go."

"In a tick." Lars enjoyed used outmoded expressions. "It's supposed to give you energy, and God knows I could use some."

"What you need is a nap," Catty snapped.

Lars took on the bewildered expression he always did when Catty opposed him. "No time like the present!" He peered at his watch. "It's just two thirty. Plenty of time for a snooze later."

"Then hurry up, and please don't chitchat," Catty said—looking defeated, as Lars always chitchatted.

He stopped before a stall and pointed. "How much?" he asked the vendor, seemingly confident that he, like vendors in every part of the globe, would know that much English. "Fif' *takys*," said the delicate-boned man.

Lars nodded agreement. The man made a show for him, spreading a paste on leaves, sprinkling tobacco and bits of the spice cone, and topping it off with a chopped-up chunk of nut in the middle. He rolled the thing up like a taco and voilà, there was the mood and energy enhancer of South Asia, ubiquitously chewed and spat out, nasty, blood-red dregs staining walls and floors like a lurid, nationwide crime scene.

Lidia had read somewhere that betel nut was carcinogenic and lots of South Asians got lip, throat, or tongue cancer. But when did people anywhere pay attention to the hazards of mood-enhancing chemicals? Nowhere that she knew of. She debated trying it too, though she still recalled her deep disappointment after trying coca leaves in the Andes, back in the day. All she'd gotten then was a sore jaw, a mouthful of cud, and only the mildest euphoria. Maybe let Lars be the guinea pig.

Lars had been atypically quick to score the betel nut taco but paying for it was another story. Catty stood to one side, shooting him looks she ignored as he mugged for a growing number of Namyanese.

Lars loved to engage with what he called the "salt of the earth" and could go on interminably if Catty would have let him.

"Lars, pay him now or I'm leaving!"

He made a small face—the beleaguered husband—and waved to the bevy of watching betel chewers, who heaved with amusement at the very pale, tall, old foreigner in an octagon-shaped straw hat that only rice peasants wore. He'd picked it up at an airport shop that morning.

The trio walked away, Lars munching stolidly.

"Well?" Catty asked, arms folded.

"Yuck!" He wiped his mouth with his handkerchief. "But there's something. Probably intensifies as you keep chewing."

"You can chew and walk at the same time." Catty sped up, pulling Lidia with her. Over her shoulder, she said, "I insist on getting some rest before dinner!"

Lars made an effort to catch up.

"You've got red ooze on your chin. It looks like blood," Catty told him.

Lars opened his mouth to say something.

"And keep your mouth closed!"

"Oh, buck up," Lars slurred.

They turned the corner and Lars's bloody-looking lower face was forgotten at the sight of a group of extremely colorfully dressed women strolling along with their chins poking out from heavy gold coils rigidly encircling their necks and jaws.

"Hinchaks," Lars enunciated with effort. "Pershecuted Northern eshnic minority. Orishinally from Mongolia."

"How many ways can men—no offense, Lars—think of to constrain women?" Lidia had been mostly silent until now, just taking it all in, feeling as if she was at a carnival. Gonyang was a Tilt-A-Wheel, and here came the clowns. Jet lag—no, life—was bombarding her. "Bind our feet," she went on. "Remove our clitorises. Strap us into corsets. Throw burkas over us. Look at them!"

"They don't shlook unhappy," Lars slurred.

"Why would they?" Catty asked rhetorically.

Lars stopped walking and regarded her. "Go on."

"Because they've been brainwashed from birth into thinking they've got to stretch their necks like a giraffe's to be beautiful. Lars, don't do your dim routine!"

"Let me digesh thish." He hawked and spit into a nearby bush. "Aren't we all brainwashed from birth? Morals. Religion. Patriotism. Really, Cat, I must say—"

But whatever he must say was lost, as they had now come upon members of their "small, congenial group," as the brochure from Trent & Koss Adventure Tours described its "guests." The Vondervilles and Lidia had met several of them already at the airport, but that had been a blur.

"Betsy Hodges," said a rather large and disheveled woman. "Have you seen the adorable train station? Oh!" She stared at Lars.

Everyone stared at Lars.

"My God, did you get beat up by street thugs?" Ward Wong, small, rather bent but spry, stepped forward.

"You poor thing!" cried Trudy Wong.

"We'll get you to a doctor. The hotel must have one. Or, where is the guide—Thira?" Barton Liu whisked out his phone.

"Thila," Catty said. "No! Lars—my husband—is fine. He's chewing betel nut and the disgusting juice looks like blood."

They crowded around Lars.

"Was that wise?" breathed Ann Boren.

"Oh, we tried it in Thailand, when Ken was stationed there. Everybody does it," said Sally Lattimore.

Colonel Ken Lattimore made a deprecating gesture. "It's legal."

"I'm going to try it," said Klaus Haynes.

"There's a bunsch of vendorsh over there."

Klaus nodded and headed where Lars pointed.

"So what's it feel like?" asked Ted Leibitz-Kai.

Franklin Leibitz-Kai tittered. "Are you stoned? Like on weed?"

"Well, I can't shay what that feels like. Never tried the shtuff." Lars chewed on. "Short of like schewing shtobacco with this shing to it. Zhing. Pleasant and dishgusting at the same time, with the shtems and woody bitz and goop. But it feels . . . good. Normally, I'm a beer and wshiskey man," he added.

Presently, they all went their separate ways. Lars, Catty, and Lidia found the bookstore Lars had enthused over while reading the guidebook; he hoped to stock up on histories of the ancient kingdom there. But the store turned out to be a shack that primarily sold Japanese comic books and used paperbacks in English, German, and French.

"Well, I'm not surprised—and anyway, we have no room for more books in the apartment," Catty pointed out with obvious satisfaction.

"In my shtudy," Lars protested.

"Your study is hopelessly crowded," Catty said, rolling her eyes at Lidia. "Let's go to the train station. That's actual history. Ten minutes," she added.

The station was a much-photographed mash-up of Victorian depot and Namyanese pagoda that managed to be both monumental and charming. Ghosts of British ladies in crinolines and parasols in the stifling heat with little dogs at their sides, husbands tightly suited, a gaggle of slim Namyanese servants trailing behind. The graceful lines and swirls of the native architecture and people as charming effects to the conquerors of the world.

"All right, it's been thirty-seven minutes," Catty said. "Let's go."

Lars turned. "Where's Lidia?"

But she had disappeared.

2

REALITY, YOU ARE ACTING so coy. Flirting with me, hugging your secrets like a child with her favorite toys. This stuff is wacked. Why did I decide to chew it? And all these people are wearing, like, table-cloths. And those women over there, chained in copper coils from their ears down to their shoulders. What's up with that? That toothless old lady is chewing in rhythm with me—united we chew, united we spit. She's probably the same age as me, but no Doctor Slotzman bridges, implants, or root canals for her; nope, she's a toothless wonder. I am feeling very weird. That time you did so much coke? Pulling an all-nighter back in college, you had to pass the final—botany? Yes, stamens and pistils. You crashed for days after that. Got a 70 on the final, all was well.

Fast train to nowhere. Lars had taken this betel nut stuff in stride, but then, he was Lars. He didn't have a track record with substances.

What a word. Everything is a substance. I mean drugs. And booze. Well, booze is a drug actually, too. My heart . . . Am I on speed?

Lidia rocked in place. She'd bought some *yoongi* from a stall and chewed for a little while, and the stuff came on strong. Now a man had started talking to her. In English. Not a Namyanese man, though he was brown skinned. She glanced at her arm, as if to check that it was still her skin—everything was so tenuous. Coffee with cream, as usual.

"*Café con crema*."

She realized she'd said this aloud.

"You all right? You want some coffee? Or water?" He had an accent she couldn't place. His voice was deep and soothing.

"I don't think so. Not all right. Do I know you?"

"Klaus Haynes. With the group. T&K Adventures. Man, you're not all right."

Her face was pouring with sweat.

He handed her a water bottle. "Drink this." He pointed at her feet. "What happened to your shoes?"

Lidia bent over. "I took them off. They were so sweaty." She lifted a bloody foot.

"Shit," he said, "you cut it on something. You need a bandage." He removed a wad of Kleenex. "Sit down."

She sat on the ground with a thump and he wrapped the tissues around her foot. The little crowd was getting their money's worth. Familiar faces then—Catty in her hat with the big, flipped-down brim, Garboesque, and Lars with knit brows.

"Good God, Lidia, we looked all over for you. Fritz, isn't it?"

"Klaus. Haynes," said Haynes. "She's fucked up, sorry, there's no other way to put it. Lost her shoes and cut her foot."

Lidia said with sudden clarity, "It's supposed to produce a mild, caffeine-like euphoria, but I'm on a fast train to nowhere."

"Did she buy it from the same guy we did?" Lars asked.

"No," said Lidia.

"Well, that could be it. I just googled *yoongi*. Here's what is says on Wikipedia: 'yoongi' . . . Oh shit. It says sometimes it's mixed with meth and some other drug they call *yibi-yabi*. In English: *Nazi speed*. Or just plain *crazy*. Big all over Asia. The laborers. And the hippies . . ."

"Hippies!" Lidia exclaimed, fast-tracking to her youth. "Is it that time again?"

Haynes got her standing up. "We need to get you hydrated and clean that foot," he said, propelling her forward.

Lars and Catty followed them—holding hands, Lidia managed to notice. They always ended up holding hands, despite their squabbles.

"So now I can start over?" Lidia looked at Haynes for confirmation and found herself staring into his eyes, almost aquamarine in a face the color of polished oak. She hobbled along. "Because this time I won't use drugs, I won't drink at all. I'll just paint." Her face crumpled. "But I have to be able to have Lily too."

Haynes shook his head. "Come on, now," he said.

With difficulty, they all squeezed into an incommodious pedicab.

"Golden Palace," said Lars.

They fell silent as the motorized rickshaw battled through a sea of movement of all kinds—a sprinkling of cars, hordes of cheap Chinese motorbikes, bicycles, ox carts, pedicabs, rickshaws, and people on foot, including a line of monks of all ages that stopped everything in its tracks as it slowly, serenely, crossed the road.

They arrived coated with dust at the gilded gates of the grand hotel. The liveried doormen tried not to stare at them as they moved Lidia, bloody tissues trailing her bare foot, through the marble halls to the ornate elevator and, at last, to her room.

Lidia fell onto the king-size bed and spread out her arms and legs, proclaiming that she was a snow angel. The counterpane was indeed snowy white.

Lidia added, "Orgy-size," and then passed out.

She slept for twelve hours.

The message light on her room phone was blinking when Lidia woke up around six the next morning. She had to shower and order coffee before she could think about dealing with anything.

When she got to the phone after that, there were three messages, all asking how she was—one from the tour guide; one from Catty;

and one from the intriguing-looking man who had, she recalled, rescued her.

She intended to call them back. An hour later, she woke up in the chair. Whatever had been in that *yoongi*, she would walk over burning coals before ever ingesting it again.

At breakfast downstairs in the dining room, she felt like a bad-girl minor celebrity as she circled the room, reassuring everyone she was fine now. Fritz—or was it Franz—wasn't there.

She sat down with her buffet selections; bland food suitable for an invalid. Except also her beloved coffee.

"Tammy Steinman," the woman next to her said. "You gave us quite a fright!"

Lidia heard reprimand, which always made her bristle—defiance was a trait she kept thinking she'd tamed after many years of sobriety. She murmured, "And myself," and was immediately distracted by Tammy's headgear, a fatigues-green Fidel cap covered in buttons and badges proclaiming, "We climbed the Grand Canyon!" and "Pikes Peak or Bust!" and "Magical Machu Picchu!" and so on.

Lars always got the nicknames in first, which made sense given his WASP background, which was stuffed with Midges and Bunnies. There was even a great-aunt Pussy, and aged men still called Chip, Tip, Topper. But she was nailing this one: Tammy Steinman was henceforth to be known as "Buttons." She couldn't wait to tell Lars.

"I see you're looking at my cap!" Tammy said. "Mementos of all the places Tim and I have been to." She beamed.

Perfect for a sketch! Lidia was glad she'd thrown a sketchbook and assortment of drawing pens and pencils in when she was packing. Minimal supplies, unlike in her youthful travels, when a large and cumbersome assortment of artist's tools had always weighed down her backpack, but enough to memorialize bits of the trip, like the Steinman cap. Hung over as she was from the *yoongi,* not to mention jetlagged and generally out of sorts, Lidia was glad that she wanted to sketch again. It had been a while.

Wearing the long piece of cloth Namyanese women and, for that matter, lots of men wore—this one a shimmering silk with a border of soft gold that surely cost more than the average peasant could ever afford—their guide, Thila, was by far the best-dressed among them. She rapped lightly on a table and they listened. Like children to a fairy tale.

The days ahead, as Thila described them, would be an endless array of wonders and delights. The Twelve Days of Christmas, the eight nights of Hannukah, the three days of Eid Al-Fitr, Bodhi Day, and so on. Then Thila had them go around the room, introducing themselves.

Retired professionals, mostly—an engineer, an entomologist, who added that it meant "bug man," to polite laughter, a legal clerk, "oil man," teacher, financial planner, principal, colonel, firefighter, documentary film producer, and one woman who described herself as a retired homemaker (did they ever retire?) A few "guests" were still in the game: an architect, a shop owner, extreme political adventure travel blogger (whatever did this intriguing black man who spoke with a German accent, of all things, mean by that? She must remember he was called Klaus), and a vlogger (again, Lidia was unsure of what that was). Lastly, Lidia, who found herself saying, no doubt due to the still-lingering effects of *yoongi*, that she had had the best job in the world.

There was a pause.

"Tell them what you do," Catty urged, leaning across the table.

"Did, you mean. Artist. Just a textbook illustrator now," Lidia said. "*That* isn't the best job in the world."

After a short pause, Thila plunged into the day's itinerary for the day: heavy on pagodas—three different ones, in fact.

"But do not worry, there will be much else wonderful to see

later," she added. "These are all close together here in Gonyang, so, must-to-see."

Klaus Haynes—who, as he'd said in his introduction, everybody called Haynes—went to the back of the bus. He was aware of the irony in this, but he wanted to be by himself. There he fell asleep and dreamed that he was having a conversation with Lidia, who fainted in front of him. It felt like a long time before he grabbed her so she wouldn't fall and hit her head. As he gripped her, he felt a jolt of masculine competence and attraction to the slightly weather-beaten, sturdy, natural beauty he was holding, with almond-tinged skin, curly hair, and a good dusting of freckles on her nose.

He told her about himself, which felt inexplicably urgent. "Last name Haynes. First names Klaus Edward, a compromise. On my mother's, the German side, the Kuttners are ancient suck-ups to some Bavarian nobles who still have some land but no money. My father . . ."

He woke up then, thinking, *Aren't I too old for this?*

At lunch, before the first—splendid—golden pagoda, Lidia at first noticed only couples at the tables. Gradually, she recognized the other singles: Very old Mrs. Hills, who'd had to be helped up and down the temple steps, as there were no accoutrements, unsurprisingly, for the decrepit and the disabled in Namyan. Then Thila, a single, at least on this job. Barton Liu, the vlogger. And Klaus, currently in deep conversation, blogger to vlogger.

And me. And I've got to get used to this. Being on my own. She hadn't gone to a party or even out to dinner since—how long had it been? Nothing besides a coffee shop or a grocery store, and occasionally to visit a few friends like Catty and Lars. Now she was in this exotic backwater, surrounded by married strangers, and Catty and

Lars had deserted her, were at the other end of the table talking to that colonel and his wife.

Lidia ate fish and rice and vegetables and smiled vaguely. *You never imagined being here, you were struggling, just getting by. Then the windfall landed in your lap from Great Aunt Charlotte's will. And Lily doesn't need you now much, she's grown and doing okay by the precarious standards of her age and generation. Ceramicist/waitperson in Cali. And you don't have any looming deadlines here. You're free for two weeks. You're not old yet. Healthy in body and mind, except for that unintended slip into chemical madness—which doesn't count as a relapse. This awkwardness will pass, don't you dare feel intimidated by this bunch. You were always the adventurous type. Strapped on your backpack and went off on the cheap, with or without a companion. Backpack, passport, and a fistful of dollars. Back in the day.*

People started wandering away from the dining room, as soon it would be time to get on the bus and see the first pagoda. But Lidia dawdled around the pretty courtyard garden and they were all waiting for her when she got on the bus. Some, including Lars and Catty, both with mouths ajar, were already asleep or working on it.

She went to the back, where Klaus was fiddling with a camera.

The back had four seats. She sat at the opposite end from him. "Hey, Klaus, thanks again for yesterday."

"Call me Haynes, everybody does." His eyes were cat-green today. "Feeling better?"

"Yes," she fibbed, but couldn't think of anything else to say. Perhaps she was going to be permanently impaired. Nonsense; she willed herself to the present and, once again, surreptitiously compared her arm's skin tone to Haynes's. This had been a compulsion of hers ever since the trip she'd taken to Puerto Vallarta with the sprawling Mexican side of her family when she was eleven. A trip that had included her porcelain-toned cousin Rosita. Who, then thirteen, had pointed out while they were lying side by side on their beach towels that Lidia was "más negra" than her. Lidia had punched her on her skinny white arm. But ever since then, she'd found she was more interested in what people looked like than she was in talking to them. She hadn't thought much about skin tones before that day, and certainly not her own, except to notice how her arms and legs glowed more in the summer. She'd noticed colors in other ways, though. On a rare trip with her father to a hardware store to pick out paint when she was seven or eight, her mind was blown by the vast possibilities the paint chips displayed for white. She'd always thought white meant "white," and so on with every other color. Now she saw that white could also be brown, blue, or red. She stuffed as many paint chips as she could in her shorts pockets to look at later. And after Rosita's comment, she realized that people's skin colors were like the paint chips: Grandma Boyle was white-bread white, Mom was pale ivory, Dad was tan, Uncle Pancho wood brown, Rosita alabaster. She would hold her arm next to others and call up colors—usually to their eventual annoyance. Except Dad: he was delighted that they were the same milky brown. He told her they were *café con crema*. Lidia wasn't sure if this preoccupation of hers was sparked by the artist in her, or if it was what led to it.

By her mid-teens, she'd discarded forever the notion of fixed colors—partly by instinct, partly by observation, and partly by accidentally happening on a TV show one night when she was bored and clicking through the then unimaginably limited range of viewing options. A soporific narrator almost caused her to keep clicking, until she realized what he was narrating: a nature show about what animals see. "The mantis shrimp"—picture cued—"has twelve color receptors to our paltry three"; "owls see a hundred times better than we do in the dark." This confirmed for her that the quality of color was as much about the unseen as the visible, the gray, yellow, pink, green, and even purple lurking beneath the surface. (To us, that is, not to the mantis shrimp.)

Klaus Haynes's arm she judged to be three shades darker than her own, caramel dusted with cinnamon sugar, with the baked-a-bit-too-long-in-the-oven look that age adds to the mix. But depending on so many factors—exposure to sun, his overall health, the angle of the light, and more important, that of the shade—she imagined how Klaus would look lighter or darker. She took in his close-cropped silver hair, strong nose, and sculpted mouth. In South Africa, he'd be called colored; in New Orleans, creole; in Latin America, mulatto. In America, Black, though referring to people as "mixed-race" was gaining popularity now. America seemed to be simultaneously embracing the worldwide fact of the browning of people while at the same time falling further into the myth of racial unambiguity.

One color she was sure about was the wrongness of his vivid blue polo shirt. A touch—no, two touches—too blue, it reminded her of Felipe. The argument they'd had, so long ago now, over his precious blue-flowered Hawaiian shirt.

After looking everywhere for it one day, he accused her of hiding it.

"No, I didn't," she told him. "I threw it away."

"Threw it away?"

"Yes, because I can't stand you looking like Jimmy Buffet."

Felipe was righteously pissed off.

What a pain in the ass I could be, Lidia thought now, sadly.

Haynes smiled at her.

At the next stop, Haynes walked with Lidia to the temple entrance where an officious man with a badge—it was always a man—stood, waving people through, once they were barefoot. A helpful sign nearby showed the picture of a shoe with a red slash through it. There were little wire cages for footwear: sandals for Lidia, sneakers and socks for Haynes. They took their shoes off and stowed them.

A few feet away, Mrs. Hills, wearing ultra-thick Skechers, was

protesting and waving her cane at the guard. Thila hurried over. The
man shook his head in a definite, bored "no." Mrs. Hills and Thila
walked off.

"Feet police!" said Haynes. "Ain't goin' to give an inch. Strict."

"Poor old thing," Lidia said, meaning Mrs. Hills. She tried to
remember if there had been anything in the thick T&R information
packet about feet rules. Yes, there had—a series of them.

They wandered through the lovely pagoda but Lidia didn't want
to linger, and Haynes didn't seem to either. They walked back down,
retrieved their footwear, and found an inevitable tea stall.

"Wish it was beer," Haynes said. "You don't drink, do you?"

"Nope. Doesn't agree with me."

He managed to cadge a Dragan and sighed happily; then, in
time-honored female fashion, she got him to talk about himself. A
rare plus: he was interesting. His work for the blog had taken him
to some of the shit storms of the world—Gaza, Iraq, and Venezuela,
recently. There were people who wanted to climb mountains, people
who wanted to eat dozens of hot dogs in record time. Why not people
who wanted to go to war zones, failing states, pariahs of the world?
Haynes had a key little group chomping at the bit for the dicey parts
of Asia, including the plum, North Korea. His angle was ironing out
the wrinkles for them—as many as could be ironed out, anyway. He
had advertisers. He was constantly expanding.

"Okay," Lidia said, "but Namyan, with Trent & Koss? Wrinkle-
free five-star hotels. Air-conditioned bus with super shock absorbers.
Etcetera. Hardly what you're describing."

Haynes laughed. "First I get the lay of the land. A nice soft tour
like this—and I *do* enjoy my creature comforts—*then* it's off the grid."
He lowered his voice. "You know how many wars are going on in
this country? The Kinhaiese, you've heard of them? Scorched-earth
ethnic cleansing, everybody knows about it, still goin' strong."

"Yes, horrible."

"Yeah, so that gets the world's attention right now—not that it shouldn't, but then? What about the Minans, or is it Menans, down in the South, animists? And most of all, the Hinchaks up north in the mountains? Near the Golden Triangle, man. Major military drug lord action *forever*. That's what I'm here for."

At that moment, the colonel—who, Lidia recalled, had said that he knew Southeast Asia "like the back of my hand; except Namyan, which is why we're here"—stopped and said, "'Scuse me, don't mean to butt in. Ken Lattimore," he reminded them. "I couldn't help over-hearing you . . . Kurtz."

"Klaus. But call me Haynes."

"Haynes, got it. I'm ex-military, Haynes. You want to think care-fully about going to that Hinchak territory. Land mines everywhere, guerilla warfare."

"Colonel, right?"

"Yes sir. The Golden Triangle was a total shit show when we were in 'Nam, and I had reason to get to know it even better after the war. Served in Thailand for a while. Probably even crazier in the Triangle now they're making meth in bulk and that stuff they call 'crazy' that sells all over Asia. And of course, the old faithful, heroin."

Lidia was only half listening now—she felt like the "crazy" might still be sparking in her brain. And she wasn't in the mood to listen to catastrophes. She drifted, scrutinizing colors and shapes around her. Colonel Ken's eyes, pale green, opaque and hard like marbles. His face was surprisingly boyish and unlined, as if the wars and attendant horrors had decided to leave their impressions elsewhere. Maybe they'd gone inside? Ulcers, alcoholism, panic attacks?

"You got a lot of stories you could tell, I bet," said Haynes.

"I'll treat you to a few over a beer one day," said Ken. "You too," he added to Lidia.

A man with a slightly crooked face—Lidia couldn't remember his name—joined them, saying he didn't know about anybody else but he needed a lie-down. Lidia yawned in agreement and Haynes said he could go for that. They got back on the bus. For all its luxury accoutrements, this trip already seemed to be mostly about getting on and off the bus.

In the elevator back at the hotel, Haynes got off at the floor below Lidia's.

"See you tonight, Hines," she said.

Without turning around, he raised a hand. As the doors slid shut, she realized she'd called him by the wrong name again.

3

AFTER THE THIRD PAGODA before dinner, at which Lidia felt like part of a group of toddlers who needed a nap—some of her fellow travelers didn't even go inside, opting to sit under dusty trees with the Namyanese who all appeared to be unemployed and not that bothered by it—and then the ride back to the hotel in rush-hour Third World traffic, dinner felt like the last act of a play that the audience just wanted to end. There was a lot of drinking. Or maybe it was the black magic of aging: senior metabolism, which could make one drink seem like two, and two, four.

Lars seemed to be one of those whose metabolism had declined. Seated between him and Catty, with Haynes and Colonel Ken across the table, Lidia followed their, at first, desultory discussion about Namyan's history as she picked at her food. By the end of Cocktail Number 2, however, Lars was impressively impassioned by both the breadth and depth of the injustices so many suffered in this serene-seeming land. "Like Cambodia in the eighties!" he declared loudly. "Rwanda in the '90s—it was the '90s, right? The world looks on upon the slaughter and does nothing!" He said this loudly enough that other murmuring conversations in the room paused. "This business with the Kinhaiese is the same, simply the wholesale slaughter of a people," he finished.

"Because they're Muslim," Franklin threw in. Which quite possibly he was, too, though nobody was about to ask.

"And what does America do?" Lars plowed on.

"Nothing. We call ourselves the land of the free. Land of the coopted, that's what we are!" Ted replied.

"Those people are *illegals*," Clint Hodges told him. "I heard about it on the news."

"Illegals? They've been here for generations. Only Weasel News would call them that," retorted Ted Leibitz-Kai.

Franklin solemnly nodded his head.

"You mean *real* news," Clint said, baring heavy teeth, the grin of an alpha primate.

"Bullshit!" Lars barked.

"Please do not curse!" Betsy Hodges's voice quavered. She was big-boned but thin-voiced and fluttery.

"You believe the fake media?" Clint asked. "That figures."

"The *facts*," Ted said slowly, "are these: Up to maybe a million people have been killed, raped, or fled for their lives in Kinhai. Because they're Muslims."

"Bleeding hearts," Tim Steinman, who'd had run-ins with Palestinians in his youth while on a kibbutz in Israel, muttered.

"Ted's right, essentially." Lidia could all but see the keen amateur historian in Lars rubbing its hands. "Not that simple, the blame, though. Never is. Have to remember who started it. The Brits back in the 1800s. Brought in serf labor from Bengal. They stayed."

"I agree with you about the British having blood on their hands in this case," Mrs. Hills said in a thin but carrying voice. "As all colonialists do. The French were even worse . . . They all diverted the various ethnicities from the real problem, which was them. I lived in the region after the war, you know."

Everybody wondered briefly which war. World War II? Maybe Korea.

"First as a teacher, then head of the Overseas School in Hong Kong. You may have heard of it. What you might not have heard about were the terrible things happening in Southeast Asia at the time. The general public back in the States didn't know."

Ah, the Vietnam War, Lidia thought. But she was wrong.

"The dirty war, the French at home called it," Mrs. Hills clarified. "From '46 to '54. Well. But elsewhere—here, too—there was plenty of killing going on." She blinked rapidly. With her small, beady eyes and jerky movements, she was like some ancient bird. And a bit three sheets to the wind. "They turned out not so clever at seeing what was going on under their noses. Ha! The hubris of conquerors! Now, I admire the British for many of their achievements, as who cannot? But as Mr. Van . . . Van . . ."

"Vonderville," Catty said in her clear voice. "He's Lars and I'm Catty."

"Yes, how do you do? Again. Well, as Mr. Vonderville says, the British brought in thousands of landless Kinhaiese from India—what was then the Indian subcontinent, I mean. A wedge in the power of the Namyanese."

"What's she on about?" Betsy Hodges asked her husband, who shrugged.

"Mrs. Hills, I entirely agree with you," Catty said. She had minored in British literature at Radcliffe (before women could attend Harvard) and—Lidia knew, because she talked about it often—had a soft spot for the novels of Aldous Huxley and Joyce Cary and George Orwell, which lambasted the Empire's rule in the tropics.

Lars stuck his oar in again. "Yet the Brits were masterful in many ways. They did instill law and order—now, Ted, I know it wasn't perfect. In the event, the blame for whatever atrocities are occurring now in Namyan must be laid at the feet of the ultra-nationalists in power."

Before anyone else could respond, Ann Boren declared, "Well, I didn't come all the way to Namyan to talk about *politics*. This is supposed to be a vacation!"

Perhaps emboldened by his wife, Ed Boren spoke up next. "Working vacation for me." He laughed a bit nervously. "Entomology! Go where the great bugs are! Let's not forget these conflict zones also destroy unbelievably rich habitats. Namyan is one of the most biodiverse regions in the world, you know. The wealth of insects here! *Eulalias*, the *Amantis aliena*, and then you have your unique *Tacus speciose*, and the *Lepidopteria*! *Abisara chelia . . ."*

"Ed," said Ann. "They get the picture."

A bit later, as he punched the elevator button, Lars asked Catty rhetorically, "What are those Hedges doing on a trip like this?"

"Hodgeses. Cliff or Clint, and Betty, or is it Betsy?"

"Mr. and Mrs. Poison," he breathed.

"And the bug man, Ed Boren and his wife . . . Amy? Ann."

"Droning on about bugs. The Bores."

"Mr. and Mrs. Bore," they said in unison.

The next day they were to be on the bus at nine sharp; there, Thila described an ambitious-sounding itinerary, having to repeat it in bits and pieces for the stragglers. To Lidia, this was—too much—like high school, with the group already dividing into the high-achieving group, taking notes and raising their hands with eager questions; the lumpen middle, going along with whatever the program was; and the rebels who were waiting for a smoke break in the woods at recess. Of course, the analogy only went so far: then it had been hormones, now it was stiff knees and bad backs. Still, now as then, Lidia was clearly in the rebel contingent, although she had been a late-blooming rebel, coming out only after she graduated from Wilton High. Then, like an indentured servant suddenly given her freedom, she'd gone wild. She'd tried to explain the perils of rebellion to difficult, teenage Lily, who'd been given the diagnosis of "oppositional thinking disorder" by a counselor who looked to be barely out of school himself. Her talks hadn't seemed to make much of an impression on Lily. Maybe it was impossible for anyone born after the eighties to understand. Sex, gender, race, drugs—everything seemed either out in the open or about to be, undreamed-of scenarios of identity, whereas Lidia and a good portion of her peers had only heard the news about free love, blowing your mind, and dropping out for the first time when they were eighteen. All of this was part of the everyday landscape in her daughter's day.

The bus idled as often as it moved, but at last they pulled up to a huge pavilion that was covered, Thila claimed, with 37 tons of gold leaf. Clearly the pièce de résistance in Gonyang. Balancing the blinding opulence of 37 tons of gold leaf on its exterior, the pagoda was stuffed inside with Buddhas but also with demons, angels, and godlets. An incredibly large number of Namyanese were waiting to get inside, quite cheerful, some picnicking in place, others playing or dozing.

"They wait," Thila explained, "to see holy relic of the Buddha, brought over from India. The bone of toe."

Barton Liu, the vlogger, who had up to then been markedly shy and retiring, suddenly became a whirling paparazzo, distinguishable from all the other tourists, with their cellphones and digital cameras, by the sheer quantity of recording gear he carried—including, notably, a headlamp device clamped to his forehead.

Barton managed to push, amiably, through to the front of the crowd, from which vantage point he snapped child monks wrapped in maroon robes, elegant and gaudy statues, and peculiar little shrines tucked willy-nilly, their lumpish little altars heaped with fruit, wood, feathers, and flowers. These were, as Thila had explained on the bus to those who weren't dozing, pre-Buddhist era deities called *nas* that the people had never stopped believing in.

Establishing himself as the historian of the group, Lars jumped in to add that Namyanese kings had tried, but always failed, to stamp out *na* worship in favor of Buddhist purism. "It makes sense he couldn't eradicate them," he added, "because those"—here he faltered—"*nats*, is it? *Thats?*"

"*Nas*," Catty supplied.

". . . deal with the basics—fertility, hunger, lovesickness, revenge."

Lidia circled a *na* altar, fascinated and also repelled, the way, she thought, life itself affected her. Unlike the elevated beauty of the Buddha shrine nearby, the *na* shrine was crude and in your face and compelling—like James Brown to Mozart, say. She knew she was going to have to draw one of these.

Wandering away, she watched the Namyanese flow by, their brown skin in shades of wheat, tan, gold, and also oak, pearl, even mahogany. She saw that Haynes was watching them too and felt suddenly close to them and to him. After all, she and Haynes were part of the brown tribe, the inexorable future of the planet, if it lasted. Also, the Wongs, Franklin Leibitz-Kai, and Barton Liu. Like the Namyanese, they didn't have to fuss about sunscreen. Papi, she thought, slender and brown, could almost have passed for a Namyanese, while her Irish American mother, part of the fading dominant white paint chip section on the color chart, had always freckled and peeled in the sun.

She walked over to Haynes. "You're not taking many pictures."

"This is postcard stuff," he replied.

They stood against a ledge in the shade. Lars and Catty joined them.

"They're enjoying themselves so much here," Catty said. "All because of a *toe bone*."

They laughed and then yawned, drowsy with heat, pagodas, jet lag. A young Namyanese man approached and spread out a mat on the ground for Lars, as he was clearly the patriarch of their clan. Lars refused with a laugh to sit, then gave in, to Namyanese merriment.

Sitting with his back against the wall, he dug into his backpack and removed his book, a history of Namyan, and turned to the first chapter, causing more ripples of laughter.

"I'd really like a smoke," Catty, who rationed herself fairly strictly to four a day, declared. "I'd probably start a riot, though." She closed her eyes.

"Better than chewing *yoongi*." Lidia yawned. If Haynes had been Felipe, she would be comfortably dozing against his shoulder. Or, more to her liking, with her head in his lap. Okay, not that—not at a Buddhist temple. She stirred and got out her small sketchpad and drawing pencils. There was an endearing child nearby. Glancing up, Lidia saw Haynes train his Nikon on a red kite that had gotten stuck behind a bemused-seeming gold-leafed Bodhisattva.

Lars at first read slowly, but picked up speed as he moved through the "pre-modern" synopsis of the millennia of incursions, invasions, and lost rulers. Namyan's fate was to be sandwiched between the two Asian juggernauts, which should have sealed its destiny and likely would have, if not for impassible mountains. He skipped to the chapter that interested him the most, the one about the last century and a half, when Namyan was colonized and deconstructed by the British before being terrorized by the Japanese and then its own military rulers. Finally, he went on to the final chapter of the book—a slim chapter, as it would have to be, about the recent infant proto-democracy, with the election of Madame. It had been, for many Namyanese, a jubilant couple of years. A walled-off state slowly being reopened to the world—which was to say, foreign money, with tourism a welcome tributary.

Lars's eyes closed, but he was thinking. Everywhere were golden pagodas, friendly, languid yet industrious people, and swarms of unintentionally hip-looking Buddhist monks, nuns, and novitiates and the formerly homeless children in their care—males wrapped in rust-colored cloth, females in pink—all with shaved heads and begging bowls unfailingly filled by the people who had little themselves. The newly elected Madame President. But all the while it was the *Damawat*, the military, who remained the most powerful force in the country, the power behind the throne, whipping up an ultra-nationalistic fervor that kept the fans of war against ethnic minorities strong. Considering all this, Lars, who had lived and worked for ten years in a very different part of the world—Colombia—felt the same helpless, depressive forebodings he'd had then.

He frowned, yawned, and spoke. "There are at least four serious insurrections going on in Namyan, one being perhaps the longest civil war in modern times."

"Oh, not now, Lars," Catty said, stirring. "It's so peaceful here." She stood up and brushed her seat. "Come on, we haven't seen half this place yet."

"That shrine with the Buddha's tooth," Lidia added.

"Toe," said Lars.

4

CATTY SOON DECLARED SHE had seen enough. She and Lidia found another ledge to lean on, while Haynes went on and Lars peered at a nearby shrine.

"It kind of feels like I'm out of purdah," Lidia said suddenly.

"Is that the betel nut drug still talking? I'm not sure 'purdah' is the right word."

"It sounds like it should be. You know, like, cut off from the stream of life."

"It's been so hard for you, this last year."

"Years."

"I know. You really needed a break. I'm so glad you came on this trip. I think that Klaus Haynes is glad too."

Catty was bracing herself for an indignant response from Lidia when Lars startled them with his classic sneeze, a trumpeting ending in a snort.

"Yes, I'm glad too, Lidia," Lars said, turning. He honked into his hankie. He always packed a stack of them, crisply ironed. "Heard anything from home?"

"Not yet."

"Well, the old adage, eh? No news is good news."

But they knew there wasn't going to be any good news from home for Lidia.

"Let's finish this temple off," Catty said with more brutality than she intended. She didn't want Lidia to start brooding again, which was why she had urged the full-on distraction of a trip. She still felt they ought to have gone on a nice river cruise, somewhere in Europe with castles, but Lars had—needlessly—pointed out that as they weren't getting any younger, they should tackle more strenuous travel now and save the "soft" trips for their dotage. He'd plied her with spectacular pictures of Namyan featured in the expensive travel brochure. "It is quite obscenely beautiful," Catty had conceded. "And maybe just the thing for Lidia, too. She's always gone for the exotic."

Trent & Koss had also painted enticing, if real estate–esque, word pictures of Namyan—the unworldly beauty of its long-sequestered, uncountable ancient temples filled with glorious art, its mysterious folkways, the unique riverine culture, all enjoyed in pristine, top-flight hotels. As Namyan had only recently been reopened to the world after so many years, it was top of Lars's list.

After lunch, it was on to a gigantic, open-air market. As a claustro-phobe, Catty clung to Lars and tried to keep Thila in sight at all times there among the surging crowds. She needed a human talisman, as it were, to keep her nerves steady.

Pushed along in the placid though implacable stream of people in the great bazaar with no end in sight, Catty squeezed her bag firmly against her side and ignored the familiar ache in her knee. The sprawl of goods—fabric, bangles, lacquered boxes, and wicker—became a blur, the unending noise made her head ache. Lars wanted to stop and look at every little thing, and Lidia had been swept away.

They came to the food market. Catty hurried past fly-bedecked slabs of meat and odiferous salted fish. Probably drugs were sold here too, she mused—opium, off in a corner—which, despite her well-born name and well-bred appearance, she would like to see. Catty had had a youthful rebellious streak, sparked by her parents. Her mother was a stickler for the rules of old-school WASPdom and her father withdrawn, probably in reaction to his Dragon Lady. Catty had been one of those young people whose balance was wildly thrown off by drink and it had been a good thing, though never spoken of in the family, when she stopped at thirty. Upper East Side AA meetings, the coat racks in winter crowded with fur coats, had even been rather chic then. Now, at sixty-five, she retained little sparks of her carousing youthful self, as witnessed by her several-cigarettes-a-day habit and puckish, subversive sense of humor. So, yeah, she'd like to see an Asian drug market. There was even a chance that she, too, might indulge in a little betel nut chewing. Once she made sure it was not adulterated like poor Lidia's.

Suddenly, before a pungent stall selling thousands of tiny dried fish, Catty realized she hadn't been paying attention. No Lars, No Thila. She the lone, tall Caucasian in a sea of small brown people. Just then she slipped on something and fell on the dirty floor, feeling a wrenching pain in her knee as she did. Kindly Namyanese people helped her up and then stood looking at her. She mimed that she was okay and began to walk, with difficulty. Someone handed her a stick. Oh, how did you say thank you in this blasted place? She smiled, she looked around helplessly. All were people of both genders in *lognis* and those black cotton flip-flops, though some of the younger men and a small percentage of girls were wearing blue jeans. What had Thila told them to do if they got separated? Catty couldn't remember. Was she supposed to go back to the entrance? She longed to sit and rest her leg.

She looked at her watch. Nearly four o'clock. "Oh shit," she said in her well-bred voice. They were supposed to go back to the hotel at four thirty. She'd have to soldier on, or rather back, and look for the group in front of the market.

Trying to hurry, she soon realized that narrow aisles cut through every which way, creating a crazy quilt of paths that confused any hope of progress. Vendors eagerly pushed their identical wares at her. Her left knee throbbed and she had the blurred sense of an imminent panic attack.

When she saw the lacquerware stall where she'd purchased a set of very pretty little bowls, she hurried to it. "Oh shit," she said again, this time as a wail. There was another lacquerware store to her right and one to her left, and they all looked the same, they all had the same pretty little bowls and so on.

The noisy, fetid building, tented like a circus, throbbed like a nightclub of her youth. There were too many people, all talking loudly in that forthright, high-pitched way Catty associated with Asian people. Many of their faces promoted the circus—or was it carnival?—image. Women who for some reason had smeared their faces with white paste in lines and swirls, like cannibals in a cheap horror movie. One of them, a woman with sandalwood-hued skin and white slashes over her cheeks, leaned in toward Catty. Much too close.

And then darkness.

When Catty came to, she was on the floor of a lacquerware stall with a small woman crouched beside her, moving a fan. A man in a short-sleeved shirt and voluminous trousers got up from the one chair, which no doubt denoted his status as owner of the shop, and handed her a bottle of water.

"Madame no good."

Catty sat up and blinked at him. "Did I faint?"

He pursed his lips. She realized he couldn't possibly know what she meant by "faint." She said, "Fell?" and mimed it.

His face cleared and he nodded.

Good God. Twice she'd collapsed. Everything ached. The woman and a little girl helped her onto a stool, where she tried unsuccessfully to get comfortable. Even if she had been in tip-top shape, she couldn't have sat for long this low, whereas the folks around her squatted, kneeled, and assumed other yogic postures with ease. An old lady in the corner was sitting easily on her haunches.

Without thinking, Catty kicked off her Aerosoles. A little girl studied them with fascination—she wore tiny little black flip-flops— and the small woman murmured something to the man in the chair, who nodded, frowning. The woman made a kind of oblation, dipped into a squat—without, Catty noticed, as much as a creak or snap— carefully eased Catty's foot into her rough hands, and applied a cool cloth and then some unfamiliar-smelling herb cream on her heels.

The gentle massage was heaven. The woman carefully wiggled Catty's toes, staring at her after each wiggle. Then, seemingly satisfied, she removed her hands.

"*Kyoe pae m r*," she said to the man.

He looked at Catty. "No . . ." He twisted his hands away from each other in pantomime.

"Not broken?" she guessed eventually. Relief flowed in place of anxiety now. The little girl handed her a cup of green tea, which Catty normally disliked, but she drank it like an elixir and smiled at the girl, at all of them. How kind they were. She would buy something from the shop as thanks, when she got up. But she did not want to get up. Her foot might not be broken, but her knee was still giving her hell. And she was lost.

The tea had revived her, however, and she couldn't take the low stool any longer. She stood and found she was able to walk. She bought bangles in gratitude.

"Now I've got to find my group," she told the man. "Or else go to my hotel."

"Hotel?" he repeated, nodding.

"Yes, but which hotel?" She put her hands to her forehead. "I don't remember! Oh, I'm so silly." And dignified Catherine Vonderville, daughter of a founding partner of a white-shoe law firm, wife of a retired international banker, graduate of Radcliffe, and member of the Cosmopolitan Club *and* Alcoholics Anonymous, began to whimper. *How silly you're being. Mother would be appalled.* The little woman wrapped a long blue-and-white cloth around the big foreign lady's shoulders. It was a simple, lovely blue, the indigo that is achieved only from natural dyes in far-off countries. Looking at herself in the small mirror behind the man, Catty realized she looked like a native, if a large native. This metamorphosis happened to her often. In Harlem where they had the penthouse, many Black people assumed she was biracial. And when she and Lars had gone to Egypt before the "Arab Spring," she was mistaken several times as Egyptian. Though there could be no doubt of her old-WASP origins, per Ancestry.com, she found it difficult to give up the notion that an indigenous American or perhaps an African slave had contributed to her olive complexion and "foreign" features.

She tried to pay for the cloth but they laughingly declined her money. She couldn't find a way to convey that she needed to get to the market's entrance.

5

IN THE OVER-DECORATED HOTEL lobby, Lars and Thila kept watch for Catty. Nearby, a local musician plucked on a boat-shaped harp. The rest of the group was in the dining room consuming the sumptuous buffet and a lot of wine, with Lidia jumping up every ten minutes to check on things in the lobby.

It had been a tough three hours. At first, Lars hadn't worried when Catty wasn't with the others when they all met outside the market to go back to the hotel. He'd thought she was with Lidia, who thought she was with Thila, who thought she was with Lars. Once it was clear she wasn't with any of them, he'd started back inside. Klaus and Colonel Ken had gone after him, and persuaded him to let Thila handle things.

"I told her to get one of those burner phones in case we needed to reach each other," Lars said, voice angry with fear. "Of course, she wouldn't dream of it. Won't even have a regular cell phone here. No need, she said. But I brought one nonetheless."

"Probably she's haggling over something and forgot the time," Lidia suggested, feeling disloyal to Catty's reputation as a stickler for promptness, per her upbringing. But she felt she had to tamp down Lars's anxiety.

Ten minutes later, Lars was sitting on the filthy pavement with his head in his hands.

Thila, though a bit pale, was coolly professional as she organized a posse of Namyanese to search the marketplace for "a tall American lady," with a reward to whoever found her. The Americans—except for Lars and Lidia, who felt she couldn't leave him—went to wait in the air-conditioned bus. A middle-aged Namyanese man arrived in a taxi and had a long consult with Thila, who then urged Lars and Lidia onto the bus with her.

"Mr. Kway will stay to find Madame Vonderville and call with date-ups—"

"Updates," someone said primly.

"—and go with Madame to hotel."

Lars stood. "I'll stay with him."

Lidia noted his unfocused gaze and was sure he was having wild thoughts of white slavery and kidnap for ransom. She put a hand on his arm. "Lars, it's terribly hot and dirty here. Let him do it."

Behind them, Klaus Haynes said, "Lars, man, listen to her. We all have your back here."

On the bus, everyone looked at Lars with a mixture of commiseration and irritation.

"She's probably in a taxi on her way back now," Betsy Hodges said heartily.

"With way too much to carry!" Ann Boren added.

Lars slumped in a seat and turned his head to the window.

Lidia breathed a sigh of relief. Who knew what Lars might say to these women if he opened his mouth.

The bus inched its way to the Golden Palace, where there was no news about Catty.

Now, three hours later, Lars paced the lobby. "Why won't you call the police. I say we call the police," he told Thila.

Thila, working her phone ceaselessly, shook her head slightly. "The police are no—"

"They must have a tourist unit, dammit!" Lars shouted.

As Thila was repeating, in her competent, soothing tones, "We are searching for your wife in every hotel and guesthouse," Lars bellowed something unintelligible and rushed to the entrance.

Lidia followed.

There she was. Their Catherine, who for some reason was encased in a blue cape, her usually neat hair sticking out all over in untidy wisps. And she was limping.

Lidia stood two paces back as Lars enfolded his wife in a bear hug, murmured private endearments and then said, practically shouting, "Where have you been?"

"Oh! I knew you'd get into a lather. I'm perfectly fine, Lars. Well, not perfectly. I got lost there—you didn't wait for me! Then I had a fall and, well, another one, actually. Lovely people helped me. But I couldn't remember the name of the hotel. So stupid of me."

"You had two falls?" Lars shouted again.

Thila approached. Lidia saw the manager, who'd been silently vibrating with fear, slip quietly away, as hotel managers are wont to do. The harpist in the corner, who had stopped plucking, resumed.

Everybody looked from Catty and blustery Lars to the short Namyanese man in shirt sleeves, trousers, and black sandals standing a few paces behind, with a bug-eyed expression.

Catty turned to him. "This is Mr. Wunna," she said. "He and his family took care of me at the market and then he drove me around on a scooter from one damn hotel to the next . . . Actually, it was kind of fun being on it, once I got over the terror . . . Give Mr. Wunna something, Lars."

Lars rooted around in his pockets and pulled out a pile of *takys*, which he handed over without looking at them. Mr. Wunna, bobbing, backed away and thrust the welcome cash into a shirt pocket. Thila, who had a headache, rubbed her temples; the manager could be seen bowing near the reception desk and the harpist now added warbling to his plucking.

Lidia hugged her friend. "We were so damn worried about you! Meanwhile, you were out having an adventure! Now I'm going to dinner, I'm starved!" Which she was, but she also wanted to leave Catty and Lars alone.

Thila said a bit weakly, "Welcome back, Madame Vondavilla," adding that she would like to "converserate" in the morning. Lidia thought that Thila's English was quite serviceable, but it could not be expected to be more than that, especially under such trying circumstances.

As Lidia headed toward the dining room, Lars pulled himself together. "God, these are great people!" He wiped his eyes.

"Really, Lars, don't be a wimp," Catty said. "Sometimes I can hardly believe you ever served in the Marine Corps."

6

"OH! THERE YOU ARE, Mrs. DeCampos—it's Linda, isn't it? My, we seem to have all the ethnicities represented on our tour. You're of Spanish descent, I take it, Mrs. DeCampos?"

"Lidia. No, Mexican, and Irish. It's Ms., not Mrs."

"Sorry. I assumed you were married. Well, of course, you're divorced."

"No . . ."

"Oh, a widow? Ah. So sorry. Losing a spouse . . . I can't imagine, must be so hard. Look at me, going on. My condolences."

Lidia swallowed. "Thank you. As for all the ethnicities being 'represented' here, what about Arab?"

Ann Boren leaned across the narrow aisle of the almost toy-size airplane. "Isn't Franklin one?" she said, lowering her voice.

"He's from Hawaii."

"Well, anyway, I was going to say we should be wearing name tags, don't you think? Look how I got everything wrong about your name! I'm Ann Boren, by the way. Ed's my husband. The 'bug man.'" She made air quotes.

Lidia smiled a bit fiercely before turning away.

Ann sat back in her seat and snapped her seat belt on (it was curious, she mused, how everybody in the group griped about the steep stairways without railings, the slippery floors, etc., but few used their seat belts on the bus.) She had an unsettled feeling, as if she had said something wrong. Well, she was too tired to ponder.

She closed her eyes and her mind drifted to her favorite project awaiting her at home: redecorating the living room. Ed had finally agreed that the BarcaLounger could be replaced, as well as that ugly coffee table inherited from her in-laws. She was going to have the couch reupholstered, too, but still hadn't decided between the blue-green or the green-gold fabric, swatches of which were affixed to the current mustard-colored cloth, awaiting her return.

Her mind drifted comfortably through the living room, and then, eventually, drifted without her noticing it to a review of the trip so far. Today—rather, tonight—was the beginning of the fifth day, yet it seemed they had been roaring around this curious country much longer. Today they were on one of those impossibly early morning flights that airlines seem to relish scheduling. But, if Thila was to be trusted, they were to be rewarded by the archeological equivalent of paradise—Gaban!

It didn't take long before the plane set down near a massive plain containing the ancient city with its thousands of stupas, pagodas, temples, and palaces. A bus took them straight to the archeological zone; a boxed lunch was provided on the way.

It was spectacular, endlessly so. They walked and walked and walked from stupa to pagoda until Thila at last called a halt, assuring them they had only "itched the top." Then they were taken to their new hotel.

With nothing scheduled for the rest of the day, Lidia felt like a kid at recess. She hurried through some small housekeeping chores—mainly handwashing her underwear, which she was too cheap to send out, and mildly reorganizing her suitcase, which always tended to look as if a giant food processor had been at work inside it. Her plan was to avoid anything to do with pagodas and Buddhas for the rest of the day, although more of them were within a short walk of the surprisingly massive hotel. No, a nice dip in the Olympic-size pool for her, and then some pages of the Icelandic thriller she'd just started—as far away from anything Southeast Asia as she could get.

As she arranged her washing on her tiny ground-floor balcony, just big enough for two chairs, Ann Boren appeared on the path outside.

"Oh hello, Ann." What was it with this woman? Was she shadowing her?

"Isn't this just so picturesque, Lidia?"

"Yeah." She glanced back at her room. "Well . . ." She was anxious to get into her swimsuit and find a lounge chair by the pool—where, she saw, several others in the group who had had the same idea were already gathered.

But Ann, who seemed determined to make a friend of her, continued to stand there smiling and Lidia, who came from hospitable folk, felt compelled to invite her to sit on her tiny balcony and sip a cold drink from the mini-bar.

"I'll just climb over this little fence!"

As Ann did so, Lidia removed her undies to the bathroom.

A good half an hour later, during which Lidia surreptitiously checked the time every ten minutes, Ann wound down a seamless tale that chiefly involved her recently "deceased" mother's many woes, with occasional queries about Lidia's own "loss," which Lidia deflected with noncommittal responses. *Blame yourself,* Lidia thought crossly, *for letting her think you're a widow. Now she thinks you're the grief sisters or something.* She did reluctantly get Ann's guilt about "Mother," though, Ann's relief that the tyrannical woman was "gone."

At last, saying "how nice it was to chat," Ann took herself off, again climbing gracelessly over the wrought-iron balcony fence. Lidia saw she had just enough "free" time left either to a) not take a refreshing dip, or b) do so but not have time to shower and fix her recalcitrant hair before dinner.

She went for option B. So she'd have frizzed-out hair. So what?

That was why Lidia was wearing her Dog Rescue cap later as she sat under the stars with Catty and Lars. They had opted out of the groaning sideboard in the hotel dining room for sandwiches by the pool bar. It was a night for headgear: Lidia's cap, Catty's black Garbo hat, and Lars's Namyanese straw hat in its beguiling octagonal shape. Curiously, Lars—who, despite his name, came from ancient blue-blood stock—could pull off wearing such a hat with panache, as his distant English forebears had certainly done during their rule over so many exotic parts of the world. The Larses of this world, Lidia thought, could don a fez, a turban, a skullcap, a what-have-you, and make it work.

Now, though, here came Ann Boren again. "Mind if I join you? Ed's feeling a little . . . you know? Off? And I don't feel like a big dinner."

"Rotten luck," Lars said. As far as he was concerned, Lidia knew, Ed Boren had distinguished himself so far on the trip as apparently only possessing knowledge—admittedly, a fund—about insects and having a proclivity for peering at things in the bush. And that wife of his *twittered,* he'd observed to Lidia and Catty earlier.

"Yes, isn't it? What about you? How is your knee?" Ann swiveled between the Vondervilles. "I heard you complaining about it, Catherine, oh, I don't remember at which pagoda? And problems with your feet, isn't it, Larry?"

"Lars," Catty said.

"Very dry skin," Lars said.

"Oh, no more sick talk," Lidia protested.

*   *

Ann smiled gamely. She felt she'd tried her best with the third wheel, Lidia, but the woman wasn't much better at conversation than Ed, who was known to grunt replies, though he knew Ann was in mourning and longed—needed—to talk about her loss. And for that matter, anything other than bugs. She'd made inroads with Tammy Steinman, but unfortunately, Tammy's Tim hovered a little possessively for Ann's taste. Betsy Hodges was nice, and though her giant husband seemed to be in a permanent bad mood, at least he didn't hover. Quite the opposite, in fact, except for tonight. The Hodgeses had been having some sort of disagreement or spat, so Ann hadn't wanted to intrude. Wasn't that husbands for you? Then she had seen the Vondervilles from afar—Catty's hat—and thought she'd just stop by their table, as they seemed nice if, well, a bit snooty.

"I have some Gold Bond lotion, if you'd like?" she said to Lars. Funny name, that. "I can bring it to your room later? Suite, I mean? Isn't this a fantastic hotel?"

"Quite nice," replied Catty. After a pause, she added, "Inside. But outside, it's hideous. Garish," she added repressively.

No one seemed to have anything more to say, so they just sat. Lars had signaled for the check before the Bore woman arrived. He longed for his bed, where he could swat a bit more Namyanese history. Catty and, for that matter, Lidia, though she was years younger than them, looked pretty done in as well.

"Thila sure keeps us going, doesn't she?" Ann said eventually.

"Oh, she does," Catty returned in her polite voice. "All this walking around interminably in the heat. And then we had to stop at that lacquerware factory today."

"All that work!" Lidia said. "Those young girls squatting there, engraving intricate designs in inadequate light. Dickensian."

Ann frowned "I thought those bowls were gorgeous? Didn't you *buy* some?"

"Yes," Lidia said. "I was just pointing out their working conditions."

"While we're waiting for the check," Lars said, "would anyone like some coffee?" Surely the woman would take the hint.

The bill came and Lars jotted down his room number, but Ann had readily agreed to coffee, so the three, who had all had politeness drilled into them from infancy, sat on. Thus they learned a good deal from Ann about Tamarinds, the senior residence in Scottsdale to which she and Ed had recently moved.

"It was hard to leave Wisconsin? But we love the desert?" Ann shivered dramatically in the cooler air of evening. "At night, Ed finds all these hairy spiders and such in the Sonoran Desert?"

"More coffee?" asked Lars.

Catty's aimed a light kick at his shins under the table.

"None for me," Catty said in her I-have-reached-my-limit voice. This was a sacrifice on her part, Lars knew, for, like the vast majority of recovered alcoholics, she rarely turned down a cup. She emitted a semi-discreet yawn. "Early day tomorrow, as usual, and we need to see to your foot. When Ann's finished."

Ann Boren said, "Oh yes, his foot!"

That's the first time, Lars thought, *she hasn't finished a sentence as a question.*

Ed—Dr. (PhD) Edward Manfred Boren—was also playing hooky from the group dinner. He'd slipped into the dining room and made himself a sandwich under the neutrally astonished gaze of the waiters, wrapped the thing in a handkerchief, and stuffed it in a side pocket of his voluminous bag, which was already brimming with camera equipment, binoculars, various bottles and bags for collection, notebooks, and pens.

Ed's happiest childhood memories had been thus: fieldwork, and then tending to the new additions of his collection in the basement of his family's modest clapboard house. He'd gone for the typical boyish treasures—frogs, snakes, bugs—but the size and variety of his collection had been atypical. Getting his first microscope on his eleventh birthday was a thrill that had never been surpassed, not even by sex, although he had found a perhaps surprising number of willing partners among the science girls, then women, who generally worked quietly in labs as assistants. Both Ed and they had been matter-of-factly grateful for the reciprocal attention.

He'd met Ann when he was twenty-nine in, of all places, a bar, to which some guys in the lab where he was then working had dragged him one rainy Friday night. Ann was with some girlfriends and caught his eye because of her wavy, copper-colored hair and calm manner amidst the shriekers.

It had been a mutually satisfactory courtship. Both were in their late twenties and had steady jobs (she as a clerk for the county probation department, he in the state department of agriculture), and in the coming years, she had achieved the status conferred by longevity and he had risen to chief entomologist, becoming known for his work in integrated pest management, or IPM—mainly with apple orchards, an important part of the state's economy. Ed got on well with the bluff orchardists who had to battle nature continually. He enjoyed the challenge of talking them around their resistance to reducing the use of pesticides. Bill Krautkramer, one of the biggest orchardists in the state, had rolled his eyes at Ed's plan to eradicate the deadly round-headed apple tree borers by removing the deadwood and brush Ed claimed harbored the insects instead of spraying before reluctantly acquiescing to try it Ed's way. He'd had the last word then—"The deer'll get mosta what the bugs don't"—but the following year he'd been, perhaps reluctantly, satisfied with his improved apple crop.

How distant those heady years of environmentalism now were, Ed mused, walking through the scrub brush at the outer perimeter of the hotel grounds. At least he'd helped eliminate the use of some of the worst pesticides, even if the world was going to hell. Since his retirement last year, he'd tried not to look back. Now he could finally travel as much as his budget permitted for new specimens.

Happy though she was with her quilting club and family stuff, Ann wouldn't dream of letting Ed go off alone "to see the world." But she drew the line at accompanying him on his forays into the bush for "bugs." So Ed was alone now, crouching at twilight behind a hedge that screened the al fresco restaurant, photographing his first *Zizeeria karsandra*, the dark grass blue butterfly.

It was a fairly common butterfly in the lowlands of Namyan, but he'd never seen it. Its design was enchanting: wheat-colored tips with lavender blue on the wings intensifying to a near true blue at the center. *Ann would like this one*, he thought as he clicked. Then, nearby, on the other side of the hedge, he heard a male voice.

"Why do some people bother coming to a place like Namyan? That woman from Scottsdale. Or wherever the hell that sure-to-be ghastly retirement village is."

"I'm sure it's because of the bucket list." A woman's voice.

"Nasty expression, that." The man again, and Ed suddenly recognized its owner: the old guy, Larry? The one who'd gone on about the Brits and those illegals, or maybe not illegals, being harassed by the government in some remote part of this remote country. History only interested Ed when it had to do with his work.

Lars, that was it. Lars *Vonderpoop*, ha!

"I for one am not going to submit to that woman's mindless chatter again. And that husband of hers, looks like he's been stuffed with his mouth left hanging open at the wrong angle. Bugs. The *Bores*."

"That's one of your best nicknames ever!" said the woman—and Ed knew who she was too, that Latina woman who palled around with the Vonderpoops.

They must have walked on, as there was silence now. *How weird to hear yourself being trashed*, Ed thought, *and maybe weirder being behind a bush looking at a butterfly.* He started to whistle because his asthma came on when he got emotional. He pondered jumping up, running after them, yelling "Gotcha!" and punching Lars Fucking Vonderpoop in the face. Crunching his nose. Of course, he wouldn't do that. Ed didn't believe in physical violence.

When his hamstrings began to ache, he stood up and coughed, as if to expel what he'd overheard.

Anyway, Ed was already convinced of the unpleasantness of most humans. The Wisconsin Department of Agriculture had included a peevish, manly female boss, a generous helping of petty coworkers, and the loutish orchardists. He didn't expect much from his species.

He stopped to peer at the leaf on which the *Zizeeria* had perched, but it had darted away. Never mind, there'd be more. What was wrong with a bucket list? He had one—lepidoptera was on it, of course, and at least one sighting of *Vespa mandarinia*, the giant Asian hornet which could kill not only honeybees but also *humans*. What if he got his hands on one and secreted it in the old man's room? One for the Latina's room, too? The horror when *Vespa mandarinia* attacked . . .

Ed stowed his stuff and went back to his room, indulging in thoughts of vengeance.

7

LARS DIDN'T MIND GETTING up early. It reminded him, he said, of his days as a Marine, which he relished, at least in retrospect. Catty and Lidia, on the other hand, liked to sidle into their day: First, they worked their way through several cups of coffee. Then, after a light breakfast, they began their day: Catty liked to putter for a bit, then plunge into her latest book for the Rad Book Club, "girls" who'd been meeting since graduating from Radcliffe in the early '70s. They only read challenging books: Feynman's *Six Easy Pieces* on physics had been a particularly tough go, but Catty had loved Whitehead's *The Underground Railroad*. Lidia, meanwhile, would on a normal morning, in her part of Manhattan, get a belated start on her latest textbook illustrating job. (Before leaving for Namyan, she had completed a chapter on ethnically diverse transgender preteens; the publisher hoped for brisk sales on that one.)

So both Catty and Lidia were finding it hard to adjust to the strict T&K time frame, above all the chatty atmosphere on the bus at the start of the daily forays.

The routine started with the bus driver's assistant, with the purple smile of a betel nut aficionado, distributing water bottles while Thila prepped them. Today, Lidia was the last to get on the bus, which meant that she missed the spiel and was forced to take the only available seat left, right across from Tammy "Buttons" Steinman.

The night before, on their walk back from the open-air club-sandwich place, Lars had broken into a lusty version of "Buttons and Bows," retitling it "Buttons and Bores." Catty had shushed him, laughing. Lidia couldn't help but remember that now.

"Did you get Wi-Fi at the hotel?" Tammy demanded of her.

"I don't know. I'm not into IT much."

"Really?" Tammy gave her the look Lidia knew so well. As if she had admitted to something distasteful—not a crime, but a substantial faux pas.

"Anyway, we're in the middle of nowhere, so to speak."

"But the brochure said we would have Wi-Fi. I'm going to make a complaint. Couldn't Facetime with my granddaughter. Very upset."

Tammy shook her head and her buttons wobbled and gleamed.

"Well, why not send your granddaughter postcards?" Lidia suggested with perhaps a trace of hostility. "Kids love to get mail. Foreign stamps. There was quite a selection in the shop at the hotel."

"Snail mail?"

"Yes. A letter with a stamp on it."

Tammy stood up. "Well, I'm going to go canvas the others."

Lidia closed her eyes, pondering what Tammy Steinman and Ann Boren—the two were linked in her mind forever now as Buttons and Bores—had been like in high school. She did this a lot, drifted to profitless imagined scenarios. They were stars in home ec, sang in the choir, and were "good girls," i.e., virgins—now such a quaint concept. Then they went to a state college or maybe secretarial school, after which they snagged sensible mates, a mechanical engineer and a bug scientist. Why the hell were they in Namyan?

The answer, though, was depressingly simple. The world was Disneyfied, a series of selfie-taking theme parks. Selfie sticks.

The night before, at the poolside restaurant, her mind tripped on,

Lars had been in a foul mood, going on about Clint Hodges—who, massive as a lineman and as adept at blocking, seemed always to be hulking in front of some beautiful faded fresco or other, snapping away, so that Lars couldn't see a damn thing. "What a bunch of Philistines. When they're not poking their cellphones at a temple, they're talking about all the stuff they just bought. But he's the worst. Rightwing clod." Lars stabbed at a French fry with his fork.

"Lars's foot's giving him trouble," Catty explained to Lidia. "But Lars, you *like* the Lattimores and the Leibitz-Kais and Barton, and the Wongs seem okay," she reminded him. "And of course Klaus," she added, with a meaningful look at Lidia.

"Yes, but those Poisons and Bores and . . . Look out!"

"What?" Catty jumped out of her chair. Lidia was impressed with her agility, given her trick knee.

"There's a huge horned beetle on your chair."

"Calling Ed Bore!" Lidia said.

They moved to another table.

"Those people!" Catty said suddenly. "Remember at the monastery, Thila was telling us about the little boy abandoned outside the gates recently? How it happens a lot. And all they could say was could they get some pictures of him."

"The world is just a theme park for their ilk," Lars said, spearing another fry.

"I love it when you use words like 'ilk,'" Lidia told him.

That was when the waiter arrived to clear the table, followed by Ann Boren.

When Tammy "Buttons" Steinman finished polling the group about Wi-Fi at the hotel—no one had any—quiet descended during the long drive, which, as Thila had promised, was a scenic one: serene plains banked by soft foothills, the wide river running alongside. They stopped at a pagoda, where Lars was barred from entering unless he removed the bandage Thila had produced to cover the cracking sole of his right foot. He said he'd be fine sitting on a step.

"You didn't miss that much," Catty told him when they got back on the bus. "All these Buddhas are starting to look alike."

"Except the *na-san*. You would have liked this one," Lidia said.

"This is the one time I wish you girls took snaps like the rest of the crowd so I could see the bloody thing," Lars groused. "What about this *na-san*?"

"I'll describe it to you," Catty told him. "Only because you're physically challenged."

"Thanks a lot."

"A nice man explained it to us in rudimentary English for a dollar. A *na-san*—lovely word, isn't it—means a house for the spirits."

"Yes, yes, I know that," Lars said.

"Don't be crabby. This one we would have missed if he hadn't pointed it out. Funny that Thila hasn't said much about them. It was behind the shrine. A not very good carving of a female face, wearing a turban with feathers stuck in it and paper garlands around its neck. But a male body."

"Definitely trans," Lidia put in. She'd become educated about the trans world by Lily's college roommate, Bart, who'd told her in kind, patient tones that "drag queen" was okay with him, but not everyone. The vast new world of gender redefinition was too complicated, she thought. "What was it the man called the spirits, Catty? Sounded like 'occult.'"

"*Acaults*. Spirit wives."

"I read something about them," said Lars. "Well, damn, I wish I'd seen that. Thila brushed me off when I asked about the ones we saw at the pagoda the first day. I bet she's ashamed of them."

Lidia shook her head. "Ignorant peasant superstitions, best kept under wraps?"

Soon they were all dozing. Lidia dreamt about weird creatures lurking in corners. One flew at her face and she woke up to find a fly buzzing.

They had lunch in a glorified wooden shack on stilts over the river that was filled with nineteenth-century daguerreotypes of solemn ancestors in the stiff Victorian clothing of their British colonizers. Everybody gulped down the citrus punch offered at the door, except Catty and Lidia, who'd found the juice was sometimes mixed with gin and then they had to spit it back into their cups. No doubt that was a very rude thing to do in Namyan, rejecting hospitality, but they were hardly going to explain that they were recovered alcoholics for whom even a drop was taboo.

The meal was now almost as familiar to Lidia as hamburgers and fries: always foot-long beans, rice, fish, murky spices. And mangos for dessert.

Lars drank the local beer and bonded with Colonel Ken, as a fellow soldier. The colonel's duty in Vietnam and something murky afterwards in Thailand had sparked Lars's interest; he'd told Lidia and Catty he was going to try to find out if he'd been with the Agency, as he called the CIA.

Catty and Lidia, meanwhile, had a reasonable chat with Sally Lattimore. She laughed about what she called her shopaholism, and in fact Lidia had noticed that she often held up the group with her purchases. Lidia thought—and knew Catty was thinking it too—that given the way Sally put away the spiked punch and wine with meals, shopping probably wasn't the only "ism" going on. But Sally was drily amusing, had long and useful familiarity with this part of the world, and a big plus for them was her lack of interest in taking pictures. Buying them, yes. As they left the restaurant, she attempted to buy one of the daguerreotypes on the wall, but the owner wouldn't part with his ancestors.

8

THEY SET OUT EVEN earlier than usual the next morning, to beat the crowds at the huge complex of pagodas at Gaban. In horse-drawn carts, they climbed foothills to a look out over the great plain, singed and dusty at the end of the long dry season. The equivalent of most of the world's cathedrals was spread out as far as they could see—walled ruins of a palace stretching for acres, temples placed like giant chess pieces waiting to be played under the blazing sun. Some of the pagodas looked like gigantic cupcakes dipped in gold; others were idiosyncratic; yet others seemed to be melting away over the millennia.

Trudy Wong wondered aloud what the difference was between temples, pagodas, and stupas. Lidia said *stupa* sounded like a Yiddish word for sex. Ward, the semi-retired architect, turning red in the face, said that a stupa had a dome, a pagoda had a tower, and temple was a general term for both. Most of the rest of them just took pictures.

"Behind that range of mountains and then others," Lars said, pointing, "live headhunters and warlords who make drugs for half the world and also tribes that follow despised religions."

"Where I'm going after this," said Haynes.

Catty raised her eyebrows at Lidia.

Around them, cameras and phones continued to click and whirr.

"Stop it, please. Stop taking pictures! Move away!" Ed Boren suddenly shouted. "There's a band of *Vespa mandarinia*! The sting can kill! I'm not kidding! Move away!"

Everyone of course did so right away, except for Clint Hodges. He moved closer to the clot of large, buzzing insects.

"Clint!" Betsy shrieked.

"Wanna get a shot of 'em," he barked.

Ed rushed forward and shoved Clint to one side. This was so unexpected that it almost made Lidia like the odd little man.

"I'm not kidding! The sting is lethal!" he exclaimed.

Clint gave him a dirty look but loped away after the group, which, shepherded by Thila, was hurriedly moving down from the platform. At a safe remove, they stopped to see ant-size farmers working in rice paddies wedged next to the foothills. There it was: timeless Asia, the tough, delicate brown tillers of grain transplanting seedlings without number before the coming rains. Cameras and phones clicked away.

Haynes handed Lidia binoculars. She saw an aged woman brush hair from her face as she bent and lifted, bent and lifted.

Not far away below, a small army of Chinese and Korean tourists was exiting a half-dozen or so double-size tour buses, followed by a few divisions of Europeans or Americans. With selfie sticks bristling like antennae, they surged toward the T&K group like giant insects.

Later, back at the hotel, after a spectacular sunset, Lars limped into the lobby with the intention of obtaining a cocktail before dinner. He saw Lidia sitting with Catty and plopped down.

"We've been talking about this hotel," Catty told him.

"Trashing it," Lidia added.

"All concrete and hubris."

Lars looked around. "And where's the fucking waiter when you need him?"

"Foot hurt again?" Lidia asked. Lars seldom used the "f" word. "Ah, here comes a waitperson."

He ordered a martini and coffee for the "girls." Once his drink came, he joined in grousing about the Gaban Imperial. "Whoever built this hotel was clearly counting on hordes. The Chinese we saw today, presumably. Too pricey, I'd bet."

"Some general's pride and joy, no doubt. The worst kind of Stalinist architectural pomp!" Catty said authoritatively. Her grandfather had been a noted architect who'd hobnobbed with Stanford White and for a moment, in her teens, she'd entertained the idea of becoming one herself before she flamed out for a while.

Lars waved dismissively at the stairways—broad enough for an imperial retinue—and the massive concrete plaza that was the view from the lobby. The two double-Olympic-size pools on the grounds were nearly always empty, as was the golf club, and the tony villas adjacent. "General Poohbah's Folly," he said.

"Lars" itself was a nickname. Just as Bertram Wilberforce Wooster was always called "Bertie," so was George Frederick Vonderville III always called "Lars." Only his mother, his headmaster at St. Paul's, his Marine sergeant, and his former wife, when she was pissed off, had ever called him George. Catty had promised not to throw his name in his face even when angry, and she'd proven true to her word.

The name had been bestowed on him by G.F. Vonderville II, due to an enduring fondness for a Norwegian resistance fighter he'd met during World War II. (Catty liked to tease Lars that maybe it was more than friendship). Lars Larson had skied his way away from Norway and the Nazis, ending up in London and working for the Resistance. There he'd become pals with G.F. II, an American intelligence officer, and had plucked G.F. out of harm's way during a bombing raid, ensuring II's first-born son his unofficial name. Again like Bertie Wooster, Lars Vonderville was a genial, old money, baddish boy who often seemed about to sneak a whoopee cushion onto someone's chair. But there the resemblance ended, for Lars, unlike Bertie, was not a dolt.

After a frivolous boyhood and rowdy adolescence, Lars was quixotically moved to join the Marine Corp for a three-year stint, and to everyone's surprise, not least his own, the Marines did turn him into a man. After that, he joined the family firm of international bankers and was posted to Bogota, Colombia, where the firm had long-standing ties to rich agriculturalists, the Latin American equivalent of antebellum plantation owners in the American South. He eventually married a highborn South American girl who gave him three sons. Marriage to Adela turned out to be a mistake but he stuck to it—had to, really, as she was a devout Catholic. He found what happiness he could in mild affairs, conviviality with old friends, and a passion for history.

Lars met Catty at a Harvard–Radcliffe reunion, although they'd already met a shockingly long time before, when she was a frosh and he was an upperclassman, then dating Catty's roommate. Their falling in love astonished everyone, including themselves, but there it was: they were soulmates. There followed epic skirmishes as Lars tried to disencumber himself at last from Adela, but the fiery Colombiana refused to consider it. When Tom Whapshot, Lars's lawyer, attempted to deliver the divorce decree for her to sign, she barricaded herself in the venerable Vonderville manse, changed the locks, and ordered in groceries. Finally, Lars and Whapshot snuck into his ancestral home through a window and confronted Adela, who was sitting on a chaise longue in the cavernous living room, chain smoking. Whapshot handed her the divorce papers for her to sign, whereupon she set them on fire with her lighter. A futile if splendid gesture, Whapshot explained: as he'd witnessed her receiving the divorce decree, it was now a done deal. She covered her ears and screamed—a sound that was to haunt Lars, but only for a short time—and Lars and Tom hurried out, this time by the front door.

Two years later, Lars and Catty went to City Hall to tie the knot. They found a reasonably priced (for them) penthouse apartment in

Harlem, which was on the cusp of gentrifying, where they'd lived contentedly ever since. Even so, it was not a union completely free of friction. There were Catty's nerves, which could play up at any time, and Lars's OCD, which expressed itself in daily hand-laundering of his underwear and shirts. In the penthouse, he had his own bathroom to festoon with dripping boxers. On the road, however, there were only shared bathrooms, windows, and balconies.

Catty said suddenly, "Do you realize you can see our balcony from here, Lars? With your smalls all over it?"

"You can see that far? You have the eyesight of a cat, Catty. Ha ha."

"It's squalid to hang your underwear where everyone can see it. Like a slum."

Lars's tactic with Catty's wifely grievances was to ignore them. If that didn't work, it was to laugh. His final resort was to express innocent astonishment. To balance these vexations, he was a steadfast cheerleader and soother of Catty's nervous temperament, which included bringing her breakfast in bed and indulging her frequent desire to retire from the world.

He was currently using a combination of the first and second variants: humorous deflection. "As you well know, it's because of my training in the Corps that I have to keep things shipshape. And speaking of drying things," he added, thrusting his foot upward, a real deflection, "that ointment the doc gave me seems to be working, see?"

Lidia, who'd had enough Vonderville thrusts and parries for the moment, turned to watch the almost invisible purples and pinks of the last of the sunset on the plain beyond the concrete plaza.

"But it's shredding!" Catty cried out.

"My dear girl. Because it's healing. The doc says it's a local fungus. Nothing in that voluminous packet of info T&K sent us about Namyan mentioned we'd have to take our shoes and socks off every day and walk through filth."

"Yes, but no one else's feet look like that. Well, no more wandering barefoot around pagodas for you anymore."

The Namyanese rule, or taboo, or fetish, barred all but bare feet in pagodas.

"Catty," Lidia said, "he's got to wander around them, that's the main reason we came here. At least they hand out sanitizing wipes afterwards. Well, sometimes."

Catty said, "Lars, it's *bleeding* at the *cracks*."

"Mere trickles. Much better than it was. Doesn't burn and itch and feels better without the bandage. Catty, I'm not going to miss seeing whatsit tomorrow."

"You are so stubborn!"

"Here's the bill," Lidia said. As much as she loved them, there were times, and this was one of them, when she wanted to flee, screaming silently, to the haven of whatever room was currently hers.

9

THERE WAS NO FOOT policeman at the entrance of the beautiful but abandoned pagoda they went to the next morning, so they were able to leave their shoes on for the steep climb to what Thila promised was a beautiful view.

Midway up, Lars stopped. "Shit!" he said suddenly. "My foot's killing me again."

"And my knee's talking to me. Let's go back down," Catty said.

Below, they joined Mrs. Hills, who after her first try, had never attempted more than the shortest flight of stairs, and Ward Wong, whose back was acting up, and Clint Hodges, who didn't say what was bothering him, though clearly a lot was. "His miserable psyche," Lars whispered to Catty as they drifted to a tea stall.

Lidia continued to climb the many steps of the pagoda, following Betsy Hodges's plump, khaki-covered rear. It felt as though they were in the clouds; a hot wind blew through the elaborately carved scrollwork. A worn, magnificent hardwood Buddha at the top took pride of place, garlanded but otherwise untouched except by time. This was rare. Like buying a wing of a hospital or museum in the States, here the rich paid for restorations of pagodas, with garish paint and even blinking neon lights added, like an old cocktail lounge. This temple had been spared. And the views from the four balconies gave four completely different scenes: one looked upon rolling, smoky hills, another the watery expanse of rice paddies in delicate shades of green, the third the great, ruined palace, and the fourth a ribbon of far-off, silvery water with boats tiny as driftwood. Lidia leaned over the last, attracted by the promise of water.

Haynes was there, suddenly. "You know, Gaban was one of the great world cities. Civilizations, really. Like Greece and Rome. Completely unknown today."

"I wish I could stay here and draw. Perfect peace."

"Yeah but think of all the restless ghosts. Wars, famine, plagues."

"Can we not talk about the dark side?" She wanted to say, *I've been living in the dark side for years and I'm sick, sick, sick of it.* What she said was, "Sorry, don't mean to be abrupt . . . Well, I'm going back down."

Getting down the steps was hard labor. There were so many, and they were so narrow, so steep. Sweat trickled down her neck, rolled between her breasts, her legs. Suddenly, something stabbed at the sole of her left foot and she grabbed for the nonexistent railing, just managing not to tumble forward before sitting down heavily. She turned her foot over, and found a nail stuck to the sole of her sandal.

Haynes sidled around her and knelt. "Jesus! All right. All right. I'm going to get it out. Hold on to me."

Lidia gripped his arm, shut her eyes, and felt a tug. "*Oh!* Am I bleeding?" She wouldn't look at the foot.

"Thank God that sole is thick."

She winced. "I'm not taking that sandal off 'til I get down."

She yelped when she put weight on the foot but slowly, holding on to Haynes, she crept down the rest of the stairs. Haynes half-supported her as she limped to the bus, where the group was waiting.

"You okay? Not pissed at me?" he asked suddenly as they inched forward.

"I wasn't. I'm not. I just, I need . . . peaceful things right now." She laughed ruefully. "Like not stepping on a nail at a fucking pagoda."

"You dodged a bullet, though. So to speak."

He helped her up the bus stairs. Everyone looked at them with that glum, where-the-hell-have-you-been, we-have-better-things-to-do-than-wait-for-you scowl.

"There was a nail sticking up on the stairs and I stepped on it," Lidia informed them. "Haynes—Klaus—took it out, it was mostly in my shoe, I don't think it pierced the skin."

"I think maybe a little," said Haynes.

Thila sprang into action with her trusty first aid kit, a foreign concept in Namyan instituted by T&K. Haynes, for the first time, sat next to Lidia, with Catty and Lars just across the aisle.

"A nail? Sticking up on a stair?" Catty said. "What are the odds? I'm just being rhetorical, Lars," she added.

"And everyone else's foot missed it," said Lars. "Why you? What cosmic slight did you incur?"

"Lars!" said Catty. "Anyway, Klaus—Haynes—came to her rescue."

"But look here. There's something about feet in this country, wouldn't you agree? What if you'd been barefoot? God."

"Lars!" Catty said again, a half-octave higher.

Lars plowed on. "It's unsanitary, this barefoot rule. Of course, you have to abide by it, but to what end? It's reduced me to a near cripple, and now Lidia . . ."

"Dreams spread under your feet," Catty said, surprising them and, judging by her expression, herself.

"What's that?" Lars asked, a little sharply.

"A poem by Yeats. It just came back to me."

"Hard little feet," Lidia added. "A poem by Neruda."

"More to the point, what do podiatrists say about it?" Lars retorted.

"It's not that bad, Lars." Lidia stood up to demonstrate, hobbling down the aisle. She fell back in her seat. "Shit. It feels that bad."

"Well, we're going around on horse-drawn carriages again tomorrow," Catty said. "You can skip whatever else is on."

Haynes handed Lidia a bottle of water. "Hydrate. Relax." He put his hand on her arm. She closed her eyes.

Back at the hotel, Catty prepared a shallow bath sprinkled with Epsom salts for Lidia's semi-pierced foot. She'd done it for Lars, too; he had meticulously scoured the tub with bleach he'd ordered from housekeeping afterwards.

"I could open a podiatrist's office by now," Catty said. "The water's quite hot, but you need that."

"Scalding!" Lidia pulled her throbbing foot away. The puncture looked fairly insignificant, but it didn't feel insignificant. "Oh, all right. And I'm almost ready to steal one of your Marlboros."

"If you must. But you gave up smoking twenty years ago."

"Twenty-three." She lowered her foot into the tub. It pulsated for a bit, and then began to feel better.

Catty heated up water in the kettle included with the room and prepared instant coffee. After adding powdered milk to the first mug, she handed it to Lidia. "Here you go."

"This is the life," Lidia said. "We are a crippled lot, aren't we?"

"You mean differently abled. Yes, we are!" Catty gave her low-throated laugh. "You and Lars with your feet, me with my trick knee, Mrs. Hills who looks like she's already expired, Ward Wong with his bad back, and—"

"Mr. Poison. With a hot poker up his ass."

"He's certainly living up to his nickname. A scowl for every occasion."

"Old redneck. My foot feels absolutely healed now, Catty."

"As the resident expert, I say don't get your hopes up too soon. Lars said the same thing. Half an hour later he was grimacing and cursing."

"Stop. I'll be fine."

10

LIDIA WAS NOT FINE the next day. She had to hobble to the tour bus at the usual departure time of 9:00 a.m. Luxury vehicle though it was, it reminded her of the school bus she'd taken as a kid, climbing in blurry-eyed, sometimes still in the dark, on chilly mornings.

Thila told them that their carriage ride had been switched to the afternoon and instead they were off to a crafts market—the largest in Namyan, even larger than the market where Catty had gotten lost. Lars, Catty, Haynes, and a couple of the others opted to hang out at the hotel but Lidia, against advice, went because Thila said there would be folk musicians at the market and when it came to recondite art, she was a moth to the flame.

"Fuck! I'm fucked," she said—to herself—at the market after learning that the musicians were at the far end of the cavernous space. But Thila found her a walking stick, quite attractive, and bargained the price down for her, and Lidia stumped her way along like Mrs. Hills, past goods that looked like those they'd seen before, until she arrived at last to the far end of the market.

As there was nowhere to sit, she leaned on her stick and told herself to suck it up. It was impossible for her to tell if the musician plucking a stringed box that was curved like a tusk was playing well or badly. And were the sour-pickle sounds he produced supposed to be happy or sad? A singer, a young girl, joined him, adding her own vinegar. Visually, they were impressive. The lute player, darker and rougher-looking than most Namyanese she'd seen, wore a sky-blue cloth around his head that stood up in tufts like horns and the brown cloth draping his loins was, Lidia thought, like a caveman's animal skin. She was enchanted and wished like hell she'd remembered to bring her sketchbook. His body curved around his tusk instrument and when he smiled, those teeth that he retained were deeply rust-colored from a lifetime of betel nut. He was the beast and the black-eyed girl, with swirls of that white paste decorating her cheeks and forehead, was the beauty.

But there was a play within the play that fascinated Lidia even more. Behind the musician and singer was a tiny dwelling, a plastic tarp draped over bamboo stilts. Before it, a tiny girl with a veil of fine black hair stirred the ground with a stick and a woman fanned a fire. The musician's family's cozy abode? Lidia closed her eyes, both to memorize the scene and to take in the unfamiliar sounds and rhythm. As she focused, they seemed to become more coherent. And full of longing.

"Would you move, would you move, would you move!"

Lidia felt a hard push from behind and her eyes flew open. She saw the little girl stop twirling her stick to stare, and she dropped her own stick, staggering, all of which happened in either seconds or a drawn-out sequence, she couldn't tell.

She jerked her head around and came face to face with Clint Hodges.

"You *shoved* me!" She noticed she was having difficulty speaking.

"Three times I asked you to move over. Three times! But you just stand there blocking the view like usual, so I missed the shot of that woman chopping the monkey's head off."

"Chopping the monkey's head off?" Lidia could but repeat.

"Yes!" intervened Betsy Hodges, pointing at the hut. "And cutting it up to boil it in that pot. *For food*," she added on a scandalized downbeat.

When life seems nonsensical, don't try to fight it; that was Lidia's maxim. She looked over at the hut and saw a bloody heap of some small animal on a plank by the cookpot. She would have the last laugh: Hodges had missed his photo op, but she would be able to draw it. But her anger surged and she wanted to punch him for laying his hands on her. She, who had never hit anyone in her life. Okay, those couple of roughhousing experiences on the playground; and the time she pinched her annoying Mexican cousin so hard she cried, and then there was the one and only time, during the height of her daughter's teenage rebellion phase, when she slapped Lily. Not hard, and it was only temporarily satisfying, quickly followed by deep shame. And she had seen fights, once between hands at Tío Pancho's ranch in Sonora, from which her mother pulled her away quickly. Most memorably, the one she saw after she'd moved to what was then called Spanish Harlem in her twenties—a street fight between two women. She heard it first, raw screams and bystanders egging them on. She'd stood on the pavement, transfixed, as one woman, with blood streaming down her face, held up a clump of her opponent's hair as a trophy. Sick to her stomach, Lidia had run away.

"Don't you *ever* put your hands on me again, asshole," she said to Clint Hodges quietly. But she couldn't do more. She couldn't hit Clint Hodges.

Betsy raised her arms in protest. Circles of perspiration darkened her camp shirt arms. "How dare you talk to my husband like that!"

Lidia swirled to Betsy. "He *assaulted me!*" She flapped her hands dismissively, retrieved her walking stick, and stumped off.

Anger gave her a power-walker's gait, with no sense of pain in her foot, not even a twinge. She felt she could have walked all the way back to the hotel on adrenaline.

* *

Later, on the bus back to the hotel for lunch, Clint slumped in a seat by himself at the back, waving Betsy away. She seemed only too happy to go. He watched her through half-closed eyes as she sat next to—and immediately began chattering with—that woman with all the doodads on her cap. Tammy. For a man his age, Tammy meant the wet dream of Debbie Reynolds at the drive-in. This Tammy reminded him of that Melissa McCarthy in the movie Betsy had tried to make him watch.

Clint closed his eyes. Maybe he had tapped that woman a little hard. Nah, he couldn't be bothered with Monday morning quarterbacking. She was always in the way, she and her snotty friends! He gritted his teeth as the sensation came over him, more frequent now, of his insides being squeezed out like an old tube of toothpaste. The only things keeping him going now were the damn pills, the beer the doc didn't want him to drink, and this last photo project. He knew it was the last one, although Betsy wouldn't hear of it.

When they arrived back at the hotel, the Hodgeses went to their suite to "freshen up," as Betsy always called it. Clint plopped down in the one armchair and waited for the lecture. (This irritated him. They'd paid for two people, so why was there just one decent chair?) Betsy sat on the spindly desk chair.

"What were you thinking?" she asked.

Hell, she knows the answer to that, he thought. They'd been married since the beginning of time, more than forty years. Clint looked at her. Like watching an old rerun on the tube. You don't really look at it anymore, just through it. She had on that blue camp shirt that was tight around her meaty forearms, those navy-blue pants with the elastic waist, and those clumpy old Skechers. She started patting her face the way she did when she was upset.

Here it comes, he thought.

"You promised you'd control yourself, you promised! What if somebody saw you do that?"

"Plenty of people saw." He sat back with a groan. "It was just a tap. Anyway, we'll never see these people again once this trip is over. Betsy, I'm tired. Stomach," he explained. Usually that was enough to shut her up. But she said, "Of course it's upset. Mine is too." Then darn if he didn't go to sleep on her, just like that. She heard his thin snore and got up from her uncomfortable chair. She'd go down to the lobby, be pleasant, bring back something Clint could eat when he woke up.

At lunch, Haynes sat next to Lidia. "So what did you see in the market? Anything worth buying?"

"Nothing new. A guy was playing a lute thing shaped like a horn. I mean a tusk. And this girl was singing. Kind of like Mississippi delta blues, Namyanese-style."

She felt eyes on her. The Borens, midway down the table. She looked back. *You were there. I saw you. And you saw what he did. And you did nothing.*

The next day, Ted and Franklin Leibitz-Kai settled into the seats across from Lidia on the bus. Still working on exorcising Mr. Poison from her consciousness, she decided to divert herself by sketching—and eavesdropping on—"the boys," which was as close to a nickname as Lars could get for the perennially youthful-looking couple.

She flipped open her sketchbook, readied her pencils, and sneaked sideways glances. Ted was all-American, fit in that blurred California way. And he was the serious one, organized and precise. Franklin, who she thought might be Polynesian or Filipino with possibly a dash of Hispanic thrown in, was zanier, a shopaholic who paired with Sally Lattimore at the frequent shopping opportunities. At their group "orientation" cocktail, Ted had informed them that they'd gotten hitched—his word—the week same-sex marriage became legal in California. At which Franklin had smiled angelically. Lidia, seated next to Clint, had heard him murmur to Betsy, "I wouldn't have clocked that white guy for a homo."

Ted and Franklin bore the faint air of resignation that long-married couples seem to, Lidia observed on closer inspection, and she remembered with a pang that intermittent sense of suffocation she'd felt with Felipe, despite all the pluses. At the moment, both Ted and Franklin were grousing.

Her pencil worked busily. Just visible from where she sat was the little bald patch at the back of Ted's head. Franklin still had all of his hair, lustrous and black. She decided he was definitely younger than the ex-firefighter.

"What did you buy this time?" Ted said with forbearance.

Lidia heard the rustle of paper.

"Christ, it's moldy!"

"It's an *antique*," said Franklin.

"You believe that? You're so . . ."

Their voices fell to a murmur, and Lidia could hear no more. It was clear from their body language that they made up quickly, though. She remembered that part, too.

"Oh, you. I feel your angry heart beating in your luscious chest." Franklin had a tinkly laugh.

Kiss and make up. Lidia shoved her sketchbook aside to indulge in a brief flurry of sadness. *Is this self-pity?* she asked herself, schooled as she was in AA's "character defects." *Because there's no one.* She sighed. *Oh, stop it. So life's unfair, what's new.*

In the late afternoon, Lidia went to the cool lobby with *Fatal Fjord*, her paperback that featured a Norwegian female detective who was also a judo expert and had the gloomy Nordic take on life Lidia found strangely comforting to read about. She had got to the bit where the prime minister was confronted with steamy S&M photos by her deputy, who the PM belatedly realized was working for the Russians, when Haynes approached.

"Haven't had much chance to talk to you lately. Been busy getting intel. You?"

"Intel?" She laughed. Like he was a character in *Fatal Fjord*.

"The trip after the trip."

"Oh, right, of course. I've been . . . preoccupied."

"Good book?" he asked.

"Not really." She wavered. Should she tell him about Mr. Poison? Nah.

Klaus ordered a beer. She watched him. He was lean, with long legs and long feet encased in those native sandals. Still fit, skin a little crepey now. Slight man boobs. Reflexively, she fingered the small tire that had attached itself to her waist after menopause and had no intention of going away. She flipped open to a fresh page of her sketchbook.

"Don't tell me you intend to draw me."

"I do."

He raised his eyebrows, ordered another beer and an iced tea for her, and lit a cigarillo. Lidia asked for one for herself.

"You smoke? I figured you were too health-conscious for that."

"I can be inconsistent when I want to be."

"Rebel, huh?"

"In my own way, yes."

Lidia drew.

"Is this gonna be porn?"

"Haynes!" Abruptly, she asked, "Why'd you leave Germany and come to America?"

"The Vaterland? Okay. Being biracial in a super white country? *Rhineland bastards*, they used to call us. And there were quite a few of us after the war, gifts of the American GIs—black, white, Asian, Latino, the whole ball of wax. Oh and they called us *koter*. Which is German for the n-word."

"Assholes. I got called 'beaner' a lot. Not the same, but . . ."

"On the same page."

"At show and tell one year, the teacher asked if I was going to do the Mexican hat dance or sing La Cucaracha." She shrugged. "I started to cry. My parents listened to *Elvis*."

He stretched out a leg. "Tell me about it. See this ankle? Scar's pretty faint now. Got cut outside a biergarten in Berlin by some skinheads. I was blitzed or I might have killed 'em. I was sick of their shit and since I had a US passport because of my dad—who I never knew, by the way—soon as I could, I caught a plane to New York."

"So you met your dad in the States?"

"Nope, never did. He was incarcerated at the time. Later, he just disappeared, another statistic. But his brother, my uncle Ted, had always kept in touch, invited me to visit. Didn't know I was coming to stay." Haynes laughed. "Long story short, he and my long-suffering aunt Marsha took me into the family. And gave me a job; they had an appliance store. Ask me anything about refrigerators, washing machines, dishwashers. There I was, suddenly living in Bed-Stuy, a blackish guy with blue eyes and a Kraut accent. Nobody knew what to make of me. And I sure as hell didn't know what to make of them. I didn't belong. Well, I was used to that. I learned English in Germany. They all made fun of my accent. Everybody."

"I think your accent's cute."

"Cute!"

"Yes, and I bet lots of women have told you that."

"Never." He smiled.

"My Mexican cousins in Chihuahua teased me mercilessly about my Spanish accent. They used to hold me down and tickle me until I'd speak 'el español como una gringa pura.' They said my accent was so *precioso*. Cute."

"And last time I checked, you were a female, so that's cool."

"Don't be sexist." *Are you flirting with him? Don't do this. You can't do this.*

"Speaking of cute, at the risk of being labeled a sexist again, those are some cute freckles. Mexicans got freckles?"

"They're from my mom's side. The Irish in me."

Lidia felt the hot tug in her stomach. She thought that had vanished from her life. Now, just like that, it was back.

"So tell me more about Mexico, your Mexican cousins. I've never been there."

"What? You've been, like, everywhere."

"Too touristy."

"Oh no. Not my Mexico. Off the beaten path. Witchcraft and food you never get in restaurants. And the art!"

"So maybe I'll go to your Mexico."

"You should, really. That's where I realized I was going to be an artist. My cousins, the ones that teased me about my accent? They were actually very nice. When I was sixteen, they took me all over the country in their powder-blue 1965 Pontiac."

"Sweet. Until it breaks down."

"Oh yeah. It did. But we managed to get all the way from Chihuahua down to Oaxaca and Chiapas. Stayed in villages, slept in hammocks. Mixtecs, Zapotecs, Tzotzils, Tzetzals. Everything is art there. The way they decorate their houses, their clothes, pots. I saw my first Rufino Tamayo paintings in Oaxaca. He was a brother mestizo. Zapotec and Spanish and whatever else he had going on. Fantastic painter, the sun was just infused in his colors. And then I saw some works by Kahlo, and later in Spain, Goya —my all-time fave—and in Germany, Beckman and Schiele—your countrymen."

"Schiele's Austrian," Haynes said.

"Hey, you know who he is! And then, when I moved to New York, Alice Neel was huge for me. I could go on and on. Be quite boring about it."

"Nah."

"Anyway, it doesn't matter now, I guess."

"Doesn't matter?"

"I stopped doing art a few years ago." She tapped the drawing she'd just laid aside. "Well, maybe I'll get into it again. But things have been… I went through a difficult time. I had to get a day job and I was lucky to find work with a textbook publisher that likes my illustrations. Then about a year ago, out of the blue, my great-aunt left me some money. Not a lot but, you know, breathing room. So here I am."

"On your own, huh? Been married?"

"Yes," she said.

"Me too, twice. My first ex-wife died a few years ago."

"I'm sorry."

"It was hard on my sons. Cancer. We fought all the time, but nobody deserves to die like that."

Go on, Lidia thought, now's the moment for you to tell him. *Say it.* She swallowed. "I—"

Haynes slapped his hands on his thighs. "Back to the here and now. You *are* drawing again. Look at your sketchbook?"

She hesitated, nodded. He leaned over, turned the pages. There weren't many. He paused at two, one of the immensely long, curving line of Namyanese people waiting to see the Buddha's toe at that huge golden pagoda their first day on the trip. The people in the foreground were sharply drawn; behind them, the line became a slow blur until the tail of the line was gilded shadow. The other was the little girl who'd been playing with a stick in the dirt at the market, her eyes wide with fear.

"I'm just getting going again," Lidia said.

"They're good. Really good."

She smiled at his suppressed surprise; as a woman artist, she'd grown—not used to it, no, but she was no longer rattled by it. Much.

Haynes put down the sketchbook and looked around the empty

lobby. Not quite empty, though. In deep shade not so far from them, with the practiced invisibility of the very old, Mrs. Hills watched as he leaned in and kissed her.

He tasted of beer and spices and she of tea. They both tasted of cigars.

They moved apart. "Sorry. Don't want to freak you out," he said.

"Oh. You didn't. Don't." But her hands shook as she thought about how long it had been.

Haynes slapped his hands lightly on his chair. "Shall we get out of this mausoleum? Take a walk?"

The hotel grounds were huge and strange and, without the crowds that were clearly meant to have been there, it could be another Gaban relic. Almost. They went down two flights of stairs, past the terraces flanking the two huge, empty pools with beach recliners garlanded with umbrellas, the blocks of suites to either side, and the expensive-looking villas carved into low hills.

After a few minutes, they came upon the flat plain that led eventually to the thousands of ancient pagodas.

"Hey, you didn't bring your camera," Lidia said.

"But you brought your sketchbook."

The birds in the scrub were loud in the busy hour near twilight, their colors as they flashed by relieving the dry season's monotones of brown and olive green. Haynes pointed out a small mud hut in the middle of the scrub.

They had to stoop to go inside and once there, there was only a long flat stone covered with bundles of wood and feathers and little mounds of fruit crawling with ants.

"One of those spirit houses?" Haynes asked.

"Must be, it's like the ones we saw in the corners of pagodas. *Na-sans* they call them."

"Wish I had my camera."

"You should come back."

They backed out of the hut and walked on a while and then they stopped and came together. He was the one who pulled away, holding her by the forearms.

"Pretty lady. Want to come back here with me later? I'll take some pictures and you can draw."

"Pretty tough to draw in the dark."

"Light's not a problem. There's a three-quarter moon tonight."

She thought for a millisecond. "Okay."

Returning after dinner went more slowly—Haynes was laden down with equipment—but there was enough moonlight to make their way.

"It's ugly, this place," he said, stopping before the *na-san*. No attempt at ornamentation had been made, no plaster or paint. "But, definitely going on the blog." They went on to a flattish piece of earth nearby, and he spread a blanket he'd brought from the hotel on the ground. "Wanna check out the stars before we crawl in there?"

"Speaking of crawling." Lidia shivered. "There were ants all over the fruit in there when we went in before. Probably all kinds of creatures in there."

"I'll be the shock troops. Look at that sky. There's a shooting star, see it?"

"I do! And the constellations are upside down! The Big Dipper, Orion. Only ones I know."

"An upside-down sky."

A memory reared up of watching stars with someone—when was it, thirty years ago? No, *forty*. She'd been twenty, a baby, with a boy she barely knew. College students, interning on a dig in southern Mexico. They'd slept on hammocks in a barn where rats rustled in the dark, eaten pretty much beans and tortillas, and fetched and carried for the one-armed, pot-smoking archeologist in charge. Lidia's job was to label bits of pottery and stow them in boxes. Occasionally, there had been bones. Human bones.

She'd loved all of it except the barn rats, this wild, mysterious place in her father's homeland. Being off the grid had been heaven— no classes, no papers to write, no drinking cheap pitchers of beer with her friends and arguing about whether to go to some party or back to the dorm to crash, only numbering finds from the stony earth. This site contained, their one-armed archeologist told them, the only *cenote*, or natural well, in the state of Chiapas, and it went on and on, huge overgrown hills containing pyramids yet to be unearthed. Surrounded by jungle.

A couple of times, they went in the archeologist's Jeep to town for supplies. Some of the peasant men at the market wore hats with long colored streamers and shirts made out of sacking with bright-striped sleeves, the women wore heavily embroidered white *huipiles* and colored yarn woven in their sleek black hair. Male and female carried loads of firewood or sacks of meal using tumplines around their foreheads. Lidia and the other students and the archeologist watched them as they ate tamales and drank beer and the local moonshine from rickety tables stamped with Coca-Cola. As evening fell, men fell with a quiet thud to the ground, sleeping where they landed.

At the end of the month, Lidia and the boy whose name she had long ago forgotten went to a cornfield where columns and bits of pyramids—stelae—lay scattered in the stalks. They smoked some local weed—she remembered it was strong—and then had sex in the field, with a vastness of brilliant stars in the blue-black sky blinking above them, almost seeming to press upon them.

Was it going to happen forty years on? Sex in a field under the stars again? They'd need to be careful about hips, knees, backs, she thought, and began to laugh.

"What's so funny?"

"I was remembering how back in college, I went on a dig—archeology site—in southern Mexico," she said. "Sometimes I'd go out at night with a candle and sit in the cornfields and draw these carved limestone pillars, just lying there, kind of glowing in the dark. Bits of old pyramids. All I need now is some Mexican moonshine and a joint and I'll be ready to go again." She pulled out her sketchbook and pencils.

"How about some wine?"

"Yeah, no, I don't drink, remember? You go ahead though." Something shifted inside her, that tug again. Other than her cat, child, and friends, who had she touched in recent years? Once, Catty had come to the apartment, and after Lidia had filled her in on the latest bad news Catty had thrown her arms around her and started to cry. It was the only time Lidia could remember she and Catty having hugged. Or cried together.

She lay on the blanket, her arms under her head.

He lay down beside her. "Look at that! Did you see it? Another shooting star!"

Then they looked away from the fabulous sky, turned to each other, and kissed and rolled around on the blanket.

11

ED HAD SET OFF for the field too, weighed down by his sturdy backpack containing notebook, pens, glass pots, Ziploc bags, hand lenses, various nets and traps for catching his quarry, two bottles of water, and one of the Power Bars he'd brought from the States.

Ann had sent him cheerfully on his way, planning to watch *Julie & Julia*, scheduled on some BBC affiliate, the first thing in English other than newscasts offered on the trip. She'd already seen the movie (though not, of course, with Hindi subtitles), but she felt almost desperate to watch it again, the tube being her major source of escape back home. Ed had urged her to agree to this trip to "turn your thoughts," as he put it, from her mother's death. But it hadn't been working that way. At any moment—while, say, admiring a golden Buddha, eating the weird food, looking at exotic handicrafts in markets—the reality that her mother was gone rose up, along with the contradictory sense of being dragged down.

Ed was no use, even watching TV with her. He had no interest in anything but documentaries about creatures, the more flamboyant and weird the better. "Nature knows how to do extravagance," he'd said just that evening during their ritual of an after-dinner Coke with a splash of rum. "But," he'd added tolerantly, "I love the plain Janes too."

Ann wanted to talk about her grief process, and about the practicalities, too—him helping her clear out her mother's stuff, for instance, which she was, of course, dreading. "Plain Janes," she repeated dully. She suspected he was talking about her as well as his creepy-crawlies. Luxurious though their suite was, there was nowhere to sit except squeezed next to each other on the upholstered loveseat, so Ed had to crane his neck to talk to Ann. And moving his head caused the right side of his face to ache more than usual.

"I've got to find a *Vespa mandarinia*," he told her.

"You already saw that thing. You pushed Clint Hodges out of its way!"

"It's not a *thing*," he said, as she knew he would. "Things are inanimate. I need a specimen. Proof," he reminded her, "for the paper."

Oh yes, the paper he was writing for the Entomology Society annual dinner. As he went on about it, she tried to let her mind drift, but unless she stuck her fingers in her ears, she was going to hear all about those Vespa thingies. About their neat, organized lives in highly cooperative, arguably *socialist* colonies in which every one of them—even the queen—fed and cared for the young. "They select their prey only from the class *Anthopilia*, kill them, chew them up, and regurgitate the pap into the babies' throats," Ed explained.

"Throats?" Ann pondered this for a couple of seconds. Well, they would have throats, wouldn't they? And stomachs. The thought made hers lurch. She had been consistent throughout their courtship and marriage in feigning interest in his bees, ants, wasps, butterflies, moths, and what have you, but it was like pushing the rock up the hill, over and over. And where she drew the line was Ed's recurring and insistent theme on the many, many similarities between insects and humans. She simply could not abide thinking of them as anything other than bugs. She sighed, more than ready for Ed to depart with his jars. Plus, the movie was about to start.

But then they got onto the topic of the various people in the tour group, and she grew a bit more animated. She was worried that Clint Hodges might be a wife beater. "I mean, he pushed that Lidia *forcefully* at the market! I hate to think what he might get up to in private!" she said. "Betsy seems a little frantic, though she's a nice woman."

Ed grunted noncommittally. Gossip didn't interest him, she knew, but who else could she talk to?

"And the Vondervilles . . . They barely talk to me," she said. "I'm done trying to be nice to them. I mean, who do they think they are?"

Walking away from the immense hotel at last, Ed entered the scrubland. It spread for miles in the soft purple moonlit night; in the distance, he made out the foothills of mountains, rising jaggedly and distantly into cloud-cloaked, eroded peaks. He hoped there would be even a modest grove out in the field, since his quarry preferred to curl under a pile of leaves or cram into a nest in a rotted tree. But failing that, he could look for coopted rodent holes.

He crept along so as not to disturb his prey, stopping occasionally to study and mark his map at likely sightings of *V m* that he could return to early the next morning. There were bound to be all manner of *Lepidoptera* too. As he paused to drink from his water bottle, he saw before him what could be a gigantic wasp's nest, but as he got closer, it turned out to be a human construction. Still, it was interesting, stuck there in the middle of nowhere. Most likely an abandoned hut. He thought he'd have a look. As he moved forward, he made out a dark shape on the ground ahead of the hut. Gradually, he realized it was a blanket with shapes on it.

A lifetime of training in stillness (like when he'd come upon the rare *Caloeciaentima juvenalis* last year on an expedition in the mountains of their new home state of Arizona) allowed Ed to creep forward without being detected. It took willpower not to burst out with something like "hey!" or "what the fuck?" in response to what he was convinced, though it was dim on the ground—the moon and starry sky had been temporarily blocked by clouds—was the sight of two *Homo sapiens* apparently copulating *en plein air.*

Rooting around in his bag, he realized he'd left his binoculars behind. For obvious reasons, at least Ed thought so, he recalled a video of the mating ritual of *V ms.* Their bodies were curled and they threw their heads back and waved their feelers for up to a full minute. And then, as the female lay shuddering, the male flew away forever. Not that different from humans, when you thought about it.

He decided to back away; he did so as noiselessly as one of those braves in *The Last of the Mohicans,* he thought. But would a Mohican yelp when he stumbled over a rock? Fortunately, Ed sustained only a bruise and muffled his cries as he continued moving until he was sure he was out of sight of the blanket and its busy occupants.

Lidia and Haynes froze on the blanket, where, in point of fact, they had not been copulating. Yet. The shrieks they'd just heard sounded like they came from a big animal. Were there dangerous beasts in this part of Namyan's bush—tigers, elephants?

And, oh God, Lidia thought illogically: snakes.

She leapt to her feet. As did Haynes.

An unpleasant thought occurred to Lidia. "What if that was a *person?*" She dropped back down on the blanket.

Haynes sat beside her and ran a hand down her arm. "That would be better, wouldn't it, than a charging beast? Anyway, what or who-ever it was seems to have left."

"Yeah, just twittering noises out there now." She shivered at a thought. "Ed Boren goes out at night looking for bugs."

"Lidia . . . We weren't *doing* anything."

"Well, I feel like a teenager caught with her boyfriend in a parked car."

"Is that a bad thing?" he said, smiling.

"It is if Dad materializes. If you're a girl."

"Let's check out the spirit hut." He busied himself with the tripod and lights and handed her candles and matches from his pack. She took a deep breath and went into the hut again. Inside, she stuck the candles around the perimeter and lit them before sitting against a wall with her legs crossed, trying not to think about the creatures crawling around, probably everywhere.

She made herself focus on the altar's flat stone, the feathers and leaves and fallen petals left as offerings. As her eyes became accustomed to the dim light, she made out something that hadn't been there when she'd looked around in the afternoon. Something on a bed of leaves, reddish, glistening.

She inched forward on her knees until she was next to it. And then she screamed.

Haynes rushed in, on his hands and knees. "What, snake, rat?"

Lidia shook her head. Clutching the sketchbook and pencils she'd brought, she started backing up. "Don't look at it."

"What?" Haynes said. "Why?"

"It's so sad."

"Will you tell me what you saw?"

"It's . . . a fetus."

"Shit. You're right."

She crawled out of the narrow opening and sat on the blanket. Haynes manhandled the equipment in through the narrow opening. Lidia heard him rustling around, and she heard more and more tiny adjustments to the apparent silence of the surrounding bush, like an ant orchestra tuning up. She wrapped her arms around her legs and screwed her eyes shut.

After what seemed a long time, Haynes came out.

"Tell me you didn't take pictures of that."

He stowed his camera gear. "I did, as a matter of fact. Yes, it's sad. But what I do is document whatever it is I find. I don't edit reality. You understand that!"

"Yes, but—"

"It's the people's temple, and that fetus was placed on the altar. It's their way of dealing with death. So I filmed it."

"It," she whispered. "It was going to be a baby girl."

When Ed got back, Ann was asleep. He watched her as he got ready for bed. She was an impressive sleeper, throwing herself into it as passionately as a child. When they were younger, he'd often wished she would throw more of that passion his way. Her cheeks and closed eyelids were downy and flushed like a child's too, and her cropped, steel-gray hair was obscured by the soft pillow she always brought along on trips. He watched her like he watched his specimens before he turned away, thinking about when he was a teenager, far more afraid of girls than spiders.

He'd been bullied from the time he could remember because of his hemifacial macrosomia; in his case, the caved-in right side of his jaw, which several surgeries had modified but could not erase. Kids, of course, had zeroed in on it in their savage way. The boys had thrown snowballs packed with rocks, slammed into him on purpose at recess, stolen his sandwiches. But girls had been worse—their secretive little packs, their giggles, and, when they got older, their erasure of him with their blank faces. He'd had the comfort of his collections waiting in the basement at home, where he could brood about payback. And there had been payback, of the sneaky variety. Kids had suspected him of being a rat but could never prove it. Now, remembering what Lars and Lidia had said about him when he was scouting for *Lepidoptera*, it came over him like thunder: a desire for revenge.

Ann stirred. "Oh, you're back. Catch any killer bees—I mean, wasps?" She yawned. "I must have just dozed off." She looked at her watch. "It's only ten fifteen. God, this trip tires me out."

"I caught something better than a killer wasp," Ed said.

"Really? I thought that was the crown jewel or something."

"I caught that Spanish woman and Klaus Haynes. *Going at it* in a field. Oh, let's just call it what it was: screwing."

Ann sat bolt upright, her eyes blinking rapidly. "Ed, what? They're senior citizens."

He knew he was fudging a bit—he couldn't be absolutely sure what he'd seen due to the dimness—but it couldn't be anything else. She'd laughed at him, and Ann. She'd *mocked them*. It was her turn.

Just one more to go: Lars Vonderpoop. He'd get his, too, soon as Ed could figure out how.

12

"WHAT ELSE HAVE YOU been up to, Peggy?" Tammy Steinman trilled at her laptop, beaming, as Tim entered the room. She smiled and cooed as their granddaughter, slumped in a chair, made lunges of excitement, pointing at her Brownie vest. "Another badge? Way to go, Sweet Pea, you're awesome." Tammy pointed at her cap. "I've got another button for you, see it?" She leaned in closer. "Oh, that's the Buddha. He's like God to the people here. They bring him pretty flowers and fruit. No, they didn't kill him, you're thinking of the Christians, honey."

Peggy gabbled and wheezed about her Brownie badges. Tammy found it easy to understand the eleven-year-old. Just concentrate, she'd told the others. But even Kelly found her daughter's speech opaque and of course caring for her was difficult, although for Tammy, Peggy's challenges had given her a new purpose in life. Tammy researched, advocated, and often paid for therapies for her only, differently abled, grandchild. She no longer convinced herself that a cure was imminent and maybe not even desirable for a person with Down syndrome: Peggy was a sweet girl and she loved her for who she was.

Tammy had her bad days, of course, when she felt weary of the whole business. Tim could tell right away when she was low and he'd learned it was best to leave her alone then. Tammy had told him once that she felt in her dark moods like the kid in the folk tale who had to keep his finger in the hole in the dike to ward off a flood and save the whole city. That she could never take her finger away.

Peggy and her dad, Mark, who was Tammy and Tim's only child, were both challenged, or differently abled, or whatever the PC term currently in vogue was. When Tammy was down, she sometimes forgot these carefully crafted circumlocutions in favor of the stark and—yes, she admitted it—cruel words of her childhood. Mark was a drunk, instead of a person who had substance use disorder, and Peggy was like one of those kids in the Jerry Lewis telethons about whom Lewis had once memorably said, "God goofed and made a cripple."

Raised as a secular Jew, Tammy believed in tradition, but as for God, why had he allowed her only grandchild to be grievously afflicted? Not to mention her only child, a sullen boy who'd become a sullen drinker. Plus a daughter-in-law who seemed to keep going on high-octane resentment. After visits with them, Tammy was hollowed out and tended to snap at Tim. A really bad sign was when she called him by his actual name, Heraclitus, which he hated. No one else but his paternal grandparents had called him that. Heraclitus Timothy Steinman Junior. Anyway, even though Tim had retired, he didn't spend much time with Tammy; he was usually at the golf club or else in his home office.

An only child, Tim had always felt like a disappointment. He'd had a needy and nervous, though kindly, mother, and a depressed, angry father who'd wanted an athlete for a son but gotten Tim, who was clumsy and preferred board and card games. For a long while, he'd had no friends. The kids at school, almost all Gentiles, had mostly ignored him, except for a few who'd picked on him when he'd been absent for the Jewish holidays. But then he'd found the afterschool math club, and acceptance.

When he graduated from college with a degree in mechanical engineering, his father had been absent from the ceremonies. His mother, though, had praised him breathily.

"We're so proud of you!" she'd told him.

"Yeah. So where's Dad?"

"You know he couldn't get out of that business thing."

Tammy had clearly been wrapping up her Facetime session with Peggy when Tim entered the suite. He had almost timed his return right, as he was in no mood to interface with his granddaughter. But "almost doesn't cut it"—he could hear his father's disappointed, scolding voice across the decades. When he didn't make the football team. When he came in second in a big math competition. When he was wait-listed at Cornell and ended up going to the University of Illinois.

"Oh look! Here's Paw-Paw. Do you have pictures for Sweet Pea, Paw-Paw?"

Tim released an audible sigh and sat in the chair Tammy had just vacated. "This may take a couple minutes to upload, all right, Peggy?"

The girl bobbed her head. Tim swiped at his phone. What he really wanted was a martini.

Another monastery? Lidia sighed inwardly. They'd seen one, surely that was enough, though they all agreed that the experience of seeing those exotic bald monks and their charges, so serene-seeming in their austere abode, had been uplifting. But, Thila explained, they were going to a nunnery this time, presumably of interest to at least half the group. A modest cluster of wooden buildings set back from a busy road, bright with, this time, rose-colored robes on women and girls of every age, all with shaved heads like their male counterparts. Ordinary black-haired Namyanese women were there too, a lot of them, chatting, coming and going with pots of food. A common scene in Namyan, where Buddhism permeated everyone's lives—except when you scraped the surface. And there were fringe groups: Christians, Muslims, Hindus, Taoists.

In downtown Gonyang, the Hodgeses and the Borens had visited the Baptist brick church with its neon sign outside that declared "Jesus Saves" in English and Namyanese. Afterward, they'd marveled loudly about the hymn books in mysterious squiggles. Lars hadn't gone, but he had read about the English missionaries who'd introduced Christianity, scoring a coup with the Hinchaks, one of the long-suffering minorities: they had converted en masse, no doubt to spite the Buddhist Namyanese who oppressed them. He'd explained all this to Lidia and Catty, along with the fact that there were some Catholics and Anglicans in Gonyang, too, and of course the Kinhaiese Muslims whose persecution was now an international scandal. But Buddhism, he said, prevailed, both in the ultra-nationalist form forged by the *Damawat* leaders, and the sturdy, apolitical form practiced by the peasants. Namyan universities had been turning out scholars who talmudically parsed the Buddha's writings and commentaries for hundreds of years. Buddhism was where the Namyanese found an intellectual scaffolding as well as a sense of the everlasting.

For a vacation or rehab, the Namyanese joined monasteries for a few weeks, months, years or the rest of their lives. Anyone, it seemed, might suddenly decide to go live in a monastery, shave their head, meditate, chant, and beg for meals on the street. Thila now told her group that she herself had spent some time in this very nunnery, as had other members of her family. She greeted the Mother Superior formally but affectionately. She led the group, after taking off their shoes, into a large, airy room where, she told them, the nuns would be happy to answer their questions.

Most of them lowered themselves awkwardly onto their rush mats; only Thila and the Leibitz-Kais assumed the lotus position. Before them, a row of rose-cloaked bald women and girls kneeled on a raised platform, smiling benignly.

"This feels like kindergarten nap time," Catty said, grouchy about her knees.

"I'm sure we are kindergartners next to them when it comes to spirituality," Lidia responded. "Maybe we'll learn something useful." Most of them had come of age when Alan Watts, Krishnamurti, Hari Krishna, and so on were popular, and she was sure some of them had done yoga or tai chi. Lidia certainly had. Her problem was she couldn't envision detachment without feeling a sense of letdown.

"You know I'd like to believe in something, but I can't," Catty said. "Raise your hand, Lidia, and impress Teacher."

She and Lidia had sparred for years, mostly benignly, about faith, God, and religion. Catty maintained that Christianity, with its Trinity, Resurrection, Virgin Birth, and Jesus as God and Man, was incomprehensible. Lidia, who to her own deep surprise had veered from indifference to regular attendance at what she always stressed was an "extremely liberal" Episcopal church, said that it might be impossible to make sense of, but that wasn't the point. She fell back on C.S. Lewis's line: either Jesus Christ was who he said he was, or he was a madman. "Well . . ." Catty had replied, with a meaningful look. But of course Buddhists had no such worries.

Before Lidia could think of a response to Catty, the head nun, in tortoiseshell glasses, said something in Namyanese in a soft but carrying voice.

"She inviting you to ask questions," Thila translated.

Catty nudged Lidia.

Just then, the first strain of "We're Off to See the Wizard" sliced through the quiet room. Tammy Steinman clambered to her feet, holding her phone. As she hurried off, they heard her say, "What? WHAT?" Then, silence.

Broken by Betsy Hodges. "I'd like to know, do Buddhists believe in God?"

The head nun smiled slightly after Thila translated. Glasses glinting, she said with practiced equanimity, "We seek to reach the divine nature within."

"Next question?" Thila asked.

"Well, do you believe in Jesus Christ?" Betsy persisted.

Whatever discussion might have ensued was stymied by sobs as Tammy stumbled in, hands covering her face. Tim jumped up and stiffly put a khaki-clad arm around her thick shoulders, clearly out of practice in doing so. Thila unfurled from her mat and hurried over to them without seeming to. Lidia had noticed how, during the small crises of this trip, Thila didn't lose her composure, although her facility in speaking English decelerated.

After a whispered conversation, while the nuns sat placidly and the group twitched on their mats, Thila said, "The Steinman grand-girl is in hospital after accident to head."

"What accident?" Betsy demanded.

"She got hit in the head and lost consciousness," Tim said. "She's in the hospital, that's all we know."

Another hushed conference. Thila said something rapidly in Burmese, then in English, "Madame Steinman ask, why such suffering is permitted of innocent dis-bodied child?"

"Disabled, you mean," said Betsy.

"Down syndrome," said Ann Boren solemnly.

Damn, thought Lidia. She wished she'd taken less mean delight in "Buttons," now that she knew she had a disabled and wounded granddaughter. She glanced at Lars, one of whose sons was wheelchair-bound with MS, but he was staring at the beaten earth floor.

The nuns, though, seemed unruffled by the scene before them. Lidia stared at the head nun to distract herself from guilt, finding her beautiful in the mostly unacknowledged way serene mature women are, the gloss of long experience rubbed into them. The nun's face was lined but shone like good old wood. In fact, all the nuns and even the little girls were beautiful and attentive but—detached. As if they had learned to float above the turbulence of life, which in Namyan included millennia of tyranny, repression, toil, want, disease, and a high mortality rate.

They waited to hear what the head nun would say to Tammy Steinman's anguished question.

The nun spoke and Thila translated. "She say, life is suffering. That it must be—ascended?"

Barton Liu, he who was forever interacting with his gadgetry and occasionally Haynes, said enthusiastically, "Transcended! Life must be transcended!" Everyone looked at him.

But the head nun had the last word, via Thila. "She say also, tend to your friend who has need."

With that, the nuns stood, bowed and filed out gracefully.

The group got to their feet. Outside, they found their shoes and walked to the bus. The air was heavier. Perhaps the long-awaited rainy season was approaching. In pounding rain, Lidia thought, those beaten-earth floors, so clean and, in places, swirled into flower patterns, would become sodden and muddy. And Ed Boren's bugs would gather in thick knots around lanterns at night, fatten on the growing crops, and reproduce at a frightening rate.

On the bus, Thila explained that rather than going on to the next stop on the tour, the legendary Lake Leini, they would return to the hotel in Gaban, which was much larger and would be able to make travel arrangements for the Steinmans. They could stop for lunch on their way, or head nonstop.

"Of course we'll skip lunch and go back," Sally Lattimore decreed suddenly with an authority Lidia found surprising. "Wouldn't it be heaven if we had something stronger than water to drink on the way?"

Up in the front of the bus, Catty declared, "Well! Poor Buttons."

Lidia shifted in the seat next to her. "I'm going to go talk to her."

Catty sighed. "She doesn't like us. But I'll come with you."

Hunched over, Tammy looked up in blank surprise when Catty and Lidia came to stand beside her. Tim looked out the window.

"We're so very sorry about your granddaughter," said Catty in the fluty, lady-of-the-manor tone she unconsciously adopted in uncomfortable settings.

Tammy blinked.

Lidia touched the woman's shoulder. "Is there anything I—we—can do?"

"No," she said, flinching. "Just *go back to that field.*"

They filed back to their seats.

"What was that all about?" Catty asked. "Go back to that field? Well, we tried."

"Very sad for the Buttons!" Lars put in from his seat across the aisle.

"Lars, she said the oddest thing to us."

"Don't repeat it," Lidia snapped. "She said it to me. And I don't feel like talking about it."

"Well!" said Catty.

"What is it?" Lars pressed.

"Please. Leave. Me. Alone." *God, that means they think . . . How do they know we were there? That noise: the beast, was it Tammy Steinman? I mean, what are the odds? But we weren't doing anything there. Oh, what does it matter? Their granddaughter is in a coma in the hospital.*

Then Lidia did something she only did in extremis: she took an Ativan that she'd tucked away from the bottle she'd brought along in case of an emergency—she had learned to have it handy during the last few years. She closed her eyes and waited for the foggy doze.

"Well, really," Catty began, "I—"

"Catty, my foot is acting up pretty bad."

"Lars, again?"

"It's throbbing." He removed his sneaker and sock, extended his foot into the aisle, and turned it to reveal the sole, no longer bleeding but still cracked like a dried-out riverbed and with little chartreuse, oozing sores.

"Lars, it's badly infected!" Catty beckoned Thila over, who took one look and said something to the driver. He made a dramatic U-turn, somehow avoiding the motorbikes, bicycles, pedestrians, and animals on the road and pulled to the side. Thila retrieved her medical kit and Catty, with shaking hands, applied disinfectant.

"We must get doctor," Thila announced.

Lars protested. "I'm all right! Just keep driving. Gotta get the Steinmans on their way."

Catty succumbed to one of her trances of anxiety. Lidia gauzily took in the commotion; she wished she had brought another Ativan to give her friend. Anyway, Catty must be taking something for her high anxiety already. Lidia well knew how she suffered from both named and nameless fears. Only a couple of days earlier, Catty had told her over iced tea, with an airiness that hadn't fooled either of them, that she wished she could get a brain transplant. "My body may be aging but it's working pretty well. But my head . . ."

"Personally? I'd go for a body transplant," Lidia had said, trying to make light of it. There were times in the past when she'd known Catty to retreat from the world for weeks at a time, ordering in food and sending out her laundry and ignoring the phone. Then Prozac and its offspring had come along and she'd gotten better. "Who would have thought forty could ever look so great?" Lidia went on. "Look, I'm sorry you're feeling blue. It will pass . . ."

"Yes," Catty responded, "and come back any time it feels like it." Rather viciously, she'd slapped the side of her chair. "I do wish I had different genes."

The driver started up the bus again. Lars closed his eyes and succumbed to a wincing doze. The others spoke in hushed tones. The bus whizzed past the familiar flat paddies of rice with peasants of both genders and all ages at work, preparing to plant a seeming infinity of rice seedlings. Ward Wong came to the front of the bus to confer with Thila. Lidia could hear just enough to know he was annoyed about the disruption to their schedule. She didn't hear Thila's response but he turtled back to his seat a minute later, frowning.

Back at the hotel, from which they'd checked out a few hours before, they had to wait to get rooms. Meanwhile, Thila attended to the Steinmans' flight arrangements. Their new rooms were smaller than before, as a large Chinese group had arrived, but no one was about to complain. Lidia sat in her little room with her book and a bottle of water, waiting for an update on Lars and the Steinmans. She wondered what Haynes was up to. She wondered if he was just an old player. *Stop*, she told herself.

She dozed off and had a dream about a delicate, bald Asian woman in a saffron-colored *logni* prostrated before a Buddha, made lumpen after thousands of applications of gold leaf (which, she realized in the dream, she had seen when awake in a pagoda). But the Buddha in the dream, she then realized, was covered not with gilt but shit. Immediately the dream shifted. She was walking in a green and leafy Central Park in Manhattan, when she came upon a bloody fetus at the base of a tree. She began to scream silently.

She woke up gasping and shivering. The cold air-conditioned room with its sealed windows made her feel as if she were incarcerated. She got up, washed her face vigorously, combed her tangled hair, put on a fresh shirt and pants, and went to Lars and Catty's room.

There, Lars lay in bed, his infected foot elevated on a mound of pillows, with pills and ointments adorning his bedside table. And beside him was a Namyanese nurse.

"What ho?" he greeted Lidia.

Catty emerged from the bathroom. "He's got a bacterial infection called impetigo. I looked it up on the web. Nasty but treatable. And of course he's dehydrated." She frowned. "He simply won't drink enough water." Catty seemed calmer, as people who are anxiety-ridden often can be in a crisis. "A doctor was here and gave him antibiotics. He says the main thing now is to monitor for fever. But it's gone down already, so hopefully he's over the worst of it."

"She was afraid it was some tropical superbug," Lars said. He looked jovial from the painkillers. "But since the doc says not, I should be shipshape by tomorrow. And by the way, Catherine, I'm hungry. Would you order a hamburger, rare?"

"You're having soup," Catty said.

Twenty minutes later, sandwiches and soup and Catty and Lidia's inevitable coffees were delivered. The nurse, Miss Cai, had a cup of tea. They watched the BBC and Lars threw bread pellets toward the set when the US President came on.

"Thug," he said.

"You *are* feeling better," Lidia said.

"Cloud Nine. Now, how long is that nurse staying here?"

"Lars, Miss Cai speaks English," Catty said.

"I beg your pardon," he said. "Well, I could use some help to the loo before you go, Miss Key."

Miss Cai stood up. "I help. I stay through the night."

"Really, Miss Key, not necessary."

"Miss *Cai*," Catty said. "Yes, necessary."

"All right, all right. But it's a bit awkward for you, Catherine, isn't it? Can you sleep with her here in the room?"

"I have two twin beds in my room, Catty," Lidia said. "You can stay with me and the nurse can call if she needs you."

"We-ell," Catty drawled, "That would be great. Sure you won't mind?"

"Of course not, I'm beat," Lidia said. "I'm just going to take a little walk later and get to bed early."

"I'll join you. I'll put a bag together and come to your room."

* *

Lidia was sound asleep at nine thirty when there was a knock at her door. Catty hurried to open it, sure it was the nurse with bad news about Lars. But it was Klaus Haynes. Holding a bouquet. A rather scraggly bunch of wildflowers he had obviously picked himself on the grounds.

"Mrs. Vonderville! I must have got the wrong room number."

"Who are you looking for?" Catty hid a smile.

"My room, of course." He fished his key card out. "Ah. Should have used my glasses. I'm down the hall."

"Right, well, good night then." Catty shut the door and got back into bed, where she resumed her reading of *The Emperor of All Maladies* for the book club. In the middle of a sad paragraph about childhood leukemia, she started laughing. Why would a man knock at his own hotel room door holding a bunch of flowers? She looked at her old friend, who was lightly snoring, and debated whether to say anything to her in the morning.

Not yet, she thought. *Let sleeping seniors lie.*

Shit, that was awkward. Holding a bunch of flowers like a pussy, and Catty Vonderville opens the door.

Haynes tossed the bouquet on a bench and went to the bar. He wasn't a heavy drinker but he could use one now.

It was still early enough that he figured some of the group would be lounging in the fat chairs by the poolside bar, but there was only a bunch of Chinese tourists, knocking them back—and Sally Lattimore by herself at a table in the corner, looking like she didn't want company.

He managed to flag a busy waiter and ordered a Dragan Special. His thoughts drifted to women, Lidia in particular, though he didn't want to think about women, he wanted to think about his upcoming trip to Hinchak country. He *needed* to think about it. He still hadn't got the visa, the crucial last piece of paper both to get in the restricted area and as insurance in case he bumped into some trigger-happy grunt who wondered what he was up to. It was hard to get, but he was close now. He'd been working on it for months with his guy at the consulate.

Back to women. What the fuck was he doing messing around with Lidia? *You're seventy-one, man, you going to die a hound dog.* Three exes—well, he and Lorraine had never formalized things, so technically she wasn't an ex. Still.

Haynes thought about Lidia smiling up at the sky, the inverted constellations and the shooting stars. Her strong, narrow hands drawing that little boy who'd been dumped at the monastery, with his little shaved head, his little begging bowl. "I haven't thought about this in a long time," she'd said.

Was she talking about fucking? He wanted to fuck her.

He should pull back.

13

AT BREAKFAST, HAYNES TOOK a seat at the opposite end of the table from Lidia and hung with Barton all day. Lars was minimally okay with his foot and Thila had gotten the Steinmans their plane tickets back to the States.

Haynes left Lidia alone all day, but at dinner, he caved and sat next to her. "All this food," she said. "I'd be happy with some bread and cheese. And this soup."

"We could take some—not the soup—back to that spirit house. Damn thing fascinates me."

"Not there again," she said, shaking her head.

"But the upside-down sky. That doesn't appeal to you?" Haynes gestured at the platters. "Anyway, you done?" He set his fork down. "Take our drinks to the patio?"

Catty caught Haynes's eye as he and Lidia left and raised her eyebrows slightly. "Should I say something to her about last night?" she asked Lars.

He shook his head. "Shipboard romance. Don't get involved."

"It's not *that*. I'm glad she's getting some attention from a reasonable male specimen. She deserves it. It's how she'll feel later. I know her." Catty fiddled with some rice and chicken. "I'm tired of this Thai food."

"It isn't Thai. Quite different."

"Tastes the same to me." She sighed.

"We'll get you a club sandwich later. Now don't fret. Lidia needs diversion."

"This *trip* is her diversion!"

"Leave it, Catherine. My. Would you look at that? *Ice cream!*" She brightened. "Well, this is a treat. I hope it isn't mango-flavored." It was.

As Lidia and Haynes left the dining room for the patio, she imagined all eyes were following them. Well, female eyes: Betsy Poison, Ann Bore, Catty, steely Mrs. Hill, Trudy Wong, Sally Lattimore, maybe Thila too. Watching them go off and thinking "couple." Lars wouldn't notice. Or care.

She regarded Haynes's lean body. In the bush, she'd been about to slide her arms down his back to touch his hard butt—she knew it would be hard—when the howl had startled them.

She said—didn't ask, determined to remember what sex was like—"Let's go upstairs."

Haynes didn't skip a beat. "Yours or mine?"

"Yours." (Whatever happened, she could leave it there. Lars had insisted he didn't need Miss Cai as a night nurse after the one night and she had her room back to herself.)

When Haynes opened his door to her, Lidia's eyes swept the room as if for hidden cameras, land mines, witnesses. *I'm doing this*, she told herself and walked into his embrace.

Later, she sighed as she pulled the sheet up to her chin, looking at the ceiling. "This is awkward, but I feel I have to ask. Do you go in much for casual sex?"

"That didn't seem casual to me." He laughed. "Nah. Too old for that."

"Okay. Me too."

They fell asleep and Lidia had one of her nightmares. She was in a bathroom and found a fetus in the toilet. She woke up whimpering. When she was about Lily's age now, mid-twenties, she went to a Planned Parenthood clinic to have an abortion. Outside the building, a dozen or so protestors had held up posters of dead fetuses and yelled at her not to go in. When she left some hours later, after the procedure, they were still there; she heard "murderer" as she made her shaky way to a cab. She'd felt nothing until she got home, where she cried herself to sleep. That seemed to be that, until several years later. Newly married to Felipe, she'd gone with him to a cottage they'd rented in Connecticut for a week. It had a pool and one morning she'd gotten up early to go for a swim. In the pool, tadpoles, their baby legs splayed out in the water, spun around, dead. Lidia had fished them out with a net, threw them into weeds and heard them plop. Then she'd thrown up, a thin, bitter stream of bile.

14

THE NEXT MORNING AT breakfast, Ward and Trudy Wong looked on as Haynes and Barton bonded over cameras and apps.

"Liu, I didn't take you for a philosopher, I thought you were a geek. 'Life must be transcended!'" Haynes made air quotes.

"I transcend every day," Barton said. "Twice a day. Twenty minutes in the morning, twenty minutes at night. TM. Transcendental meditation?"

Trudy and Ward exchanged looks. They were, always, glad to see Barton interact with people. Still—Klaus Haynes? That bothered them. Not the black part, not really, they were liberals. It was the German thing. Ward's uncle had died fighting the Germans in World War II.

"At least he's not a Nip," Ward muttered. Members of Trudy's extended family had suffered at the hands of the Japanese invaders in Namyan during the same war.

Trudy gave him the look. Though she agreed with his assessment, she strove to keep the past in a box, while Ward kept pawing through it. They were the kind of couple that thrives on their opposing natures. After all, it was her family, not his, that had lost two of its members to the Japanese invasion in Gonyang, still called Goonran then, during the invasion in 1942. Why couldn't he let things be?

"We must stay positive for the reunion," she said. The American relatives of the Takoye, as the Chinese-Namyanese community was called, had finally been allowed visas to the country. After the tour, for the first time in many years, they would all be together for Chinese New Year. Which was why they had come to Namyan in the first place.

"I just don't like the Krauts and Japs."

Trudy sucked in her breath. "You've done business with them."

"That's different."

"Klaus seems to be a nice man, even if he . . . well. It's good for the boy to be socializing." She resumed eating.

"The boy?" Ward muttered. "He's in his forties!"

For some time, much too long in Ward and Trudy's opinion, Barton had been a typical American hipster, living in a rundown house in San Francisco, his roomies techies and pot-smokers. But recently—after getting involved with this TM business, which was probably a cult but seemed to have done what nothing else so far could do for him—he had moved out of the Animal House place to his own small apartment in Oakland. He had cut his hair and become serious about this vlog business. So maybe they could relax now. He'd been a constant worry as he grew up, a solitary boy who didn't like to leave his room. His dad, a gambling "fiend," as Ward called him, had bailed on Ward's sister, Huan, and their infant son and Huan, never very stable, had flipped out. She said she couldn't cope with a baby and begged Ward and Trudy, who had no children, to care for Barton. She never took him back and eventually they'd adopted him.

Trudy had defended Barton at every turn because of his birth parents. His lackluster grades, except for math and science; his lack of interest in sports or girls. He would have spent all his time on his laptop if they'd let him. Trudy had worried that he was gay, but Ward had thought he was just not interested in a relationship with anybody.

He'd hoped Barton would become an engineer, maybe join Ward in the business—architect and engineer, a good combo. But Barton had been all IT, until he pinned all his hopes on "The Undetected."

It sounded like a cop show, Ward told him.

"Nah, Dad, it's all the stuff people don't normally see," Barton replied.

Klaus said now, "Barton, why don't we think about collaborating in the future? What I do seems perfect for 'The Undetected.'"

Barton finished thoroughly chewing his toast. "Hmm. As a matter of fact, I have been thinking about that."

Trudy sighed.

Lars lounged around his room in his dressing gown, plugging away at *Fallen Umbrellas*, the 500-page Namyanese history he'd brought along. For breaks, he practiced walking with the crutches Nurse Cai had supplied. They were too short and he felt like a wounded crab as, dressed at last, he limped around the lobby. He fretted about his damned foot putting the kibosh on the group's plans. Stuck one more day in Gaban. Meanwhile, they'd had their fill of ancient pagodas, they were choking on them, they told Thila—not in so many words, but she got the picture and cobbled together a trip to a tea plantation and then a (French-run) winery. That Lars regretted missing.

The Steinmans, he heard, had been at breakfast. Everyone had consoled them before they left to be driven hundreds of miles back to Gonyang's international airport.

A couple of hours later, Lidia was also reading *Broken Umbrellas*—borrowed from Sally Lattimore, who had finished her copy—on the porch of the tea plantation. Their group, she thought, could be divided into those who wanted to read *Broken Umbrellas* and those who didn't—the curious and liberal versus the self-satisfied and conservative. Of course, if she were to express this idea, she would be roundly criticized as an elitist.

She turned to the last chapter first, a habit she had with nonfiction, and skimmed to the end, where the dictatorship was described as having been checked at last, but not checkmated: the future of the ancient kingdom was, as usual, in doubt. The Damawat was still mighty.

She turned to the middle section with its photographs. A young woman being manhandled by uniformed men at a tea shop, the caption explaining that she'd been discovered printing a broadsheet against the government, "a crime against humanity." Another photo was of a caricature of generals dancing upon the giant feet of an enormous reclining Buddha. The caption said the artist who drew it languished for years in the infamous old Namyanese prison for a double whammy: "desecration of the state" and "desecration of the Buddha."

A hard, pale sun bleached the sky and even on a shady verandah with sunglasses, Lidia's eyes quickly tired. She shut the book and wandered to the other side of the pavilion, where there would be tea soon. She sat on a ledge, lit one of the pungent cigarillos she'd bought at a market stall, and thought about the calm, cheerful Namyanese in the context of their suffering. That last chapter had depicted them, or a good number of them, as being far from "detached" Buddhists in their treatment of the ethnic groups that nibbled away, like mice, into the territory the Namyanese had claimed from ancient times. The Kinhaiese villages had been razed—their crops burned, their women raped—by the tens of thousands. And in the north, drug barons harvested death on a scale commensurate to the appetite of the West. Meanwhile, at the other end of the improbably serene-seeming land, the *na*-worshipping Menans continued their civil war that had gone on now for seventy years, one of the longest in the world.

And here I sit, feeling sorry for myself half the time. Countless people in this one corner of the world, pretty corner though it was, had lost, were losing, would lose, everything. At one time, she had been an artist who depicted reality as unflinchingly as she could. But now? She illustrated textbooks and dabbled at best in her own work. She remembered the "dark rooms" of Goya's late period. She'd seen them at the Prado in Madrid when she was a recent art school graduate who didn't know, until she saw those excruciating masterpieces, that she needed to translate confusion, rage, and fear onto the canvas. Goya drew war and madness and suffering as she had never seen it before. Not even Picasso's "Guernica" was as wrenching for her. And Goya, producing his greatest works in his old age, had been banished from his country. Which proved that his work had achieved its aim.

Lidia had wanted only to create something within breathing distance of the master's work. To pull off the scabs. But of course, America didn't jail its artists, it co-opted them. And she had done some decent work, she knew she had. But she had let that go.

Maybe she should talk to Haynes about going with him on the Hinchak trip. Maybe that would get her going again.

Thila approached.

Lidia had left Broken Umbrellas open to the two photos.

"I join you?" Thila said.

"Please."

Thila smoothed her *logni*, black silk today with a red-and-yellow-striped border. She folded her hands. "That is a famous book."

"This." Lidia tapped the first photograph sharply. "I didn't know about the troubles in Namyan. But you know, my father's family is from Mexico. Long, violent struggle by the farmers for their land, now the cartels—drugs."

"I am sorry, I do not know about this history. Mexico, this is your father's country?"

"Yes. And as I say, Mexicans know about suffering."

"Like we here. We custom such things." Thila brushed again at her *logni*. "But you know now in Namyan we win some freedoms. After so many many years. Before . . . What is that word when you are in a small place and you can't breathe?"

"Claustrophobia."

"I cannot pronounce! That was the way before. Everyone was watched." She leaned forward. "When I was so young, my father, a professor of chemistry at the university, invited some colleagues to our house for dinner. At that time, professors were not trusted by the rulers. They were watched. It rained that night—like, you say, dogs? So, the streets could not be passed and his colleagues remained the night. Two days later, they were all arrested at the university. Why? It was not lawful to meet when not approved by authorities. There were spies on every street. Looking for anything to, to . . ."

"Repress the people? Take away their freedom?"

Thila nodded. "All the professors went to the prison. Many intellectuals there."

"Oh Thila, I'm so sorry."

Thila shrugged. "It was our reality."

Thila was eight when her father disappeared. She remembered her mother crying, months later, when they had to sell the family shrine: a beautiful Buddha, hand-carved tamalan wood gilded with gold leaf. At ten, she saw *a pay*—her father—again. She was coming home from school (her uncle had scraped together the fees, had brought them vegetables, they were forever in his debt). *A pay* was sitting under the acacia tree on the street with some men, chewing betel nut. Thila recognized him by the seersucker suit. When he became a professor, he'd had two seersucker suits made: one of blue stripes, one of brown. They had remained covered in paper in the wooden chest in the one room of their house that they now lived in, the other rooms rented out. Shoes he hadn't cared for, preferring his flip-flops. Thila wondered if she was now seeing a shabby ghost masquerading as her proud father.

In a way, she slowly came to feel after, he *was* dead. What if he hadn't urged his friends to stay in the house the night it poured rain? But he was hospitable, which was why the *yasesayo*, who was particular about his patients, had agreed to come and heal him when he was released, though *a pay* was a marked man now.

Whatever illness had followed him when he came home from the prison was beyond the *yasesayo*'s medicine, however. Mostly her father raged or sat under the banyan tree chewing *yoongi*. Rancor replaced reason in the home. The paper screen that divided her and her sister's sleeping mats from their parents at night could not block out the sounds of their arguments. *You are a scholar,* her mother whispered furiously, *don't act like a peasant.*

Lidia grimaced sympathetically as Thila continued, "My father lost everything because of *one night with friends.* It was worse for so many others, the peasants and other—tribes. But my sister and I gained an education, thanks to our uncle. And now, since elections, people have hopes for the future. So I am happy to be tour guide for Trent & Koss Adventure Tours."

There followed one of those awkward silences when so much has been revealed and both speaker and listener, unnerved, are anxious to move on.

"We go soon to the hills after the tea for lunch and the tasting of wine," Thila said presently.

"I don't drink alcohol," Lidia said. "But I'll sit and enjoy the view, read my book, it doesn't matter."

"And you meditate." Thila smiled slightly. "I have seen you do that. But . . ." She inclined her head, looking at the cigarillo.

"Can't give up all my vices. Bad habits? Guess I'm not ready for Nirvana yet." But Lidia stubbed out her cigarillo, which was suddenly objectionable, even foul.

As she had drifted over to her, Thila now drifted away.

Needing to process what Thila had told her, Lidia walked down neat rows of tea bushes laid out as far as could be seen. Men and women and, yes, children, plucked tea leaves very fast and, over and over, flung them into deep woven baskets. Repeat. Namyan was like that: wherever you looked, a country of people who seemed peaceable and accepting of a hard lot, but were they? Lidia had seen no violence, no outbursts. But she felt it must be there, the iron fist behind the tourist curtain, the simmer of injustice. She just couldn't see it.

Haynes was walking also, ahead. She ran up to him. "Hey!"

"Lidia De C."

"Your blog trip. I want to talk to you about it."

"Sure. Let's get out of the sun first."

"Good idea."

But there was no chance to talk back on the verandah. There were two free chairs left at the long table—beside Catty, who was next to the Hodgeses. Lots of pots of different tea on the table.

"You two! Well, you haven't missed much," Catty said grumpily.

"We're wondering how Lars is doing with that poor foot of his?" Ann said, leaning over from a near chair. "Mother had a bad infection in—was it her right foot, honey?"

"Mmm," Ed said.

"This stuff tastes like leaves," Clint said.

"Green tea is very healthy, you know," Catty said.

"Rather have some of that stuff they chew," Clint said.

"*Yoongi*? That's easily arranged," said Haynes.

"Clint told us he thinks it'll help his hip," Ann explained, rolling her eyes slightly. "Mother had problems with her right hip, didn't she, Ed? Made it painful to walk."

"Is there any ailment your mother didn't suffer from?" Lidia blurted.

"Well!" Ann said.

Clint pivoted to Catty. "About that yong stuff, what's in it?"

"You'll have to ask Lars, he's the expert," Catty said, brittle.

Betsy took a sip of green tea and gulped. She carefully put down her cup. "It's cancerous. I mean, not this tea, those yongo-pongo things. Stay away from anything cancerous."

"Chewing betel nuts once won't hurt you," Lidia said. "It's what they might put in it."

"Yes! And have you noticed what it does to their teeth?" Ann queried. "Those awful stains? Mother's gums turned bright red when she got gingivitis. At this rehab place after the stroke. Bed sores too. Well, I said to them, I'm going to write to the Health Department and the governor. Expect a lawsuit. I took her back home that very day."

Ed said on a sigh, "Ann."

At that moment, Thila approached them and said it was time to go back on the bus. Fortunate timing. Otherwise, Lidia thought she would have snapped.

15

AT THE HOTEL, LARS enlisted a porter to find him a walking stick, for which he tipped handsomely, and abandoned his crutches. He hobbled around the grounds for a while before sinking into a chair in the shade and ordering a beer.

He was glad to be alone; he didn't want people around to witness his feebleness. Certainly not Catty. He was not ready for the dotage stage in their relationship, though it seemed possibly to be pouncing upon him.

Theirs was a winter romance against which his children had lobbied vigorously. His first-born—Lars III, always called Young Lars—had told him that he and his brothers thought a man of his age had no business breaking up a family. Lars replied that age had nothing to do with it and furthermore, it was none of their damn business. And in time, the boys had come around.

Happening upon Catty at his fiftieth Harvard reunion (Radcliffe for her, of course, as it was then still the dark ages before women were allowed to attend Harvard officially), had been the best thing to happen to him in a long, long time. He'd recognized her immediately. A splendid woman! He intended to be shipshape for her unto the grave.

So he was determined now to put his best foot forward—ha! At least they'd gotten a handle on the infection and he told himself his foot felt better. He drank the beer proscribed because of the antibiotics, but just the one. Then he had to pee, a fairly incessant need now. He pulled himself up and tapped his way gingerly to the elevator to go to his room, pausing mid-journey to admire one of the intricate flower petal designs—mandalas, weren't they?—created afresh each day by invisible hands, outdoors in the dirt, indoors in massive planters.

What a lovely way to spend your time, he thought. God, how could you not love these people? These flower-loving, attractive Namyanese people, always under the heel of one autocrat or another. Of course, it was only a matter of time before the Chinese engulfed them. Yet they'd fought them off for centuries, maybe longer, and then, recently, the Brits and the Japanese, and finally, the generals. Now at this moment they had a chance—slim though it was—at some kind of self-rule.

Lars's review of historical malfeasance chased by beer led to a pleasant nap, after which he went downstairs again, where the group had just gathered on the verandah.

"How were the libations at the winery?" he asked Haynes a bit plaintively.

Haynes shrugged. "Beautiful vineyard. The wine not so much. I see you got rid of those midget crutches."

"Yeah, foot's better, thanks."

The Dragan Special they ordered arrived in ice-cold glasses. Yes, he was having another, damn it.

"At least the beer here is good," Haynes said.

"Not like your German beer, though."

"Not possible."

Lars wiped tiny beads of perspiration from his forehead. "Look, this is a bit awkward, something I feel I must say. You know that

Lidia's a close friend of ours. Well, Catty's first, but I've known her quite a while too. Well, you know that."

Haynes set down his glass.

"She's a bit . . . fragile right now," Lars continued.

"I see that. She didn't want to talk about it . . . You know, my wife died too. Well, ex-wife."

"Haynes, not my place to intrude, normally. But I have to tell you, Lidia is not a—"

"Lars!" Catty said, appearing suddenly. "I have been looking for you everywhere. I kept imagining you were lying at the bottom of some stairs or temple. Not in the room. No note. And here you are, defying doctor's orders and quaffing beer."

"Here I am. Large as life."

"How can you get well if you don't let the antibiotics work? Really, Lars."

When he turned back to Haynes, the man was gone.

Clint Hodges downed his Dragan, also medically forbidden, on the balcony off his room, watching the foothills darken to azure, navy, black. He thought, as he routinely did, about mountains he'd trekked as a younger man—the Himalayas, the Andes, the Rockies, the Zagros in Iran, and, his personal favorite, Yanar Dag, the burning mountain in Azerbaijan. His job as an oilman had taken him to deserts and wetlands, mostly, and he knew the desert and the swamp peoples well, the tough farming people and the small-time wheeler-dealers, grifters and thugs who go wherever oil is. The ingenuous, sometimes outlandish agricultural methods that the farmers clung to and their peasant magic that spit in the eye of their inhospitable reality. But Clint was a product of the Alleghenies and always preferred rugged hill folk. He got to whatever mountains were around every chance.

In his early thirties, after meeting Betsy McLean on a furlough in Oklahoma City, his trekking had, of course, slowed down considerably. He'd been ready to settle down and she'd been a home-body even then. They should have had kids. Clint would have trained his sons, even daughters, in the ways of mountains.

He'd left the balcony door open a crack to let some air into the canned air-conditioning of the room and heard Betsy stir from her nap. After forty-plus years of marriage, he could predict what she was going to say. And his reply.

And she said exactly what he expected, and he pretended not to hear.

"Huh?" he said.

She came on the balcony, closing the door to the room with a snap behind her. "I said, why'd you leave that door open? You know they got mosquitos here, and Lord knows what else. Last thing we need is to come down with malaria or something." She smoothed down her thinning, graying hair. In the restaurant she was waitressing at on the day they met, her hair had been thick and rebelliously curly in the heat. Brown with red glints.

Clint picked up his beer.

"Tell me you at least closed your eyes for a while. You didn't just sit there with a beer can. You know what the doctors said."

"I rested." He never wanted to hear what the doctors said again.

"Beer, Clinton? And on an empty stomach, too. Dr. Morton told you—"

"Will you stop hounding me?" He stood up. "I'm gonna go take some pictures."

Betsy looked at her watch, a plain, sensible band. A long time ago, while in Wyoming—those were some mountains—he'd bought her a Pawnee bracelet of worked silver and turquoise made into a watch-band. Betsy had put it in the safe in the den, said it was too valuable to wear for every day. She'd worn it maybe twice after that.

"I guess I'm cranky," she said. "It's just—"

"Okay," he cut her off.

"Well, supper's at seven thirty."

"Plenty of time."

Clint put on his Padres cap, hitched his camera to his shoulder, and plodded from the hotel out to a nearby stupa. It was shaped, he thought, like a dick. At its base was a pretty, yellow-flowering bush. He grunted down to one knee and snapped it. For the pretty waitress with the red-brown curly hair.

The place seemed deserted, which suited him. He decided he was up to climbing the stupa stairs. He cussed the sign with a red arrow slashed through a shoe, sat on a step, laboriously removed his New Balance sneakers and athletic socks (he refused to wear those compression stockings), and left them there, frowning. So far, nobody's shoes had been stolen on this jaunt, but you never knew. He'd raise holy hell at the hotel if he had to walk back in his bare feet.

Going up, he got that toothpaste tube squeezing sensation in his gut. Shallow breaths hurt less. He was going to do what he wanted; Betsy could fuss all she wanted, the doctors could lecture him, the world could see him as a mean old cuss. They'd cut him up and filled him with poison. For what? The pain got worse and it still came down to he had maybe a year left.

There was no railing, so he stopped often on the steps to catch his breath. Finally, at the top, there was a funny little statue poking out, low-down in the shadows. *One of those voodoo things*, Clint thought, *voodoo* being his catch-all for the worldwide web of peasant superstitions. He raised his camera.

Just then those New York snobs came around from the other side, blocking his view.

"This is a damn good *na*, isn't it, Hodges?" Lars said in that fake-jovial voice of his. The wife gave him a quick glance and looked away and the Spanish one didn't seem to see him at all. *Na to you too*, thought Clint. They bent over, peering at the thing, giving Clint a good view of their backsides.

"Black as night, this little statue. Can't tell, is it male or female?"
Lars went on.

"Probably neither," the Spanish one said. "They go in for a lot of
gender-bending."

Miss Know-It-All, and she's always *in the way,* Clint thought.

As they moved on—thank God almighty—the other woman in
her witch hat said to him, "Enjoy."

Enjoy what? he thought.

Back at the hotel, Clint asked Betsy what that witch hat woman's
name was again and Betsy, of course, knew right away. Catherine,
but everybody called her *Catty*. They sure got that right, she added.
Betsy was proud of her memory; it had, she always said, made her an
excellent waitress.

"She and those two other ones blocked my shot again," he said. "I
should be out looking at mountains."

Of all things, Betsy had won the grand prize at the silent auction
fundraiser for the new roof and siding at First Baptist back home.
The prize was an all-expenses-paid trip for two, donated by Emory
Small's travel agency, to Namyan, a country nobody knew anything
much about except it had an active Baptist presence. Clint had been
surprisingly agreeable after he'd read on Wikipedia that the highest
mountains in Southeast Asia were there. Up in the Golden Triangle
region. Man, those would be interesting. No oil, though.

Too late, he'd learned they wouldn't be going to the Triangle. Betsy
had pointed out that anyway, she wasn't about to let him go traipsing
around in the high altitudes in his condition.

16

NOW THAT THEY WERE two days behind schedule, what with
getting the Steinmans off and waiting for the all-clear on Lars's
foot, the only way they could see legendary Lake Keini was to drive
overnight on the bus to make up the time. They set off at 9:00 p.m.,
giving Mrs. Hills the long back row with pillow and blanket, the rest
of them making do with their seats.

By morning, after they'd breakfasted on noodles at a roadside
stall, the countryside had begun to get lusher, and soon they saw
the long lake glinting beside the road. A tribe called Nitha, Thila
told them, had arrived there seven or eight centuries or so ago after
getting kicked off their land in some tribal war. There were enough
Nithas to take over the lake from the few folks already there, and they
called the lake Leini after one of their deities. As all the surrounding
land was fully inhabited, the Nithas, a clever folk, dredged up the
rapacious water hyacinth that clogged much of the water, piling up
the weeds repeatedly until they had enough floating earth on which
to grow crops above the water. And they fine-tuned the art of fishing
in weed-clogged water, twisting one leg around an oar to steer while
kicking water weeds out of the way with the other. On the water's
edge, they built stilt-houses.

From the bus, the group watched the Nithas' descendants work on their floating farms and dance their boats around until late in the day, when they turned off onto a manicured expanse exuberant with plants and flower mandalas, two-story buildings scattered around the grounds. At the lobby, a white man and Namyanese staff shining with professional joy greeted them. The Namyanese padded off with their suitcases in all directions. The white man offered them cocktails on the verandah in a French accent. Dinner was from seven thirty to ten.

Everyone but Ken and Sally Lattimore went straight to their rooms for a shower and change of clothes. Sally lingered in the lobby. She could use a cocktail or two but she knew she'd be apt—okay, certain—to stay on if she did, planted in the same grubby clothes, through cocktails three and four and so on. The rest of the evening would become a haze.

She turned to Ken. "I'm going to the room to shower."

"Don't you want to wet your whistle?" he replied.

Trust you with the passive-aggressive bon mots, she thought.

"Well, I'm having a drink, I'll be there in a bit," he said. And the thing of it was that he would have only the one. He just didn't get it.

Their room was on the second floor of one of the buildings, small but prettier, more Namyanese-inflected, than the luxury behemoths they'd stayed at so far, with two tiny, exquisite flower mandalas on their little bedside tables. There was a view of a slice of the marsh and the glittering lake and Sally saw a small boat approach the shore and tourists get out.

She had her shower. Sally believed in hot water and hot drinks as an antidote to heat, as those who've spent time in the tropics (and have access to hot water) do. She put on her pale linen pants and a fresh top, fussed minimally with her face and hair, stuffed some money in a pocket, and exited the building.

Instead of taking the walkway to the lobby, she turned up the flower-filled drive, noting how much of the flora was familiar from

Thailand, her home for five years, back when Bangkok had not yet become de trop. She and Ken and the boys had lived in officers' quarters on the compound, of course, with the golf club at the center of everyone's social life. But after a year or so, she'd grown tired of the bland sameness of that life. She was a college-educated (psychology major) sorority drop-out, one of the countless young people in the '60s and '70s who fell between the cracks of straight or hippie and came to marriage with vague expectations of being more than a wife and mother. She kept somewhat busy at the compound with volunteer work, but could not shake off a growing sense of it all being pointless, the routine of ferrying the three boys around, lunch at the club with other wives (where drinks, at least, were part of the routine), volunteering for organizations that collected clothing and school supplies for needy Thai children, and boozy weekend dinners with the husbands.

Ken had been a good husband—solid, dutiful, good-looking. But he was often away and when he was around, he tended to find reasons not to be with her. Oh, call a spade a spade: they hadn't had sex more than half a dozen times since the kids were born. But he was a good father, enthused over their endless games, helped them with their math problems. Also, he took the family to interesting parts of the country on vacations. And the boozy Saturday night dinners at the club. Still, Sally wondered if he was up to the usual mischief, the Thai girlfriend thing. She assumed he was. When he was at home, she gave him lists of things to do with the crisp tang in her voice of the officer in charge. Perhaps perversely, it was Ken's readiness to unclog a drain or caulk windows (or whatever other task she devised) that confirmed her suspicions about his unfaithfulness. Most of the tasks could have been done by servants.

It got to where she had to find something new. Get away from the compound. At first, a couple other officers' wives, friendly, hearty women, had gone with her to the upscale hotel bars in Bangkok.

Occasionally, they ended up for a laugh at places like Cheap Charlie's, in an alley past Patpong's long parade of girlie bars and massage parlors. After several such nights out, however, the wives started making excuses. So Sally started going on her own, which had actually suited her better. She felt freer to study the wildlife, as she thought of it. She liked watching the higher-end bar girls, any one of whom might have been a companion for her husband, beautiful and tiny and wanton.

On her adventures, Sally was streetwise enough to pay one of the Patpong boys to accompany her. The kids got some cash, food, and alcohol-free drinks, and she got protection. The heat and dust parched her throat, the smells were fetid, and the shouting in Thai was impenetrable to her beyond the basics. Street thieves were plentiful, and occasionally she had stuff stolen in the street despite her young companions. Once her handbag was slit open and her wallet taken. Another time, her camera was tugged away. But for Sally, in a nice linen or cotton dress, these were annoying inconveniences. She needed freedom and then she needed escape, even if she couldn't say quite what she needed escaping from. She tried Thai sticks. But what she really liked was whiskey.

Over time, she became friendly with a Thai manager at the Mandarin Oriental. He became her companion on night crawls, taking her to places she hadn't known existed. She felt safe with Virote, who was a riot to be with and always made sure she got home safely. On one of their pub crawls, he suggested they visit a "she-boy" bar, as the Thais called it. And there, at the bar with his arm around a pretty she-boy, was Ken. Sally rushed out before he spotted her.

She didn't know what to do, so she did nothing. It was the early 1980s, way before the gender-fluid concept, let alone its acceptance, and well before "don't ask, don't tell."

She could have destroyed Ken's career and their way of life if she wanted to. No chance of that, but a week later she had told him she wanted a divorce. "An amicable divorce," she emphasized. "I know what you are."

He'd slapped her, not hard but it stung. "You know nothing. If you do that, I'll fight for the kids. And I'll win."

Slowly, Sally had downed her whiskey sour and set down the glass. "I don't think so," she said and cradled her cheek.

"Oh, I do think so," Ken said. He reached for a file nearby and took out photographs of her and Virote in a room at the Mandarin Oriental.

"Bastard." She had nothing on Ken but what she'd seen. Should she too hire a private eye to tail Ken and his she-boys? Then what? It would ruin everything, not least of which the boys, to find out what their all-American dad was doing.

They came to an understanding. Ken was approaching the pinnacle of his career, they liked each other well enough, and there were the kids. They could "go their own ways," Ken said, as long as they used "discretion."

Sick of Bangkok, Sally counted down the days until they could leave Thailand. At home she filled her time with wine and whiskey. The understanding between spouses lasted and solidified.

She walked on the edge of the road with no goal. Sally liked Namyan. It hadn't achieved that frenetic mix of greed and resentment that becoming a tourist destination had turned much of Thailand into, in her opinion. It was hard to imagine *this* place as a major world drug producer. The Thais had always complained about Namyanese cartels dumping opium and meth across the border, but they were the movers. Everybody made money off the product, everybody but the addicts. Money and misery. *Give Namyan time*, she thought as an ox cart creaked by. She bent her head in greeting to the young driver, whose answering smile showed missing teeth, those that remained a purplish black. She imagined his simple life of rice and vegetables for breakfast, lunch, and dinner, with the odd bit of fish thrown in. *Yoongi* for a numb high, family picnics at pagodas. Was he hopeful about the future, greedy for Western stuff? She had noticed that some rickshaw drivers had cellphones.

She passed a tiny tea shop and then appeared a pagoda, a complex of several little buildings and a pavilion with flower offerings. Boys were playing soccer in the dust around it. She walked around the pagoda and started climbing. A boy yelled something and pointed at his feet. The no-shoes rule, oops. Sally folded her hands and bent slightly at the waist. Off with her sandals, on with the dirt. Black soles again.

She stepped to the flat top, beside a modest statue of the Buddha and surveyed the little courtyard. Suddenly, she felt the world tilt. She slumped down and looked at her hands. They were shaking. *This again? But I've got it under control.* Anxiety pursued her, a patient predator. She needed a drink.

It would have to wait. She got up and went to the edge of the little platform. The boys playing soccer had left but she felt a terrible self-consciousness, as if they were hiding around the corner of the pagoda, watching and laughing at her. *Stupid me to come here.* She got up, brushed off the seat of her pants, and willed herself down the steps. The sky was no longer transparent. Soon, it would fill with darkness.

The darkening sootiness of the evening as she walked quickly back to the hotel increased the nameless dread that clung to her, a film of fear. Sally made herself think of the warm glow of the hotel verandah, with waiters bowing over trays of drinks and steaming plates of Asian stew. She hurried to the lights, laughter, chattering voices, booze. She smoothed her hair and stepped onto the verandah.

Ken saw her immediately and waved her over. "Oh, *there* you are. Where'd you go? The river?"

She sat down and shook her head and reached for a glass of wine. The little burst inside, lovely release. She drank deeply, set the glass down. "I took a walk down the road. Some boys playing soccer by this little pagoda actually played feet police with me when I started climbing up in my sneaks."

She took up her glass again, finished it, and poured herself a second. Ken said nothing. They were so past it now.

17

To GET TO THE lake from the hotel meant a twenty-minute walk to a footbridge that flanked the marshes where water buffalo grazed. From there, they climbed into small boats with local helmsmen after Thila cautioned them about the dangers of the deceptively placid-looking water.

"Each year a boat with five statues of Buddha passes along the whole river," she said. "Very big boat, so all people can come pray to Buddha. But sometimes people drown because they do not take care. When they fall in the water, it takes them away."

Lidia almost raised her hand—after all, Thila was their teacher, wasn't she?—to ask why life vests weren't provided. *Silly me*, she thought. *Safety and, more to the point, liability, don't exist here.* Floors slippery as glass, steps without railings, treacherous water— caveat emptor.

Having dawdled, she found she was stuck with the Borens and odd Barton in the last of the boats. "I Ku," their boatman said, bowing very slightly, showing the obligatory stained teeth. This seemed to be the extent of his English.

It became cooler as they chugged into the wide lake. Birds stalked the ripples and colorful laundry waved from the railings of the stilt houses on shore where women and children came and went. Ku tacked in and out of spots thick with pretty pink and lavender water hyacinths. Barton filmed and shouted above the motor's roar that the plant was considered very wicked. The Borens also snapped away. As they zipped past a fisherman netting a large red fish, Barton stood and leaned over the side, camera whirring, and the boat tilted sharply. Barton scrambled for his footing and Ann shrieked. He sat down with a thump.

Presently, they docked beside a market built on stilts over the water. Lidia was last out, behind the Borens. Ann said, "I'm going to tell Thila he stood up in the boat. Endangering our safety like that!"

Of course you'd be the snitch, thought Lidia. *The kid who runs to teacher.*

Ed shook his head. "He's learned his lesson."

"He almost tipped the boat over!"

Barton was ahead of them, working his camera, reunited with the Wongs.

"Is that a—yes, it is!" Ed said and darted off the path, camera aimed. "A *Triodes aeacus*! First one for me. Come on, Ann. Slowly."

"Is it one of those flesh-eating things?" Ann folded her arms.

"It's a *Triodes*, Ann, a golden birdwing butterfly. Marvelous markings."

Ann went and Lidia felt compelled to follow. As they got close, the butterfly fluttered away in a flash of bright yellow wings and red throat.

"Gorgeous!" Lidia said.

Ed turned and looked at a spot next to her. "Well of course it is." He walked away.

Snitch and Grouch Bores, she thought. To her surprise, she was a little hurt by Ed's snub.

At lunch in a well-appointed stilt-house restaurant, Thila, no doubt prompted by Ann, repeated her warning about the lake. Lidia darted a look at Barton. Fiddling with his head cam, the particularly geeky-looking device he strapped around his forehead to leave his arms free, he appeared not to be paying attention. But his face reddened.

They were going to continue upstream, stopping at traditional crafts shops along the way where, Thila said, there would be "good shopping opportunities." Someone groaned.

Back at the boat, Lidia, the Borens, and Ku got in. There was no sign of Barton. The other boats took off. The sun, high in the sky, sliced through the sunscreen on Lidia's face, arms, and legs and especially the back of her neck. The Borens, of course, were protected by their sensible hats with flaps at the back and sides—which, she had to admit, provided the protection her baseball cap did not. She dug out her sunscreen again and chugged from her water bottle.

"Let's get going, with or without Liu!" Ed said, fuming.

As if on cue, Barton loped up and swung himself in. "Sorry, sorry, sorry," he mumbled. "I was shooting some—"

The engine sputtered and roared to life, cutting him off.

They zoomed across the expanse of the blue-gray water late in the day on the return to the hotel, after stops at a boat maker and a lacquer umbrella maker with all the miniature boats and lacquer umbrellas they—which is to say, mainly Sally and Franklin—could wish to buy. Lidia was in a sunburnt daze, longing only for a cold drink in her future, as Lu slowed again before a particularly luscious plantation of tomatoes, peppers, beans, sunflowers, and other, unrecognizable, plants. The farmers were using giant wooden rakes, heaving tangles of weeds onto their plots, when an errant stiff breeze jostled the boat and Barton, again standing and leaning over with his camera, toppled in, as quietly as the time baby Lily had fallen into a public pool and sunk like a stone.

Lidia had been over that moment countless times. She had been distracted—but by what? What was more important than eternal vigilance of your toddler? Be distracted for one moment, and that was enough. Other children and adults were in the pool; still, it was Lidia who was first to see the blue frills of her two-year-old's swimsuit vanish underwater. It seemed to take an eternity for her to take this in. The second eternity was the time it took for her to leap into the water and scoop up the choking Lily. The lifeguard came and had to pry Lily from Lidia's arms. The baby sputtered and cried lustily; she was fine. But Lidia was overcome with her failure to protect her child and fled with her, buying her ice cream, lemonade, a Barbie doll. And she wouldn't let her near a pool for the rest of the summer.

Barton was not drowning. He was floundering in a thick tangle of weeds, his safari vest ballooning around him, his hair plastered to his scalp. He shouted, "My Canon! The Handycam! Jesus—the film! Fucking hell!" Ku continued to cruise calmly forward, deaf with the motor's roar, unaware, as Ed crawled to him and with bold gestures, got him to turn around and go back for Barton, who crawled in with Ed and Lu's help.

"Oh. My. Lord," Ann said. "You did it again."

A long red slash glistened below Barton's many-pocketed, now drenched khaki shorts.

"Who's got a towel?" Lidia shouted.

Ku somehow understood; he tossed her a cloth and she wrapped it around Barton's leg.

"You could've capsized us!" Ann said.

"Not now, he's in shock," Lidia told her.

Barton sat up, sodden, his head in his hands. Ku handed back a bottle of water from the cooler.

The other boats circled around, the boatmen and Thila engaged in a lively-sounding conversation. Everyone was looking at Barton. The Wongs wanted to come onto the boat but Thila talked them out of it.

A blanket was found and flung around his shoulders. He looked like a refugee.

"Send someone down there to find my camera!" Barton yelled. "Please!"

"Too much weeds to find it," Thila shouted back.

"But you're okay," Lidia reminded him. "Stuff can be replaced."

"It was thoughtless of you, leaning over the boat like that—again," Ann said.

"Very foolish," Ed added.

"After what Thila reminded us at lunch!" Betsy shouted from her boat.

"He's lost his equipment! His film!" thundered Haynes nearby.

"His own damn fault," said Clint.

"Oh, leave him alone!" Trudy wailed.

"Now we go," Thila said.

Barton did not appear for dinner that night, a delicious seafood risotto and Namyanese salad with mango ice cream for dessert. Everyone either avoided talking about him or had other things on their minds. Betsy was upset about the quaint hotel and complained to Ann in ringing tones that easily carried to the rest.

"No internet again! And that mattress sinks in the middle! Plus no washcloths. Why didn't we go to the General Shangri-La like it said in the itinerary?"

"Because of the change of schedule, and I think it's a perfectly charming place," Catty called from the next table in the brook-no-nonsense tones of her ancient, by American standards, pedigree.

"Yummy food!" Lars added, forking in more Namyanese salad. "Philistines," he whispered.

Haynes laughed and Lidia smiled. Catty and Lars could—almost—always entertain her just by being themselves. Since the bequest from Great-Aunt Charlotte last year, Lidia for the first time in her life had her very own pile of mad money. But the dynamics between her and the silver-spoon Vondervilles hadn't shifted. When she and Catty had become friends in the '80s, Lidia had described herself as a "starving artist who's now just a struggling artist." Scraping by on low-paying jobs to pay the rent, she on principle had never turned down free food and drink. Which was why she'd been at the fancy party for some artists' collective in SoHo, where she'd met Catty, one of the patrons or sponsors or whatever they called the money people.

But Catty, with whom she'd drifted into small talk that quickly became amusing and then astute, belied her appearance and her background. Lidia learned that she worked as executive producer for an important, kick-ass documentary filmmaker, "mostly as his go-fer," and it was clear Catty saw through the pretensions of the frenetic self-promoters jostling arms with them. It was the era of Warhol, punk rock, punk art. But Catty knew her art. She could talk intelligently about Lidia's heroes, Frida Kahlo and Francisco Goya, and she had her own loves—Vermeer, Constable, Van Gogh. A friendship was born.

Thanks to her trust fund, Catty had a perfectly appointed, if small, apartment on the Upper East Side, where she regularly had Lidia to dinner—in order, Catty said, "to get a decent meal into you once in a while." There was no question of reciprocating. Lidia barred anyone but fellow struggling artists from her humble tenement door and had no money to take Catty out. That is, until she married Felipe Suares and achieved the Upper West Side version of precarious middle class. And now she had the bequest.

But even if she had been left millions by her great-aunt Charlotte, which she hadn't, she would never have Catty's patina. Most of the time, Lidia felt little class envy because their long friendship had schooled her on the downside of being Old Money. Catty had had to pry herself loose from the many social expectations that girdled her from the cradle: perfectly run households; flawless manners; flawless gardens; flawless everything, really. No, Lidia did not envy her old friend that.

After their mango sorbet and coffee, Catty said, "I think we should mingle a bit."

"Find out about Barton, you mean," Lars clarified.

"Is he okay?" Lidia asked Thila.

"He is resting," Thila murmured.

"Trying to get on Wi-Fi, last I heard," Haynes put in. "Very spotty, as we know."

"It wouldn't be if we were at the General Shangri-La," said Betsy Hodges, who had edged into the conversation.

"Yup," added Clint.

Lidia turned slightly so that she was facing away from the Poisons. "How is Barton feeling?"

"Pretty upset," Haynes said.

"The doctor gave him the antibodies for, um, prophetically," Thila said.

"Prophetical antibodies!" Lars repeated with delight. He'd remarked more than once on the trip how he loved the twists and turns of Thila's English. "Well, I should stop in and see how the old prophet is doing."

Lidia thought Lars shouldn't joke about poor Thila's uneven command of a foreign language when she had had so much worry because of them. Lars's foot. Her foot. The Steinman drama. And now Barton. What if Barton had drowned? That would be down to Thila, wouldn't it. On her watch.

"His aunt and uncle are with him now. They try to find replace for camera and so on."

"Under control, then." Betsy yawned. "I'm off to bed—on my lumpy mattress."

"Mine is perfect!" Catty said regally.

"Mine too!" said Lars, Lidia, and Haynes in unintended unison.

Haynes added softly in Lidia's ear, "Your place or mine?"

"Oh, mine. But I'm awfully tired from all that sun," she whispered.

"Are we already at the too-tired-tonight stage?" he whispered back.

Thila said suddenly, "French people who come to Namyan are mad keen for this hotel."

"Even the diplomatic Thila has her limits," Lars murmured admiringly.

"So we just have to rough it, like the French do," Lidia put in.

Impervious, Betsy Hodges walked off with the last word. "Well, even the French must want Wi-Fi."

Almost the last word.

"Ha!" Lars said. "Read a book!"

He then drifted away to join Ken, inevitably now called "The Colonel," for a nightcap. Soon the two were sharing a joke, laughing like schoolboys.

Catty, Lidia, and Haynes lingered.

"More coffee?" Catty asked Lidia.

"I really shouldn't," Lidia said. "It'll keep me up."

Haynes smirked slightly.

"It never bothers you, though," she said, ignoring him, to Catty.

"Never," Catty said.

Another burst of laughter from the Colonel and Lars.

"Lars is getting a bit pickled." Catty made to stand up. "I'm going to collect him. Haynes, you're not drinking with the boys?"

"I'm a two-beer man," he said.

"I'm annoyed that my husband seems to have forgotten that he is too. Well, I guess he's blowing off steam about his foot. See you tomorrow."

A roar came from Lars.

"They are having fun," Lidia said.

"Not as much as we're going to have," Haynes said.

"Promise?" Lidia said.

18

CATTY WAS HAVING BREAKFAST in bed, the inviolate trio
of banana, toast, and coffee (when, as rarely happened, there were
no bananas, she would accept berries)—which Lars delivered, after
which he returned to the dining room for his own meal. The buffet
there, though less lavish than those provided by the luxury chains,
was delicious. But having fewer options was another sore point for
the Hodgeses and Borens, who made sure to let Thila know there was
no sausage, white-bread toast, or strawberry jam.

Lars devoured scrambled eggs, grilled fish, fruit, and a croissant
and was getting ready to go back for seconds when Lidia arrived.

"Sleep well?" he asked.

She yawned. "Not really."

Lars hesitated, plate in hand. "Lidia, I know about, well, *you know.*"

"What?" she demanded.

Lars mumbled something unintelligible even to himself and
headed for the buffet.

Haynes came in, gave Lidia a sunny smile, sat down, and poured
himself a cup of coffee from the pot on the table.

"*Guten abend,*" he said.

"*Buenos días*," she replied curtly. She was well and truly pissed off at him.

Haynes cocked his eyebrows.

She was about to kick him in the shins under cover of the table but thought better of it. "Here comes Lars."

"He's gone to sit with the Lattimores," Haynes said, sipping his coffee. "What's up with you?"

"*What's up with me* is you told Lars about—us. Now he's probably telling the Colonel and Sally, and I can't bear it if Betsy Hodges and Ann Boren find out. Oh God, and Thila."

"Will you listen to yourself?"

"Last night, I had this dream: everybody in the group was standing in the room, watching us, you know . . ."

Haynes burst out laughing, one of his hearty beerhall laughs, startling at a breakfast buffet. He leaned over and touched her nose. "You mean having sex?"

Lidia looked down. "Yes, if that's how you want to put it."

"And how would you put it?"

Lidia choked slightly as she swallowed some coffee. "Well, *having sex* seems clinical. Making love," she mumbled. "Oh, never mind." She wanted to flee, she wanted to be back in her slightly cramped one-and-a-half-bedroom apartment on Amsterdam Avenue on the Upper West Side of Manhattan.

"I did not tell Lars about our *passionate affair*, but I did tell him I think you are a lovely woman. And he said you're, well . . ."

"*What?*"

"Fragile."

"Fragile?"

"Good morning, Klaus, old man." Lars was sliding in across from them with his second, half-eaten plate. "Good chow, have you dug in yet?"

"About to. I'm just telling this stubborn friend of yours that I said she was lovely and—ouch!"

Lidia had kicked him in the shins.

"Yes, of course! Highly attractive woman!" Lars agreed stoutly.

"Stop talking about me as if I'm some—exhibit!"

Lars chuckled. Lidia stalked away, imagining that Ann's and Betsy's eyes were boring into her back, which pissed her off further. She could imagine all too well what they would say about her and Haynes sneaking into each other's rooms. WTF (as teenage Lily and her friends had messaged each other constantly), *we don't sneak. We're simply two adults who enjoy each other's company carnally. WTF? Half the planet makes sex tapes and hooks up and I'm still this repressed creature struggling to throw off the pre–Summer of Love Mad Men '60s. Gloves to church and skirts to school, never pants, and good girls don't go all the way, and if by some fluke they do and get caught out . . .*

"Everything all right, Haynes? Lidia looks upset."

"Damned if I know. Women."

Lars nodded sagely. "Let sleeping dogs lie, eh? On another topic, The Colonel and I got to talking about Liu; as you know, he's absolutely distraught about losing his equipment and film. Refuses to leave his room. What a fiasco. We thought we'd go have a chat with him, try to get him to buck up."

Haynes said, "I wouldn't right now. Word is he's feverish. That lake is probably like a sewer."

Lars polished his plate off. "Oh, God. Speaking of which, going to hit the head."

He rose and headed toward the elevators in the lobby, where he found Lidia slumped before a freshly drawn mandala of pink petals at the base of a madly blooming Burmese honeysuckle vine, its trunk as thick as a tree.

Lars paused. "All right, Lidia?"

Lidia jumped and rounded on him. "Not really, no."

"No. You looked like you might cry or hit someone in there. Well, Klaus."

"Or you. I'm mad at both of you. I know he told you about us. Just do not tell Catty."

"But what is this? You're the best of friends! Anyway, she may suspect something . . . Not much gets past her."

"Lars, will you sit down with me? Just for a minute, I know you have to pee." She pointed at the bench. "I will tell her. When I'm ready."

"Jesus, Lidia, she'll get it. We both do."

"Lars. How long have you known me?"

"Fifteen years? Twenty?"

"Eighteen. And it was always with Felipe . . ."

"You don't need to justify what you're doing. Christ, it's been a terrible situation for you. Terrible."

"I want, I need, something normal," she went on, as if she hadn't heard him. "Haynes and I . . . went for a walk in the moonlight. Then we lay down on a blanket and looked at the stars and, you know, goofed around."

"*Outdoors?* Wasn't that, well, risky?"

"Oh, nothing *happened.*" Then, "Am I crazy, Lars? Having a fling at my age?"

Lars chuckled. "People are attracted to each other at any age. Look at me and my bride! Anyway, I consider you to be a girl still. Look, I have to—"

"Go, go. No, wait a sec. I need to know. It *was* Haynes who told you about us, wasn't it?"

Lars felt a lie was justified here. "No. I assure you. I divined it all on my own."

She sighed. "All right. I forgive you."

"More to the point, forgive yourself." He hobbled off.

19

LYING FLAT ON HIS back in bed, Barton watched the white floor-length curtains at the windows dancing in the slight breeze. *Gui,* he thought in the Mandarin of his childhood, *nas* in Namyanese. *Ghosts, spirits, imps, elves* . . . He imagined he was watching a creature with thick white makeup, heavily drawn brows, and a pert cherry mouth, swaying in her white robes. He sighed and turned to the wall, where a sleek black—thing—was next to the—thing—he was lying on. How, he wondered idly, could he remember the word for "ghost" in three languages but not these familiar—things?

Now a sound came from the black thing. He swatted it to make it stop and a disembodied voice spoke to him. Barton wanted to say something. Instead, he closed his eyes.

His grandmother was singing *Xiao xingxing* to him. He was a little boy and *zumu* was his favorite person in the world. He opened his eyes to find people—he remembered that word—staring at him from the end of the thing. Lying place?

In case they were thieves who had come to rob him, he said, "*Ni xiang yao shenmea.*" Then he remembered. *Everything of value* was lying in the lake, in the slime, in the ooze, in the fucking flower weeds. In Lake Leini. He threw up and presently felt a sharp prick in his arm and then something being attached to him.

* *

"He's delirious!" Trudy wailed. She and Ward had run to Barton's room when they'd gotten the call that Barton had spiked a fever. Now they pressed against the wall, intently watching the nurse. Ward put his hand over hers and squeezed. She squeezed back the slightest bit, then pushed away and started combing through her russet-brown (dyed) hair, a nervous tic she had.

"What's going on?" she wailed again.

Thila was there too. She spoke to the nurse and translated, "She gives medicine for fever."

"Why the hell isn't the *doctor* here?" said Ward.

"She's coming, Mr. and Madame Wong, please to not worry."

But it was clear to Trudy they had reason to be worried. Even the hotel nurse, who was well-trained and well-paid by Namyanese standards, had flushed cheeks and twitching hands.

Barton moaned. The nurse checked his temperature again and had a rapid conversation with Thila and the dapper hotel manager who had just arrived.

Immediately, the manager got on his phone, no longer the polite and deferential man they knew. He began shouting.

"They must to bring special plane," Thila told the Wongs.

"A medevac?" Ward barked.

Trudy began to cry.

Thila had never faced this level of emergency as a tour guide. There had been health crises before—notably, the elderly Chinese man whose wife found him slumped over the toilet, dead from a heart attack. Trent & Koss Adventures Tours prepared their agents for such eventualities. But Barton was not old, and he had had an accident under her watch.

Thila chewed her lip, not noticing until blood trickled out and splashed onto her hand. She had to stay calm. She could hear her father's voice from the time before he came back from prison and gave in to despair. A vigorous scholar, he'd liked to use the anglicisms he'd learned from his English literature professor, a Brit who'd managed to stay on after the coup—"buck up," "pull your socks up" (amusing, he pointed out, in a country that wore flip-flops), "don't give up the ship." Up, up, up.

Thila blotted her lips. She would buck up and pull up her socks and defend the ship with her last breath. No one must guess at her fear and—this surprised her—the anger that coursed through her as they fussed over Barton. The care these Americans assumed was theirs by right—and they received it. Had they medevaced her grandmother out of her village when she was bitten by a *mwebwe* viper? Or the babies who wasted away from dysentery? Only the top out-of-sight in Namyan got that level of care, or any medical care, come to that, aside from the *yasesayo*'s herbs and incantations.

She went out of the room and called the head manager in Gonyang, who groaned and cursed when she told him what had happened.

While Thila was on the phone, the doctor, an elderly Frenchwoman who spoke medical Namyanese with a strong accent hurried in. The Wongs flew to her. She waved her hands, turned to Barton, and soon gave a stream of orders to the nurse.

Yes, she said at last, turning to the Wongs. He had to get to a hospital.

Trudy moaned. "All the family is coming next week for Chinese New Year in Gonyang!"

"He may recover by then," Ward said, but weakly.

Trudy waved a hand wildly. "And I don't trust the Namyanese with him. They resent us Chinese because we are successful. We need to fly him out of the country!" She was too upset to worry about being polite.

The doctor said nothing, but her lips tightened.

* *

The copter's arrival hours later was a dramatic drop into a patch of land behind the hotel bordering the marsh, the lake glinting just beyond. Quickly, Barton was carried on in a stretcher, as the old French doctor conferred in shouts with the medevac personnel. She was afraid he might have contracted necrotizing fasciitis, in which case they would be lucky to save him and certainly have to amputate, though she said nothing about this to the Wongs.

Thila had arranged for a car to take the Wongs to Gonyang. She patiently explained to them over and over that it would take a while to get to the hotel. They sat in the lobby, bags packed in a fury, and waited, rigid as portraits.

20

THE NEXT NIGHT, a festive dinner had been planned for the group at an alfresco restaurant a few miles from the hotel. No one, of course, was in the mood for celebration, but they went.

At the restaurant, white-clad tables lit with hurricane lamps were set near the lake glimmering through the reeds that came to the edge of the lawn, and a family of ducks that seemed to have settled in for the night nearby quacked sleepily.

Wasn't it a shame, Betsy queried at once as she sat down, that the Steinmans, the Wongs, and Barton weren't here to enjoy this beautiful setting?

There were murmurs, head shakes, and a subdued response to the waiters who immediately brought around cocktails. Soon they perked up after the first sips, even laughed a bit. It was a beautiful setting to take in, drink in hand. Even abstemious Lidia, Catty, and Thila unwound with their faux mimosas.

Yet Lidia was restless. She hadn't talked to Haynes since the Barton fiasco, which had kicked up the guilt lying in wait like the mist now settling on the lawn and shrubbery of the restaurant. She left the group and wandered around. If only she could sit with her sketchbook by the reeds and draw the duck family bobbing gently on its reed bed for the night, their beaks drawn to their chests, the babies with mama; a perfect life. She was overcome by an appetite for physical pleasure that had flared up in her again. The only thing she knew to do was to wait it out. Strangely, she thought, it had also opened her up to art again.

At a pagoda that morning—for inevitably, they'd gone to another pagoda—she'd come across several men drawing and selling drawings of Buddhas, fishermen, monks. Tourist factory stuff, except for one man's. She'd pointed at his drawing of a small boy holding a slingshot, laughingly crouched behind a row of monks. It reminded her of her brother Tomás. Always getting into trouble. "I'll take that," she'd said. "How much?"

After handing him the *takys*, she took out her sketchbook and box of colored drawing pencils and drew an old woman standing nearby, her eyes crinkling, her expression sturdy, her *logni* faded to a dusty lavender imprinted with stars. The Namyanese artist nodded and smiled and began drawing the woman too. He and Lidia traded strokes like musicians: faces, hands, feet. She shared her pencils. She forgot herself. A little audience gathered to watch.

Finally, Thila approached. "Miss DeCampos! How beautiful! I see you make new friends. But now please, we must to go."

Lidia had given the unfinished sketch to the artist before hurrying off.

Now she left the ducks and went to the table, where everyone else was sitting. She saw Haynes laughing between the Lattimores and the Leibitz-Kai's. She took the one vacant seat left, next to Betsy Poison, who seemed to be lecturing her husband in a whisper.

"All right, all right," he said with a rusty growl. *Like the Tin Man in need of oil*, Lidia thought. Actually, he sounded like Felipe had, as if he were corroding from the inside.

Lidia slumped into her seat. "Madame," said a waiter, bowing to her as if she were some kind of pasha. "Beef, chicken, fish."

"Oh, fish, I suppose."

It was always a long evening when you were the one, or one of the ones, who was not drinking, but tonight, sitting with the Hodgeses, it seemed endless. She ignored Mr. Poison completely, of course, per her pact with herself. Why hadn't Catty and Lars or Haynes saved her a seat? Well, not Haynes, as they'd agreed not to fan the flames of speculation by sitting together at meals: her idea, not his. What a dumb, uptight "rule," she thought now, the kind of self-imposed censure she'd had ground into her. A working-class Catholic school girl who had to wear *white gloves* to school, until senior year, when she and a few others dared to go with naked hands. She'd have to rise to the occasion for the next couple of hours. But wasn't she an expert in riding out spaces of time? Grim watches in institutional settings when time was like a black dog. And here, at least, she could watch the bruised shades of night fall upon the long brown lawn, hear the dream-honks of the slumbering ducks, look at the varnished-silver lake as it merged with the darkening sky. Eat, nod, smile, ignore Mr. Poison. Think about a sketch: these waiters when they were home at last, squatting on earthen floors, hawking betel nut, slurping tea. Kids running in and out between their long brown feet, women bent over smoky fires. Their faces: pliant, jocular, free of the demands of white tourists.

Betsy, neatly deflating this modest fantasy picture, brightly said, "You never drink the wine, Lidia. Are you teetotal?"

"It upsets my stomach. Here, you have mine. Please."

"Oh, I couldn't. One glass is plenty for me."

An old AA fortune-cookie adage sprang into Lidia's mind: *One drink is too many and a thousand are not enough.* Lidia hardly ever thought about the non-drinking thing anymore, but found it interesting that occasionally, as now, the notion of downing that glass just for spite popped into her head.

"All packed for tomorrow?" Betsy asked. Lidia was about to attempt a response when Ann leaned over.

"Isn't it something how jammed the suitcases get?" she asked. "All these knickknacks! I told Ed he's going to have to sit on mine to get it shut." She took a good swallow from her wine glass.

"Yes," Lidia said. *Yes, no, sure, you're kidding.*

The waiters came with another platter. Dessert. Which would probably be mangos. And was mangos.

"Coffee?" Lidia asked, plaintively.

"Yes, Madame."

"Have you been shopping your way through Namyan?" Ann suddenly asked her.

Surprised that Ann was still acknowledging her existence, Lidia said politely, "I bought a lovely pen-and-ink drawing."

"Oh, that's right, the artist thing. I just love art. The Impressionists! Manet's 'Water Lilies'. So beautiful."

"Monet," Lidia murmured. Ann seemed to have been imbibing a bit more than usual. "Actually, I find that painting disturbing. If you really look at it."

"Disturbing? 'Water Lilies'?" Ann straightened her shoulders.

"The thing is, I was very near-sighted as a child, and then when I got glasses, it was so disconcerting to realize there was another way of seeing that I'd known nothing about. Much too sharp-edged at first, instead of the creamy blur I'd taken for reality. I mean, *everything was too much to look at.* Too vividly detailed and in your face. And the upsetting question—I couldn't formulate it at that age, of course, but still, it was there: so, what was real? What I'd always seen without glasses, wasn't that my particular reality? Glasses were, I don't know, like a drug. You know? Sharply altered my perceptions. Of course, I soon got used to them. But, back to Monet . . . It happened to him when he painted 'Water Lilies', except in reverse. He was losing his sight then and a new reality was revealed to him, murky and soft-edged. It must have been strange and upsetting at the very least, the world seen so gauzily—for an artist, I mean. That's the sense I get from his paintings of that period. The *anxiety* that comes over you when you can't rely on what you've always thought was real."

Ann blinked.

Lidia picked up her coffee cup. The coffee was surprisingly good, smooth and strong. Ann's expression was one Lidia had seen before when she'd opened up to people who didn't get it, the "what the fuck?" look. But why should she have to stick to their boring, quotidian script all the time?

"I guess you artists just think differently," Ann said eventually. "Well," she added with relief, draining her wine glass, "Thila's giving us the high sign!"

They all tried, as older people do, to conceal the effort it took to toil up what was quite a steep hill—with no staircase—to the road where the bus waited. And they were tired, from the general relentlessness of travel, the Steinmans and Barton, the fancy dinners and abundance of booze. Thila, by far the youngest, and Ted and Franklin Leibitz-Kai, who worked out regularly, and Lidia, who was "only" sixty, managed the climb okay, but the rest of them huffed and halted frequently.

Last, as always, came Mrs. Hills, broad-beamed in cotton trousers, jabbing her cane at the slope as if it were an affront—which, arguably, it was—to her mortality. She finally accepted the arm of a waiter who, after being scolded by the manager, had come running after her.

21

"I HEAR YOU GOT ON the internet. Still sorry we stayed here?" Lars asked the Hodgeses and Borens at dinner the next night, their last at the lake. The hotel offering was a deceptively simple meal of perfectly grilled fish, pommes frites, Namyanese-style salad and, for once, no mangos.

"Very spotty," Betsy replied, "but I finally got through to Tammy. Her granddaughter's out of critical now and they think she's going to be as okay as, well, she can be."

"What a relief." Catty fiddled with her cutlery. "We haven't heard anything new about Barton, though."

"Let us pray for him." Betsy bent her head and plunged into the "Our Father."

After a frozen moment, a very thin chorus accompanied her. Not Ted, who was Jewish, or Franklin, who was Muslim, or the Vondervilles, lapsed Episcopalians. Not Mrs. Hills, either, whose beliefs Lidia wasn't clear about. Even Lidia, an unlapsed Episcopalian, declined to participate.

Catty murmured afterwards to her, "If we were going to pray, I think it should have been something Buddhist."

"But, oh ye of little faith."

"Of no faith."

142 Linda Dahl

All but Catty and Lidia resumed drinking wine or beer or mixed drinks after their amens. Lars, glowing after his second cocktail, leaned in on Catty's right. "Wasn't that the pip?"

"I'd rather we'd prayed that Barton has a competent medical team," Lidia said.

The group was swallowing the last of their drinks when Thila at last appeared. As if this marked the start of musical chairs, they all stopped moving at the tense expression on her face.

"I have news. Mr. Liu is changed to Royal Asia Hospital. I must go there to help operations."

"Operations?" Ann squawked, sounding like a parrot. Lidia had noticed she'd been pretty free with the wine again that evening.

"Logistics," Lars supplied.

"Therefore I have another guide to the many sites in Dalayman until I may return. Mr. Phyo, our driver, will also assist."

Amid the voices, anxious, curious and, a few, querulous, Colonel Ken's cut through. "Good that you're going; the Wongs will appreciate the support. But I suggest you choose a contact person among us to keep everybody up to speed."

"You, Ken!" Lars said.

"Second that!" Sally shrilled—also, Lidia thought, rather like a parrot.

The last leg of their journey to the city of Dalayman meant a long bus ride around the lake and east into the interior, where they'd meet Thila's replacement. The bus driver, Mr. Phyo, did his best to point out interesting sights along the way, which consisted of stopping the bus and pointing. Lunch was at a pizzeria of all things. Papa Aung's featured lemongrass-flavored marinara sauce and was popular with the European trekkers. Then they went to the hotel, one of the luxury chains Betsy and Ann loved.

A young man with a wispy hipster beard and clothing that might have come from a vintage shop in Bed-Stuy was waiting for them in the lobby.

Even the new guide's name, Revo, was hipster. They had time to "clean," he said, before meeting him in the lobby to "go view the sun descend."

"Have you heard from Thila?" Ken asked rather sternly. "We are anxious to know how Barton Liu is doing."

Revo was at once gravely conciliatory, that quality perfected in countries used to being oppressed by external players. "Yes. Miss Thila, she say she shall call when at hospital. Too much traffic still. I please to tell you next."

The gorgeous sunset viewing took place at an ancient palace, a mercifully short drive from the hotel. The palace was a great, red and tan, rambling edifice—vine-choked, abandoned, and melancholy, with some beautiful, faded carvings and a long once-grand walkway around it. Lidia was surprised to learn that a part of the palace, battered and worn as it was, was still in use as government offices, plus the usual food and tchotchke stalls.

As it was late in the day, the place was pretty much empty of the dreaded fleets of buses that conveyed Chinese and Korean tour groups from their less grand hotels. Revo's attempts to tell them about battles won and lost soon stuttered to silence as they wandered off in various directions, snapping photos and peering at the crumbling perimeter. The palace had been renovated in part, in a slapdash way, with bright red bricks crammed into otherwise opalescent walls, such that the potentially magnificent place had been withdrawn from consideration as a World Heritage site. The cherry on the top was a neon sign, winking like the pink martini glasses above 1950s American bars, in what Revo told them had been a king's private stupa.

The sun set in molten red behind the ruins and they went back to the Wi-Fied hotel, done, cooked, over it.

News came about Barton: he was resting and the doctors were considering options. (Revo had looked up the English for "options" in his pocket dictionary.)

"Options?" Clint said. "I'll bet those Wongs are moving hell and back to get him on a plane to the States."

Sally, who had gotten an early start with cocktails on the terrace, tittered. "The Chinese were like that in Thailand. Always got their way."

Ken leaned in. "Sally . . ."

"You know it's true. Very aggressive."

Revo's face began to perspire. From a recess of his mind there popped up one of those colloquial expressions that his English teacher in college had delighted in parsing for the class: *hot seat*. He was in the hot seat. He should stop this *trash talk*, but how?

At that moment, the dignified bald old man stood up and demanded more details about Barton Liu's condition. "Options? What options?"

Haynes chimed in. "Yeah. Because we know it's something damn serious."

"Give it to us straight, fella!" growled Clint. "Are they're gonna amputate or not?"

Ann gasped. "Oh no!'

"If it's a flesh-eating disease, they're gonna have to," Ken said.

"Flesh-eating?" Ann screeched.

Revo, who felt as though he were in a bad dream, started edging away. "Please, we do not know these things!" he said.

Everyone ignored him as Colonel Ken took charge. "Look, but we can't speculate. We know it could be bad. We just have to hang in there."

"He's right," said Ted. "Thila's very competent. Let her do her job."

Revo let out a sigh. He would make an offering to the Buddha in honor of the resolute words of these two men. Despite the fact that one of them had lost serious face by having a publicly drunk wife, and the other called another man "husband" and they'd been seen *holding hands*. (Men and women never showed public displays of emotion in Namyan, let alone two men! Of course, they were Americans.)

"Look at the symptoms! They're gonna cut off his leg," Clint stated, then swigged his beer.

Ted said tightly, "As a firefighter and EMT for twenty-five years, I've seen pretty much everything. Look, doctors can call it wrong, but they usually don't. Thila will tell us what she knows from them when she knows! So stop talking about cutting off his leg!"

The Lattimores, Leibitz-Kais, Haynes, Catty, Lars, and Lidia left shortly after that (Mrs. Hills having long since decamped). The rest stayed, sharing lurid details gleaned from their devices about flesh-eating diseases, as Revo squirmed.

Their time in Dalayman rolled by in a listless haze like the last days before school lets out for the endless summer. Before their last meal there, Ed sat in his hotel room, nursing a Coke. Ann had gone downstairs. He edited some photos on his phone for that piece he was still working on for the Entomology Society dinner. Clicking through, he came on a series he'd forgotten taking. It must have been automatic, his long training in the field. Hesitate and you lose the shot. These were of those two in the field near that hut. He peered, got out his magnifier. He still couldn't tell for sure if they were copulating.

His thoughts turned to work. That day he'd only been able to spend an hour in the field, but he'd been rewarded by the sighting of an *Aspidimorpha sanctaecrucis*, the Golden Tortoise beetle. Ann chided him, though not so much after all these years, for not being more of a "people person." Ed protested that he liked some of his fellow entomologists, and of course he loved his two children, and his grandsons. Peter, the younger, ten, liked to go on hikes with him and point out wildflowers and such to take pictures of. Ed planned to get him a decent camera for his next birthday, though Ann thought he was too young for that.

He drained his cola. He hadn't talked much with Barton, but there had been an unspoken sympathy between them in their shared passion for the proper working of their equipment. And once, trudging up or down some pagoda, Barton—he had an eye—had pointed out a swarm of yellow moths, for which Ed had been grateful. But that wasn't what moved him about Barton, he knew. It was the shared catastrophe of the body. He fingered the right side of his jaw.

Hemifacial microsomia could be quite disfiguring; he had been lucky compared to many with his disorder, but still, he always tried to avoid looking at the slightly caved-in right side of his jaw, except when he shaved, and managed to forget about it for the most part. But now, Barton's impending loss of a limb revived his childhood terror of being in the hospital for that lower jaw reconstruction surgery.

22

FINALLY, REVO HAD SOME news. His lack of familiarity with English made it something of a cliffhanger. "The illness, it is . . ." A dusky blush reddened his face as he paused to look at notes. "Is . . ."

"Necrotizing fasciitus?"

Revo looked up. "Not."

"Well, what is it, man?" Clint bellowed.

Colonel Ken strode up and peered at Revo's notes. He shook his head. "It's written in the Namyanese alphabet. Can you spell it out in English, Revo?"

"C—e—l—l—u—"

"Cellulitis!" several of them said simultaneously, as in, "Bingo!"

"They not cut the leg," Revo added.

Catty took a pensive sip of coffee. "What a relief."

"It's good, but he's not out of the woods yet," Ted cautioned. "He'll be on heavy antibiotics. And hope for no complications. It's not a quick recovery."

"Let's send him a get-well card!" Betsy said.

"Good idea!" said Ann.

"Those two never fail to appall," Lars muttered to Catty and Lidia. They had wandered to the shady side of the pool area, as the group had the morning off. They were in that mood that comes over children at the end of a hectic day with too much sugar: they were wired but wanted to do and learn nothing, certainly not one more Namyanese fact or sensual impression. They flattened their loungers and lay motionless. Very soon, Lars's gentle snores pierced the silence.

And then Catty broke the silence, turning to Lidia. "You haven't told me a thing about you and Klaus."

"I haven't told anyone! Except—Lars. And why I told him, I have no idea. LARS!"

Lars scrambled awake, his book, *Finding George Orwell in Namyan*, slipping to the concrete. "What?"

"Did you break your promise to me?"

"Which promise are you referring to?"

"Don't obfuscate. Yes or no."

"Well . . . She guessed it," Lars said.

"It's obvious," Catty said.

"It isn't! We—*I've* been very careful. And it's, well, it's nobody's business."

"Oh, nobody cares, Lidia. Except the busybodies."

"Mrs. Poison and Mrs. Bore," Lars clarified needlessly.

Lidia put her face in her hands. "Oh, hell, *they* know?"

"As long as you've been enjoying yourself, who cares?"

Lars edged nearer. "He's clearly a nice enough fellow."

"Oh, go away, Lars," said Catty.

"Well! I will." He grinned. "Speaking of which, there he is, in a pair of natty swim trunks. Think I'll see if he wants to join me in a cold one."

"You will not!" Catty told him. "Lidia doesn't want you to. I'll go with you," she added. "As a sacrifice for the greater good."

Lidia smiled at her friend in thanks.

After Catty took Lars away, Lidia went over to Haynes, iced tea in hand. Her expensive swimsuit claimed to be a miracle but her tummy was stubbornly resistant to even miraculous girdling. Well, what did it matter? He'd seen her in the altogether.

She couldn't help assessing him in his swim trunks. Older men tended to be mostly scrawny or swollen. Klaus didn't fit either of these categories, thankfully, but still, she thought, if he'd turned up in a Speedo, it would have been a game changer, despite his reasonably smooth skin and muscles. The only thing out of proportion about him was his very large feet. And who cared about feet other than foot fetishists and the feet police? That his well-preserved brown body looked good, even with the flippers, perversely annoyed her. All the more likely that, even at his age (and when do men, most of them, ever accept the fact that they've aged?) he could well be the kind of macho creep who goes blithely from woman to woman. She wondered how she'd managed to suppress this well-worn fear until now.

"Wondering where you've been hiding, lately," she said, instantly counting it as a bad move. *Don't show your cards.*

"Yeah, I've been on the phone constantly, mainly with my son-in-law in the States. Kwami's an infectious disease doc so the Wongs wanted him in on the conversation, maybe fly him out . . . That isn't going to happen, though." Haynes stretched and yawned and suddenly looked his age. "They've got it figured out now, thank God. I wasn't *avoiding* you," he added.

Lidia couldn't get her game together. She was obscurely aggrieved, off-kilter. Well, for good reason: she was going to be leaving Namyan soon, he was going to a mine-strewn civil war zone. This was it. "You could have checked in with me."

Haynes stroked her cheek. "Well, what're you doing later?"

"Hm. I thought I'd go climb another pagoda."

An hour later, she lay beside him in his suite, which was exactly like her own but felt very different because the air conditioner wasn't on.

A hot breeze stirred the sheer curtains at the window, as did a table-top fan.

"How the hell did you get the window open?"

"Called the engineer. Made him take the bolts out and bring a fan."

"That is so Haynes." She reached over and kissed his dry, firm lips. "I am so hungry."

He waved a hand. "There's fruit, nuts, wine. Fancy water for you." He got up and improvised a plate with a towel. She watched him, settled now by sex, possessed by the marvelous if unfamiliar feeling of not needing to do anything or go anywhere. This, she mused, was the impending end to their whatever-it-was. Not a relationship. Hook-up, Lily's generation called it. She pictured Haynes in his youth, wearing a 'fro, rolling a joint, hypnotizing women with his green eyes and strange accent.

"Back in the day, did you wear a 'fro? And/or bellbottoms?"

He shook his head. "Neither. You?"

"Sewed a little American flag on the butt of my jeans. Papi made me take it off. He was steamed."

"Little hippie." He set down the towel, arrayed with red bananas, mangos, and almonds. They ate.

"I told you," he continued, "I was selling appliances. Played handball, listened to soul." He shrugged. "I did smoke some pot."

Lidia nodded, chewing. She was feeling deliciously drowsy yet energetic, the way she sometimes did when she meditated. She leaned back against the pillows, full of healthy food.

"But you and refrigerators? I can't see it."

"It was a living. Okay, I quit, eventually. Saw a photography show at the Schomburg. Gordon Parks. It blew me away. Then I saw another one. Peter Matthiessen, snow leopards. That was it, I got a camera, took some classes. Started working for Sears, you know, babies, kids. Mostly lame stuff but I was learning. Wasn't easy—well, you know that. Went from a regular paycheck to nothing. Drove a cab for a while." He shook his head. "Blew two marriages apart. My uncle died before I quit the store, he would have chewed my ass for leaving." He smiled. "And I still maintain there's nothing wrong with selling refrigerators. Better than drugs."

"Except you stopped," she said. "My papi never did. He worked in a factory all his life. The plant, I should say. Not on the floor. He wore a shirt and a tie. Management, first in the family. Came home after work and fell asleep in front of the TV after supper. Mom waiting on him, us. He was happy when he went fishing. I didn't want that kind of life. It wasn't a bad life." She yawned.

"Sleepy?"

"Uh-huh."

Soon, Haynes was gently snoring, but despite wanting to, Lidia couldn't fall sleep. Then she thought about the last time with Felipe and couldn't push the memories away. She brought him his old CD player and a bunch of his favorite music, some Latin jazz. She put on Eddie Palmieri and he broke into a smile. He hadn't known who she was anymore, but he remembered his precious music.

When she woke up, it was the middle of the night, and Haynes was sitting cross-legged on the bed, balancing another plate of fruit and nuts on his knee.

"I ordered a pot of coffee for you," he said.

"I'm glad I met you, Haynes."

"I'm glad I met you."

"Can I draw you? For real this time. I'm going to call it 'The Fruit-eater.' There's some Gauguin in your tough hide."

"Do I have to sit long?"

"Not long. I'll ply you with mangos."

23

WHEN REVO TOLD THEM they would be going to another pagoda, something about a sleeping Buddha with giant feet, there were widespread groans.

"But this one's a must-see! Five stars," Lars said, looking up from his guidebook. "The giant feet are mapped out with 108 'auspicious characters.'"

"Hmmph," Clint said.

"What a peculiar number, 108," said Catty. "Do they explain why?"

"No," said Lars.

"As my grand-niece says about everything, *whatever*." Catty shrugged. "I'm going to get another coffee. Lidia?"

Lars waved a hand. "You girls go. I'm going to read up on the auspicious characters. By the way, where's Klaus?"

"Shouldn't we wait for Mr. Haynes?" Lars asked Revo ten minutes later on the bus, as the driver prepared to leave.

"Oh, Mr. Hah-nes not come. He go away."

"Go away where?" Lidia almost hissed. She'd left Haynes sleeping after she started her sketch, which soon gave way to lovemaking again.

"Mr. Hah-nes and Laddymores go to Gonyang."

Revo avoided her eyes. He was, Lidia realized, embarrassed. Oh, good Lord, who didn't know about their liaison? "Yes, of course," she said crisply. *So there*, she told herself.

For once there were only a few steps up to the entrance where the feet police stood next to a large but fairly orderly pile of Namyanese sandals and tourist shoes. It was a massive white pavilion with several small shrines, like a cathedral with saints' niches. At the far end was the pièce de résistance, a gigantic, gilded Buddha lolling on his side, with an expression of perfectly gleeful detachment. The soles of his giant feet were indeed mapped out in a grid of red and gold segments. Lidia went to a plaque nearby that, in almost digestible English, explained the 108 auspicious characteristics of the Buddha. So arbitrary and so finite. And again, why the feet? Wasn't the head supposed to be the seat of consciousness? Though when you thought about it, it was the sinews and bones and knuckles of the feet that held up the whole package. The head made contact with the air, sky, but the feet made contact with Mother Earth, wherein bodily suffering resided: Lars's suppurating foot, Lidia's pierced sole, Catty's trick knee, Barton's infected leg . . .

Dozens of people circled the massive resting deity. Cameras clicked. Lidia tried to imprint on the artist's part of her brain this huge Buddha at rest—like God, she thought, on the seventh day. She knew that her lack of reaction to the news about Haynes leaving was simply a delayed response. Already, a stew of feelings was starting to simmer.

High-pitched yelling pierced her musings and Lidia followed the commotion to the other side of the pavilion, where a foot policeman seemed to be berating a young Asian woman. Beside the woman, who didn't seem to understand what was happening, a young man was rooted to the spot.

Finally, the policeman stalked away. Lidia approached them. "Um, do you speak English?"

In a tiny voice, the girl breathed out, "Yes."

"Well, what was going on? Happening? Why was that cop—policeman—so upset? Upset?" she repeated.

"Because we go in that small temple. To look." She pointed tremulously at a shrine with its statue of the Siddhartha Gautama. "That man puts hands on me. Rough. I don't know what I do! He keep to shoot." The girl began to cry in hiccups.

Lidia whipped around. She saw no gun on the glaring man nearby. "Do you mean shout, maybe? Speak loudly at you?"

"Yes."

Lidia noticed a placard at the side of the shrine. Beneath the curlicued Namyanese script, it said in English: No Female Allowed. "Oh dear," she said. "Look at this."

The girl sucked in her breath. "I do not see this."

"I almost made the same mistake at another temple. Apparently, each place has different policies—rules? Made by men, of course. Some think that women are a polluting influence—do you know that word?"

The girl shook her head. "No, please."

"Unclean. Not clean."

The young woman cupped her hands around her face and moved her head back and forth.

"That guy was being an officious prick—uh, bad man. Not very Buddhist, to my mind. Not at all. Look, it probably happens all the time with tourists."

"You are kind to help us." The boyfriend shook his head in disgust and, no doubt, shame. "We go now."

"But have you seen the Buddha with the giant feet? You have to see it, just around the corner. Come on, yes, come with me, it's all right."

She led the reluctant pair to the recumbent mass, but as she was explaining that "auspicious" meant "lucky" (close enough), the Japanese woman drew in her breath sharply.

"He here!"

The two made tiny head ducks to Lidia and hurried off, the cop behind them. Lidia glanced around to make sure no one was looking at her then stuck her tongue out at the gaudy feet-worshipping statue. *Please*, she thought, *enough about feet forever.* She went outside.

Many in the group habitually returned to the bus before the appointed time, except for Mrs. Hills; a wild card, she might get there very early or very late. Franklin and Sally, who always looked for a shopping opportunity, and Betsy and Ann, who got caught up in whispered conversations, tended to be the regular late arrivals.

Lidia was usually fairly prompt about the bus, but today she wanted to be alone to clear her head, to think about Haynes's vanishing act. She found a shady spot, leaned against a column, and closed her eyes. But apparently, there was no escaping the group; Ann's voice pealed from somewhere out of sight but nearby, "And did you see how she looked when Revo said Klaus Haynes had gone to Gonyang?"

"Those two, carrying on like teenagers." Betsy Poison.

"Can you believe it? Ed saw them in a *field*, carrying on. *You* know—having *sex!*"

"Ladies, ladies." Franklin. He sounded both amused and annoyed. "I mean, we all like to gossip, but—"

"She's just telling us what her husband saw," Betsy said huffily.

"Well, *I* say, good for them, they're certainly old enough to do what they want," Franklin replied. "Come on, it's time to go back."

Lidia waited until there was silence. When she was sure they'd gone, she kicked a stone hard. A bird flew up, squawking. Maybe it was mating season and she had disturbed a nest. Mating, sex! Perfectly normal, she and Haynes . . . last night. The odds, she thought, were astronomically high that Ann and Betsy—and Ed, don't forget Ed, the source of the fabrication—had not had a good fuck in decades. If ever.

Lily's voice, she of the gender-fluid present generation, floated into her mind. *Hey Mom, why do you care what those old farts think?* And Franklin had stuck up for her, bless his heart.

But I do care, Lidia thought, *because he left without a word.*

She steeled herself, shades on, chin erect, to go to the bus. Mercifully, she found a seat in the back, ripe for brooding.

But here came Catty. "What was the kerfuffle about with that Japanese couple?"

"Oh, the poor girl polluted a shrine. Didn't see the sign forbidding women to enter. You know, like a bathroom figure of a female, with a slash."

At that moment, the Hodgeses got on and moved back to seats just in front of them. Almost immediately, they heard Clint snoring. Betsy glanced around, narrowed her eyes at them, and then pivoted forward, though not before Lidia shot her a smile like a gunshot.

"What did you think of the 108 auspicious aspects, Betsy?" Catty asked in her best, carrying, lady-of-the-manor voice.

Betsy turned her head minutely in their direction. "Those big old feet? Seems like childish nonsense to me. These people are just like children with their Buddhas, aren't they? Child-size, too."

"We must seem like the Hulk to them," Catty shot back. "Anyway, doesn't every religion seem nonsensical to outsiders? For that matter, to me. But I have to say, I much prefer looking at Buddhas than a man wearing a crown of thorns nailed to a cross."

"Well, we Christians don't use the crucifix, we use the cross."

"Catholics use the crucifixion and they're Christians," Lidia inserted, reluctantly. She should know, she'd been forced to go to mass until she left home.

"No, they're Catholics," Betsy responded obscurely.

Lidia persisted. "And these people the size of *children* are smaller than us because they've been malnourished for eons. I think their religion is a beautiful tradition. Even the Buddha's feet. The 108 auspicious signs. It gives them hope. I'm sure we can all use some hope."

There was one of those flat silences and then, to Lidia's amazement, Betsy's moon-shaped face scrunched up and tears coursed down her slack cheeks. "Hope? Don't talk to me about hope." She glanced at her husband, head lolling. "My husband has cancer." She let out a half sob, half hiccup.

Lidia, who knew intimately the devastation a terrible illness causes for all concerned, felt an unwelcome rush of sympathy. This trip was meant to be an escape, a reprieve from that. But it hadn't gone away.

"Well, I'm very sorry," she said, trying to mean it.

Betsy's face reddened. She glanced swiftly at her husband. "I shouldn't be talking about it." Her face twisted.

But you're still the Poisons, Lidia thought.

24

In GONYANG, SALLY FELL gratefully into an overstuffed chair, shopping bags at her feet. All she needed to buy now was another suitcase to cart all the extras home. She stroked the firm yet soft fabric of the flowered chintz arm of the chair, smiling at the golden Buddha close by. Chintz with Buddhas—the Brits always left their mark, seen and unseen, on their former colonies.

"Care for a drink?" she called out, seeing Klaus Haynes.

He sighed and sat down with a thump in an identical chair.

"Tough time at the consulate?" she asked.

"Yeah. Hurry up and wait. But they keep saying it's almost ready. What're you having?"

"A Bock. Ein-something."

"Bock Einbecker? Man, that's one of the best German brews—how the hell do they have it in Gonyang? Waiter!"

"Order three, will you? Ken's coming any minute and I'm almost finished with this one." She sighed. "We missed seeing the huge Buddha with the huge feet in Dalayman."

"But you have your own Buddha now."

"True." Determined to buy a Burmese Buddha, and not just any old Buddha, Sally had done her research before setting foot in Namyan. The best ones were in a half dozen or so exclusive boutiques and she'd nabbed her favorite before they'd set off from Gonyang on the tour—a small, exquisite jade figurine. She'd put down her deposit, planning to secure it at the end of the trip. Then—the recording had only come through on her phone when they'd finally gotten service in Dalayman—the owner of the boutique left her a message that he'd been made a better offer. It could be, probably was, a trick to up the price, but she wanted that figurine. She called him back and protested, wheedled, begged, and bargained until he said he'd hold it for her—at a new, higher amount, but still less than he'd started with. Then, when Ken said the consulate had texted Haynes to get back to Gonyang right away for his precious visa to the war-torn hinterlands, she'd convinced Ken they should go with him so she could seal the deal. Hurriedly, they packed and left with Haynes in a rental car he'd somehow finagled in a land without Hertz and Enterprise.

After another round of Bock Einbecker, Sally sashayed to the elevator.

Hope she'll make it up to her suite. She may just fall over like a stone, Haynes thought, lingering with Ken. Despite her sharpness or maybe because of it—it reminded him of his aunt and other memorable Black women he'd known, including Ellie, his first wife—Haynes appreciated Sally's sass and the many useful tidbits she'd picked up on maneuvering in Southeast Asia. Still, he felt a sense of unease about her. And again, why *did* Ken always put up with her shit? She'd called him a dolt, a dummy, and an ass, all in less than an hour.

Lidia, disheveled and disheartened, sank into a chintzy chair too, but in the lobby of the hotel in Dalayman. "He left without a word!" she said dramatically.

A faint flash of anxiety crossed Catty's face. "Well, we'll be on our way to Gonyang soon. You're sure to see him there."

"I don't want to. Anyway, you know all he thinks about is getting to Hinchak territory." She drooped. "Catty, what have I been thinking?" "You said Dr. Fried told you it's healthy to have *diversions*."

"Fried was encouraging me to *draw* again. I don't think he meant— well, Haynes." She put her head in her hands. "Am I an awful person?"

"Of course not. Listen, I think that young man is looking for *you*. He's saying something that sounds kind of like your name."

"Letta for Liya Deca," said the young man in the sailor whites in which this hotel decorated its lower staff.

Lidia flagged him down, took the letter, and opened it as Catty gave the boy a coin. "It's from Haynes."

She read:

Lidia, I got a call that the press visa which I must have to go to Hinchak territory is coming through so I had to get to the US Consulate here in Gonyang immediately to arrange it. As you know, I've been really hoping for this, so I hitched a ride with the Lattimores—that's another story. Don't know when I'll be leaving the capital but I really hope I see you before then. If not, please know how much I enjoyed your company. I still think you should have come with me. Maybe next time?

—HAYNES

P.S. Read the next page when you have time. I'm working on this for the blog.

Page 2

Persecution

The Namyanese are the largest ethnic group in Namyan, but depending on what you read, there are between 40 and 135 (maybe even more) smaller distinct ethnicities. Many have been fighting for years, even decades, for independence against the well-trained and ruthless Damawat, the powerful Namyanese military force.

Best-known of the civil wars, though there are many more, include these: the far north nominal Christians; a headhunting tribe; and the Muslims in the southwest, now mostly wiped out or banished. The British, when they took over Namyan in the mid-1800s, encouraged many seeds of destruction with their well-honed divide and conquer tricks. After the Japanese had pillaged and burned the country in the Second World War, the Brits "gave independence" to Namyan in 1948. But there was no independence for the people; instead, coup after coup fattened the Damawat, which tightened control of the wealth of the nation—jade, opium, amphetamines, timber, land and serfs. Hundreds of thousands of men, women, and children have been forced to work for the Damawat, many of the women as sex slaves. Many thousands killed.

I might have chosen to go southwest where the Muslim Kinhaies suffer abominably—that is, those who remain. The world's attention is on them now. But not on the Hinchaks in the north. Converted to Christianity when British Baptist missionaries arrived in the 1800s, but not to worry, they worship the nas too. Hinchaks have been at war with the Damawat for at least seventy years. One of the longest civil wars in modern times. The Damawat wants control of their mines (gold, jade, amber) and the only advantage the Hinchaks have is that they know every inch of their land. But they are greatly outnumbered in every way and somewhere between 100,000 and 200,000 Hinchak peasants are caught in the middle, living in refugee camps or hiding out in caves. More of them are dead. There are many landmines where I'm going and constant guerrilla fighting. I am going to film this cruelty, greed, and rapaciousness, which I know something about from my own heritage.

Wish me luck.

Haynes

"The last leg of our trip," Lars said cheerfully as they approached the plane to Gonyang two days later. He no longer felt even a twinge when he walked. To celebrate his foot recovery, he'd bought Namyanese black cotton sandals at the hotel shop, which carried large sizes not available in markets, at king-size prices.

But Catty's trick knee gave out on the steep stairs up the plane and she had to be more or less shoved up and onto the aircraft, where, humiliated and in some pain, she downed two Advil. Scrunched in her seat, she pulled down her Garbo hat.

Lidia was behind Catty and Lars on the small plane. As she half listened to the rise and fall of their voices, Catty's strained, Lars's soothing, a sharp sense of loneliness washed over her. She peeked around her seat. Sure enough, they were holding hands again. Complaining and comforting: the stuff of intimacy, knitting a world around them. The throb and hum of the plane soon lulled her into listlessness, as did the thought of icy, gray March in Manhattan, where she'd be within forty-eight hours, maybe less.

The trip was basically over, she thought.

She was wrong.

25

THEY WERE BACK IN Gonyang, back at the Golden Palace, with the rest of that day and the next as "free" time to catch up on any sightseeing they'd missed and then to pack for the usual middle-of-the-night airport run.

Like many of them, Carolyn Hills opted for a nap. She lay on the bed in her room, which blended with all the other rooms she'd stayed in, trying to doze through the afternoon. Not that she seemed to sleep anymore. It was as if she had an invisible swarm of insects buzzing in her head. She'd read somewhere that butterflies in Namyan were good spirits. Carolyn, who had a private whimsical side, lay picturing an army of *nas* as butterflies, emissaries of rest and peace. But even the lovely image, along with a Percocet, didn't make much of a dent against her attention-grabbing rheumatoid arthritis.

Carolyn counted backwards from one hundred. She thought of other calming things. She monitored her breathing, remembered that her grandniece had given her a CD of relaxing nature sounds (Carolyn wouldn't dream of an iPod), but she had no idea where her relic of a Walkman was in the tangle of her suitcase.

Eventually, she threw off the covers and stood up. Reaching for her kimono on the chair nearby, she slipped on the highly waxed floor and down she went. She heard a crunch as she landed on her face.

Carolyn was familiar with the stages of pain after a fall. In fact, she thought, she could have written a useful pamphlet or blog— what an ugly word—or Twitter feed—even uglier—for the elderly. By which she meant her set, the later eighties and above. At first, you feel surprised, then nothing. This period is very brief, followed by high-voltage jolts and often a cascading agony. Next, you might vomit or pass out. If you're lucky, you manage to make enough noise so that someone hears you. The lucky few will be wearing those medical alert devices. But most people will lie there helplessly. As she now lay.

You moan, whimper, curse, pray. You assess the damage. If, as she had, you've smashed into a hard surface, you grasp the wounded part(s), trying to figure out if something's broken.

Carolyn was also angry. She would *not* lie in the pool of bodily fluids that had been released beneath her. Slowly, she wrestled her body onto its side. She pressed and pushed up to a ragdoll position, grateful for the spurts of strength from her indignation. She was angry at herself. For slacking off the tai chi and chair yoga that helped her with balance. For letting her aches and pains become dictators after a lifetime of rock-climbing, motorcycle racing, skydiving, and practicing Eastern disciplines of strength and flexibility. She was angry also at these hotels, so slick and slippery, so handrail-free. So cruelly indifferent to the elderly.

Carolyn Hills slid back to the floor and passed out.

She woke to the sun on her face, streaming through the curtains, and gradually worked out that it had to be the next morning. She desperately needed to get to the bathroom. *YOU ARE INTREPID*, she reminded herself as she inched toward the bedside table where the phone was.

Between her efforts, she found herself admiring how time seemed to hang in the golden dust motes illuminated by the sunlight coming in through the window. She remembered a dream just before she woke up—or *came to*—probably triggered by the light. Another sunny day. A day that began joyfully. Easter Sunday.

She was wearing a new, cream-colored dress with beautiful smocking and scratchy crinoline and shiny black Mary Janes and she was in church, swinging her legs when she felt a warm trickle down her leg, into her frilled white socks and the new Mary Janes.

"Mama?" she whispered, "I had an accident."

Her mother took her by the arm, out of the big room and down some stairs, gripping hard. Carolyn didn't cry until Mother said, "For shame, Carolyn, a great girl like you soiling yourself like a baby! On Easter, too!"

How old was she? Three? Four? *Oh, the shame of it. The shame of it*, she thought, eight decades on. *But what happened to the beautiful sunlight?*

Later, after the kind people—a nurse and Thila—had gone and she was in her bed again, clean and bandaged and medicated, Carolyn began to cry. It was only a banged-up nose and some bruises. Nothing serious, like a hip. A broken hip could take her out, she knew. Not a nose. But she sobbed with the shame of it.

The frustration! She longed to be on the trail again, in a splendid pagoda, on a clamorous street, the East she had craved and made her home for many years. A good life. She conjured up Hong Kong in the 1950s: glamorous and strange. The immaculately run international school, where she met Louise, the newly arrived Classics mistress. Louise's hair, black as an Indian's (they could say things like that back in the day), always struggling out of its bun. Her peals of laughter. The fun they had at those festivals, the gongs and wild wooden flutes, boats full of flowers, the rice balls, and painted paper dragons writhing down the narrow streets. Laughing, tipsy on rice wine that glorious afternoon when they had pledged their troth at some food stall. Brushing hands in the hallways. Loving one another.

Carolyn slept. She felt much better when she awoke, and rang for a sandwich and tea, waiting by her window until it arrived.

Entering the room, the servant carefully placed a silver tray on the coffee table, bowed, and said, "Okie, Madame."

"Oh, lovely fruit too. Won't you have a cup of tea?"

He looked almost as if she'd struck him in the face, she thought.

"I'll tell the desk you were helping me."

He eased himself onto the edge of a chair. "Okie, Madame."

"What is your name? Mine is Carolyn Hills," she said slowly and carefully, remembering the difficulties of her Asian students in Hong Kong with the peculiarities of English.

"Htun. It mean the success in Anglis." Htun grimaced slightly, perhaps ironically.

"Well. I hope you have much of it," Carolyn told him heartily. "Success."

They drank tea in silence for a bit. Then Htun said, "Madame, I can ask you one thing?"

"Ask away," she said.

"Where you live?"

"In New York City. Well, a part just outside the city proper. It's called Riverdale."

Htun nodded eagerly. "I dream always go Unite States. Madame know Indinapoli?"

"Indianapolis? I don't. It's a very big country, you know."

"Plenty Namyanese people there. Best place for me," he said with a wistful smile.

Carolyn could think only of strip malls, hard winters, and rusting, empty factories.

"Other say I crazy for this dream. To educate as radiation technic, like my *tu*. Is son of my *ma*, sister above me." There seemed to be tears in his eyes. "Yet, how I go?" He rubbed his thumb over his fingers. "For the airplane."

He's hitting me up, she thought placidly. *He must think I'm rich. Of course he does. Staying at this hotel. Being American.* She almost laughed but didn't want to hurt his feelings. "But I have a just-adequate pension and Social Security," she wanted to tell him, "I have had to save up for several years for this trip. No eating out, no new clothes. Coupons. Oh, I'm a lucky, lucky woman, but I've got nothing to give you, my good man, except a nice tip."

What she said instead was, "Keep studying English—it's good already—and do your job well. Job? Work? I'll talk to the manager and tell him how much you helped me. Perhaps he'll give you a promotion. Better job, more money."

Htun clearly wasn't digesting all of what she said, but he looked happy. She found her handbag and dug out $10 US.

"Thank you, Madame, thank you, Madame."

"Best of luck to you."

As Carolyn ate her chicken sandwich, she felt irritatingly guilty. *But why should I feel responsible for Htun/Success's future? He has a job; he must get lots of tips.*

But she did feel guilty.

The left side of Catty's forehead had a cartoon bump where she'd smacked it against the side of the shower, and her right ankle had twisted as she slipped and fell. After she crawled out, the shower continued to wastefully stream behind the slammed bathroom door. But this was no time to be environmentally conscious.

She flung on a bathrobe and dialed 0, dripping water onto the polished floor.

In delightful Namyanese-accented English, the receptionist cooed, "How may I direct your call, Madame Vandavilla?"

"There's a giant hornet in my bathroom!" Catty yelled. Into the silence that followed, she said, "Insect! Bad!"

"Please, I send someone, Madame."

The Golden Palace in Gonyang had gone all out for their soon-to-depart T&K guests. Gift boxes on their pillows containing raw silk scarves, hers a lavender-pale orange mix, Lars's gray with a gold undertone. Tea cakes had been delivered in the afternoon and chocolates had been left on the pillows the previous night. It was shocking to be lathering with high-end, hotel-supplied body wash and be confronted by a monstrous bug waving daggerlike claws at her. Oh, where was Lars? Well of course, schmoozing over Dragan Specials downstairs.

Living up to its high-end reputation, the hotel sent up a team right away. First to arrive was a young man in crisp khaki shirt and pants, all but kowtowing. He held aloft a pole with a net on the end in one hand and a can of probably carcinogenic bug spray in the other and was followed by a manager-type in what looked like Armani. Both were solemn as pallbearers.

"In there!" Catty pointed to the bathroom door, around which steam was seeping. "It has pincers—oh, never mind, just get it out."

The manager bowed. "A thousand apologies, Madame Vandavilla."

The young man opened the bathroom door cautiously while she and the bespoke manager waited at the far end of the room. They heard bumps and thumps, the toilet flushing. The young man emerged, holding the pole, and said something in Namyanese.

"So sorry, these insects we never find here!" the manager said emotionally. "Very strangely!"

"Well, what is it? I want to show it to Dr. Boren, he's an ento—bug scientist. Insects."

"That one is *Kina yeme ouk.*"

"Very sorry," said the boy. "I put on toilet."

"It's on the toilet?" Catty cried out.

"What's all this?"

Catty whirled around. "Lars! Now you show up. A nasty, huge insect with pincers came at me in the shower and of course then I slipped and hit my head and maybe sprained my ankle. These nice men came to get rid of it. They are saying it's on the toilet!"

Popeyed, Lars whirled around. "Kill it, man!"

"He mean *in* toilet," the manager said.

"Thank God," Catty said. "But what if there are others—I don't know, babies? You must check."

The Armani man said something to the khaki boy, who returned briefly to the bathroom.

"I send nurse for you?" he queried.

Catty almost laughed as she touched the egg-shaped bump on her forehead and gingerly moved her ankle around. She'd seen enough health professionals on this trip, thank you very much. "Just an ice pack."

"Certain." He whipped out his cellphone and spoke rapidly. "They to bring ice now." He bowed for about the fifth time. "I am deep sorry. We never have such thing here until now," he repeated. He steepled his hands. "Please you accept champagne."

Catty sank into the plush armchair beside the king-size bed. "No thank you! Coffee would be great."

Minutes later, there arrived an ice pack, a pot of coffee, a flower arrangement, and slices of cake. Catty took some Tylenol. Lars reconnoitered the bathroom and emerged, declaring "All clear. Perfectly safe."

"I'm not going back in there until I absolutely must."

There was another knock on the door. The young man with the net again. He was netless this time, but bore more gifts, an assortment of fruit and wine, and hovered over their placement.

"Please take the wine," Catty told him as he backed away. "We don't drink wine." True enough. Lars was a beer or martini man. "Lars, give him a nice tip, please," she added.

"Madame, I can no."

She drew herself up imperiously. "I insist! I won't hear another word!"

It was at such times that Lars especially admired her.

Ed picked up the hotel phone on the second ring. "Hello?"

"Ed? It's Catty Vonderville."

He hemmed and hawed. Why should he talk to Mrs. Vonderpoop? Part of the cabal that had given him and Ann that hateful nickname. But when Catty said something about a poisonous *insect* that attacked her in the shower—"big and black, with pincers, and hairy"—he was all attention. "Did you preserve the specimen?"

"No, the guy who came flushed it down the toilet. But the manager told me what it was. Something like keen. Then emma or yemma. I don't remember the third name."

Ed was on his entomology translation app. "Keen?"

"Or kino, maybe."

"Kina. OK. Then—emma, yemma . . . yeme. Here it is: *Kina yeme ouk.* Arachnid order *Scorpiones.*" A pause. "Poisonous but not as deadly as some other scorpions, although infants and the elderly are at highest risk."

"Well, that's a comfort!" Catty said tartly.

"Death is unlikely," Ed went on, "unless the immune system is seriously weakened. You do know there are at least 2,000 species of scorpions? Only thirty or forty can kill humans."

"Except for infants and old people! Great. I'm sure the hotel doesn't want to admit there are more of those kinos lurking here, ready to kill all the old people."

"*Kina yeme ouk.*" Ed closed the app and began writing in his notebook, which was always close by. "Well, good sighting," he said, jotting down the new entry. He closed his notebook.

"Ed, there's something else, as we're on the phone."

"Another sighting?"

"You could call it that. But it was very unscientific. Inaccurate. And hurtful. You know that field that you told everyone you saw my dear friend Lidia, umm, cavorting in. On?"

"Mrs. Vonderville," he hedged.

"I'm referring to the night you said Lidia was in a field with Klaus Haynes."

"I saw them, they were in the field. On a blanket. Rolling around and, you know, must I spell it out to you? It was almost a full moon—good for research—and I saw them. I have excellent night vision."

"You were mistaken and Lidia is mortified by this base rumor you've spread. They were looking at the stars and smooching a bit. Whereas you told everyone that they were . . ."

"Mrs. Van—Catty? I am a highly trained observer." Ed paused. This was his chance. He was going to do this. "To change the subject, you and your husband and your friend called my wife and me a spiteful name."

"Well, I'd say it was well deserved!"

They hung up at the same time.

A few minutes later, Ed slammed the door of his room and marched down five flights of stairs, red of face and muttering under his breath. He marched out of the ornate entrance, collided with a doorman who was helping Mrs. Hills up the steps, and kept going.

Another one who was *hinat rara*—crazy—thought the doorman as he recovered from his collision with the rude American. These foreigners! They didn't seem to know basic, inviolate rules. Strong emotions were never to be displayed, but they did so all the time! Appearing in public partially unclothed! He had heard horror stories, about younger foreign women, especially, although some of the old ladies also went in pagodas in short-short pants and blouses without sleeves. And foolish! He had seen a foreigner bend over and pet a street dog. It was his fault he'd had his face bitten, what did he expect? At the Pacific Palace, a colleague had sworn he'd witnessed a woman slap her husband in the lobby. At a family outing to Swigon Pagoda, he'd personally witnessed two young white women sitting with their toes pointed at a shine before he hurried his family away from the obscenity. Beyond hope, these Europeans and Americans. They broke taboos like they were chopsticks.

26

As THE REST OF the group fiddled around in Dalayman and Sally Lattimore bargained for her Buddha with the wily shopkeeper, Haynes was alternately fiendishly busy or bored stiff. He and the Lattimores had gotten to Gonyang late—tired, dusty, and hungry—eaten immediately at the Golden Palace, then gone to bed.

This morning he'd been up with the sun, determined to nail the elusive visa. He arrived at the American consulate a half hour before it opened, only to be confronted by a long line of Namyanese supplicants. When he finally was called, it was all he could do not to get in the face of the smirking girl behind the desk with the Buddy Holly hipster glasses, a mousy blonde with a southern accent who he strongly suspected to be a racist.

"Mister Hay-inz?" she said, somewhat imperiously. "Oh ye-es, you've applied for the Restricted Regions Visa. You need to go to that office. Yes, you have to! And once you get it, come back here. Yes, here. Now if you hurry, you can maybe make it before siesta. It's on the other side of town."

Haynes took the wad of paperwork, forcing a smile. Because he needed Ms. Buddy Holly.

Traffic to the Restricted Regions Visa Department was as thick as the water hyacinth in the damn lake poor Barton lost his equipment in. When he got there, an ugly concrete building, it was shuttered. A sign said it would reopen at four. Of course, he couldn't read Namyanese, but one of the many people waiting had enough English to help him out.

He bought a bowl of spiced vegetables and chapatti-like bread from a vendor, and washed it down with a lukewarm Dragan. He sat under a tree—there were no benches—along with some Namyanese men. His long legs and particularly his size 16 feet, splayed out in sandals, made him feel like a freak. At least this was the "real" Gonyang. Maybe in five or ten years, maybe thirty, but eventually, it would all be gone. These micro lives—the hawking of betel nut, the *nas*, the crowds that waited for a little magic to rub off from seeing the Buddha's toe bone—soon they'd all be on cellphones living virtual lives. But for now, everybody, men, women, children, and animals, shuffled along, time not yet another commodity. Somewhere nearby were the seedy Victorian buildings he'd seen the first day of the tour, with Lidia in her bare feet, one of them bleeding, stoned on "crazy." He really wanted to see her again before he left Namyan.

When he woke up, the pockmarked door of the government office was open. Haynes swore lightly at himself for falling asleep and dusted himself off. He went a few steps before he realized something was different. He was lighter.

It was the absence of his Canon. He had folded his arms tightly around it while he dozed, but it was gone, the old slice and grab trick. Shit! He'd all but handed it over to thieves by falling asleep. You *Trottel, Blodel, Dummkoft*, his mother's voice echoed, gravelly from smoking so much. You forgot to shovel the coal, you cut school, you hit Karl, you eat too much, you grow too fast, you are like your no-good father. At fourteen, gangly but strong, he had wrenched the leather belt from her. "*Es ist deine verdammte Schuld!*" He was done. In the middle of the night, he threw some clothes in his rucksack and most of the Deutschmarks his grandmother kept hidden, or so she thought, in the wardrobe. Hallo Berlin.

Why was this shit coming back to him now? He clenched his teeth and shook his head. *Just get the damn visa, Haynes.* He had a backup camera, of course he did, in the safe of the hostel he had contrarily chosen today to stay at instead of the Golden Palace. It wasn't as good as the Canon. It would have to do. Nothing was going to stop him.

Surprisingly, nothing did stop him once he was inside the building. He was plucked from the doleful line of people—Namyanese and, he was interested to see, a fair number of ethnic minorities—clutching paperwork in this purgatory of hope suspended. Waiting for someone with superpowers, waiting for the key to open and escape the stink of memory trash.

Haynes was shown to a corner desk where a small, unsmiling man's skin color was, he was amused to see, exactly the same as his. It didn't seem to provoke any fellow feeling. The man avoided eye contact as he picked up some paperwork and then left to confer with a colleague.

The two of them looked at Haynes with the blank, self-important gaze petty bureaucrats everywhere have perfected, willing their supplicants to concede that their fate is in the bureaucrats' hands. Haynes made a quick, possibly rash decision. He had a stash of *takys* and newly minted dollars in the money belt that, thank God, the thieves hadn't found, probably because it was strapped around his calf. He crouched by the desk, withdrew a bunch of twenties, folded the wad, and strapped it on again.

With a flash of paranoia, he wondered if he would be mugged outside for the rest—a considerable amount to an American, a fortune for a Namyanese. He longed to get out of this place, its pungent smell of desperation.

Hang in there, here comes toast brother, he told himself, as the little man sidled back and sat down at his desk. Haynes sat too, on a stool not built for Western behinds across from him.

The clerk shook his head. He had wattles, which rippled, as he said, "No."

"No? No what?"

"No bisa." Head shake, wattle ripple again. "Off the limit. Bisa deny." He slid a paper across the desk.

Haynes grabbed it. There it was: DENIED. Dated—today. He couldn't make out the signature of this asshole.

"What's the explanation for this?" If they were going to deny it, they could have said so at 10:30 a.m. Something must have gone down in the past few hours. Not waiting for a reply, Haynes leapt up, sending his stool flying. A small security man with a big gun at his hip edged toward him. Haynes raised his arms. "Sorry. Going."

He found a pedicab. He told the driver the Golden Palace. Maybe the T&K people were back. Maybe Thila could help. Also, there was Lidia. His mind jerked to her, he remembered her sitting on some verandah, curly brown hair and freckles. White jeans and a colorful shirt. She liked colors—well, she was obsessed with them. That smile that held something back, that forthright body. He saw her at a pagoda, drawing a three-legged dog lying in a patch of shade, and the boy monk who'd tripped and spilled the contents of his begging bowl, and the old woman smiling, her stumps of teeth stained black from a lifetime of betel nut. Lidia . . . She was bound to be seriously pissed with him.

He changed his mind and had the taxi go to the consulate. The hotel could wait. After a brief wait, he saw Ms. Buddy Holly again, who told him there'd been fresh intel about a serious skirmish in Hinchak.

"Fresh intel?" he shouted. "You couldn't have told me sooner? Now, when can I go?"

She wasn't having it.

He threw up his hands and left, hailing another pedicab, where he pounded the seat, cursing. At a red light, the driver turned around and stared at him. Haynes pulled himself together.

When he went in the hotel, he thought it was miraculous timing. There was Lidia, standing there by herself.

"Lidia!"

She turned and then quickly looked away.

Haynes didn't blame her. He moved toward her. "Can we talk?"

Now she did look at him.

"Look, I had to rush back to Gonyang. The consulate told me the visa was going to be on but it would only be good for a week, starting tomorrow. So I had to go right away. I did write you. Did you get it?"

"Really Haynes? You couldn't spare five minutes to tell me good-bye to my face?" She laughed. "I felt like I'm sixteen again, when Allen Valdez dumped me right before the prom."

"Who would do that to a beautiful woman like you? Can we talk? For a minute?"

"Well, I've got to be somewhere."

"Man, they turned me down, Lidia! Denied the visa. Said they have *new intel about skirmishes.*"

"Oh, Haynes. I am sorry about that."

"Look, have a drink with me?"

She gave him a long look. "I'm busy."

"The thing is, I didn't know how to say good-bye to you."

"Oh, that's simple. Good-bye, Haynes."

She walked away and started punching an elevator button.

"Fuck." He decided to go get fucked up.

27

IT WAS THE LAST day of their "Miraculous Namyan" tour. Thila as usual got up at dawn, spread her rush mat on the floor, meditated for ten minutes, then fetched the green tea that room service had left outside her door. Washed and got dressed in one of the *lognis* and blouses T&K provided. Double-checked arrangements for the day on her phone.

Everything seemed to be going blessedly, unusually smoothly on this final day, an irony that didn't escape her. Mrs. Hills had left a message that she was feeling better, so cross that off the list. No one else had fallen, chewed betel nut spiced with "crazy," wounded their feet, fallen in a lake. She even had time to doze for a bit before breakfast. Americans, she'd learned, called this a "power nap." So like them! Determined to dominate everything.

Falling into the buoyant zone where daydreams and dreams mingle, Thila found herself in the old family apartment, on the far side of Gonyang. A *may* squatted, chopping vegetables on a wood block on the dirt floor—thin but puffy, always at work, her black eyes seeing "nothing but the bad," as Thila's sister Nyunt put it. Nyunt slumped on the narrow bed in the space she shared with Thila, a science textbook balanced on her crossed legs. Nyunt was twenty-two, Thila twenty-four. The daydream switched: she and Nyunt were explaining to *a may* why she would be happier living in the village, surrounded by the generations, the familiar fields, the local stupa. Her daughters would come to visit regularly. But, as always, *a may* shook her head. No, she would stay in the cramped rooms she hated. She would keep her daughters close.

Thila's eyes flew open when the room phone rang, just as she was thinking *family: steamed buns that stick to your teeth.* Though soon she would not be living with *a may* and Nyunt. She would be living with Emile. A total secret as yet. She had met him a year ago on one of the first tours. Thila's introduction to the world outside Namyan had followed six months later—during the rainy season, when the tourist season came to a screeching halt. Emile had paid her fare to Stockholm. He was a tall, serious man, a pediatric cardiologist. Thila had never heard of pediatric cardiology, let alone known anyone whose heart had been treated. She'd never imagined that hearts the size of (she imagined) nuts could be sliced open and fixed. Emile did that.

She'd also never imagined that she would love a pale foreigner, that when she went to Stockholm they could hold hands, hug, *kiss* in public. Now she and Emile had planned a future together. Thila could not leave Namyan, she supported *a may* and Nyunt in pharmacy school. But Emile had found a way to come to her. It wouldn't be long now.

She picked up the phone. "I have bad news." It was T&K's Country Director of Operations. At first, Thila didn't register what he'd said and had to ask him to repeat it. "I'll be in touch as soon as there's an update," he ended.

"*Rah yasype, rah yasype, rah yasype,*" said Thila, falling on the bed. Shit, shit, shit.

Fifteen minutes and several phone calls later, she raced downstairs. Was her karma so bad that every day of this tour must bring something more negative, more terrible? As a tour guide, she had experienced plenty of crises; the Chinese man dying on the toilet was at the top of the list, but there was also the wife who caught her husband in bed with a maid (stupid maid!), and the man who was stung by a scorpion in his private parts while putting on his pants. His shrieks brought a security guard crashing through his door with gun drawn. A few people who drank too much and lost their money or got lost. Sprains, flu, nausea, nerves. But this trip!

Klaus Haynes and the Lattimores had been thrown in jail.

The group, except for Franklin, who had opted to leave early for a day of shopping, milled around the lobby, wondering where Thila was. She was never late. And this was their very last day. In the middle of the night, they'd be boarding the plane for home. They intended to squeeze the last drops of Namyan into a last hurrah.

Lars spotted Thila as she came in the lobby, phone clutched to her ear, free hand waving like a frantic flower, and penguined over to her.

"Thila!"

His voice was unexpectedly deep and authoritative. She halted, phone still pressed to her ear.

"We're quite behind schedule."

She ended her call then and looked at him speculatively. This amiable, elderly American was, she realized, also a man who would not take no for an answer. She had known such men on both sides of the dictatorship. And that's what she needed now.

"Something bad has happened. To Mr. Haynes and the Lattimores."

"What! Are they hurt?"

"I don't think so. But they are in trouble."

"Well, what?"

"What I know is they are in the prison."

"Prison!"

"Do not say anything to the others, please," she implored. "Not yet."

"Good Lord, Thila, I've got to tell Catty. And—Lidia." Lars peered at her. "You'll get them out?"

"Please, you must to help me."

"Of course. Anything."

"But we must go now to the Boulder Pagoda."

"What? Absolutely not. We'll go to the American consulate. Storm the gates if need be."

"Mr. Lars, the consulate works now to free them. But I cannot cancel another of the program. Some complain already to the Head Office because of the delays before. Head Office say I must continue to Boulder Pagoda. It is best photo op of trip."

Thila twisted her hands, which were damp with perspiration.

He gulped. "In that case, give me what information you have and I'll go there."

"Please yes, thank you. I have phone." She gave him the number.

"I'll call you as soon as anything breaks," he promised.

Breaks? she thought. *It is breaked already.*

28

CLINT PARKED HIMSELF NEXT to Thila, in the choicest first seat of the bus for getting pictures through the panoramic front window.

Happy that this was the last day, he turned to his wife, behind him with Ann. "This boulder thing, the best photo op of them all," he said. He'd checked it out online—a giant rock, painted gold and topped with a little pagoda, teetering at the edge of a cliff, seemingly defying gravity. As close to a mountain as he was going to get.

Lars got on the bus and frowned. "Hodges, would you mind moving back a seat? I need to confer with Thila."

"Nope."

Thila turned, cheeks flushed. "Mr. Hodges, important you move, please."

"This is outrageous." Clint huffed his way to the back, pausing to turn and shoot venomous looks at them.

"Well, I never," said Betsy. She followed him, along with Ann.

When Catty and Lidia took Betsy and Ann's just-vacated places, Lars leaned over the seat.

"Now keep this under your hat," he said. "Klaus and the Lattimores are in the slammer!"

Color and sound faded from Lidia's world. It had happened when tiny Lily sank like a stone into the swimming pool and when Lily was fifteen and Lidia found a bottle of pain pills stuffed under her mattress, and, most recently, when the doctor gave her Felipe's diagnosis. A protective cover of numbness that wouldn't last long.

Catty spat out, "WHAT?"

At the same time Lidia said, "IN JAIL?"

"Shh! It's clearly a fuck-up. I don't have details but the consulate is working on it and Thila wants me to, well, run interference for her. Help with the consulate, I gather. Girls! We have to stay calm."

"I am calm!" Lidia wailed. Catty clutched her arm as Thila tapped her microphone.

"There is unfortunate news," she said.

"Oh, for Pete's sake, what NOW?" Ed demanded. Gradually, they fell silent.

"Mr. Haynes, Mr. Lattimore, and Madame Lattimore are detained for a law breakage."

"Law breakage?" Ted said.

"Detained where?" Franklin asked.

"Get in touch with the consulate," Mrs. Hills advised.

The Bores and the Poisons said nothing.

"What happened?" Catty snapped.

"The Head Office say they disturb a dharma hall in Gonyang last night."

"What does that mean?" Lidia implored.

Thila cupped her forehead with her hands as the voices rose. "Is common for Buddhist people to meet for ceremony in dharma hall. Sometime music, dance, sometimes other things from old times. Was big . . ." Her English was fleeing, they could almost see it flying away, smaller and smaller. "Big fight. Police say they disrespect Buddha."

Catty pronounced, "But that's absurd!"

"Unfortunate, maybe much wine and then touch Buddha with

feet . . . such a thing. Now not easy to get from the jail. This is all I know! But counselor and T&K office work without stop on this matter."

"Of course, the consulate will get them out!" Mrs. Hills said stoutly.

"Meanwhile, we go to the Balanced Golden Boulder Pagoda. I keep up the news."

Lars stood up. "Well, group, I'm staying here to man the phone and see what else I can do . . . I've an idea. Ted, Franklin? I could use your help. Join me?"

Ted exchanged a look with his husband. "Yes, okay, sure. But you don't need both of us. Honey, you go to the boulder thing."

"I guess I will," Franklin said. "Good Lord! Just be glad this is not a Muslim country," he added.

Lidia, who'd found she was crying a little, wiped her eyes.

Catty looked at her. "This is just the worst."

Lidia hesitated. "I feel terrible. Haynes and I . . . Well, it didn't end well yesterday."

"Well, how could you have imagined this? Now look, Lars had to deal with some dicey stuff when he lived in Bogota for the bank. Americans busted for drugs, ransomed by one of the armies or cartels, and he'll help."

"But Lars was a banker."

"And money is power. I simply can't imagine how they got themselves into this."

"Poor Sally! She must be freaking out."

"Maybe we can smuggle in a flask for her."

Lidia shook her head. "How can you joke about this?"

"Gallows humor," Catty said. "Well, maybe the wrong term. You know what I mean."

"Maybe I should stay here with Lars."

"You'd be miserable hanging around the hotel. And Thila will tell us when there's any news."

They lapsed into silence. Lars and Thila were talking, alternately, on her phone.

Presently, Catty said, low, "Just to get your mind off this, I want you to know I told off Ed Bore. That scurrilous rumor he spread about you and Klaus."

"Shit, Catty, who gives a fuck about that. He's in jail. I can't . . . I have to try to see him."

"We're flying out tonight," Catty reminded her.

Lidia put her head in her hands.

After Thila ended her phone call, Lars and Ted headed to the hotel and the bus took off for the Balanced Golden Boulder Pagoda Seemingly Defying Gravity.

An old Namyanese saying came to Thila: "The rice paddy is drained dry."

She didn't know the English equivalent: "The shit has hit the fan."

Huddled over a pot of coffee, Lars and Ted discussed "the situation," as Ted called it.

"We could put in another call to the consulate," Ted said doubtfully.

"Well, they said they'd call here as soon as they had intel." Lars pecked tentatively at his phone, to see if there was any kind of news. Nothing.

Ted drained his cup. "Beneath the sweet smiles and flowers lie the shadow men," he said.

"Quite the philosopher-poet, Ted! To what do you refer?"

"This Filipino poet Franklin turned me on to. When we went there to meet his extended family. Once. Never again. Some of them were nice but a lot more were homophobes. And of course, it's a political hornet's nest."

"Yeah. Same deal in Colombia. Lived there twelve years," Lars explained. "Beautiful country and people, fucked up as hell."

Lars's phone thundered the first four bars of Beethoven's Fifth and he shot up. "Consul! Thank you for returning my call, sir . . . Oh, I see." He scribbled a name and number on a napkin. "Ah, there's always another meeting, isn't there? Appreciate this very much, thank you." He disconnected.

"Key guy's unreachable on some island in the Pacific, if you can believe that. We have to rely on . . ." He peered at his napkin. "Ms. Kittering. Who's in a meeting now."

Ted stood up. "I'll talk to the manager here, maybe he'll have some ideas. Would you order more coffee?"

Lars did so, fiddled some more with his phone. Still no news.

Ted returned. "Got some info! Word is they smashed up a Buddha, drunk."

"What Thila said, more or less. But it doesn't sound like Klaus."

Ted looked at Lars and shrugged. "Sally, though? Franklin told me a couple of stories about when they were out compulsive shopping and she got looped."

"Well, anyway, we know how these feet police are. Martinets. What the fuck were those guys up to?"

"Beats me. Your friend Lidia seems distraught. Oh, everybody knows about her and Klaus."

"Well, I don't know what you heard. Ed Bore made up some story about the two of them being, well, *in flagrante*, in a field in Gaban."

"Sally said Boren told her he was out collecting butterflies and practically stumbled over them going at it on a blanket."

Lars looked sharply at Ted. "Total canard," he said.

Both men suddenly laughed, in short bursts.

Ted tapped the side of his chair. "What a fucked-up world. You know, I think while we wait, I'll go for one last swim. I'll have my phone handy, of course."

"Right. And I'll go up to the room for a bit."

* *

Lars was happy to plop down in the slice of shade on his balcony with *Finding George Orwell in Namyan*. Silence from the consulate. About an hour later, he and Ted regrouped for lunch. More silence. Until now, Lars hadn't particularly warmed to Ted, who seemed to him one of those American men who chases after eternal youth. Polo shirts a size too small, well-muscled but with the inevitable wrinkling of age, tight jeans, and a well-disguised but indisputable comb-over. Lars believed, or thought he did, that one should age gracefully. Imagine Catty's response if he tried the tight T-shirt and jeans routine!

Lars had been something of a bad boy in his youth, a fan of fast cars and motorcycles, a little trouble with the law at frat parties. After Harvard, the Marines had purged him of these tendencies and then, his tenure in the family firm and especially becoming a parent had expunged any remaining rebelliousness, at least overtly. He could not approve of an AARP-eligible man who dressed like James Dean. On the other hand, as Ted was a gay man, by Lars's way of thinking, his striving for eternal youth was understandable. Though he could not have said why this should be, exactly.

But Lars now got that Ted was a stand-up guy, someone you could rely on. After lunch, Ted worked the phone relentlessly, trying to get Ms. Kittering. When he couldn't, he managed at last to find someone at the consulate who could shed some light on the situation.

"So, this dharma hall they went to is known for rowdy parties," he told Lars. "People drink and chew whatever that crazy shit is and there have been fights. Mostly, they make a lot of noise and annoy the neighbors. The consulate guy says there've been plenty of complaints about the place staying open after curfew. So maybe there's some leverage there. Not their fault—wrong time, wrong place."

"Damn good work, Ted. Dammit, though, will that get them out?"

"Well, this guy, Tom Begin, Began, seems to be the eager young man low on the totem pole, says our guys did get physical. The worst is, Sally climbed on a Buddha *with her shoes on.*"

"Shit. What is this thing they have about shoes? Bare feet, think about the crap that's on the floor. Petri dish. Look what happened to me."

"Be glad we're not in, say, Saudi Arabia. Religion! I don't mean to offend . . ."

"No offense taken. I'm a card-carrying agnostic."

"Lapsed Catholic here. Back when I was an altar boy, women had to cover their heads in church."

Lars sighed. "So what next? Meet with this Begin guy?"

Ted leaned forward. "He says bottom line is, get them a good lawyer. Namyanese."

"Right. He suggest someone?"

"Working on it." Ted shrugged. "Probably gonna cost them plenty."

Working Google, they came up eventually with a few other cases of Westerners who were currently languishing in the actually medieval Gonyang prison. Two were in for drugs. Gonyang might be one of the world's largest illegal drug producers and exporters of meth and heroin, but it was Nixon on steroids if you used them in the country. "But get this," Lars said to Ted. "Here's a similar case to ours, this Brit who owns, or runs, a bar here. He posted a psychedelic image of Buddha on the bar's Facebook page. Two and a half years, he got! For insulting religion. Says he's been in nine months, lost fifty pounds."

"Shit. Must have had a lousy lawyer."

"Maybe, maybe not," Lars said. "The Damawat buys a lot of the Buddhist honchos off, pumps them up with ultra-nationalist bullshit. What can the elected leaders and their minions do about that?"

"Right. Let's hope Haynes and the Lattimores can raise a lot of cash," Ted said.

The group agreed that the Balanced Golden Boulder Pagoda was a spectacular finish—or would have been, if not for the latest flaming fiasco. They were relieved to head back to the hotel with no more wonders of the world left to see. The bus was completely silent.

Suddenly Franklin said loudly, "Listen to this! Al Jazeera. 'Angry Namyanese stormed into a dharma hall at midnight, demanding that the loudspeakers be turned off. The law states that they are to become silent at 9:00 p.m. A fistfight broke out. One man, who refused to give his name, told this reporter, "We can't sleep at night, we are having problems staying awake at work." Mr. Ha Hyo Ung declared, "If the Buddha Himself were alive, he'd be deaf from all of this racket." A fine was imposed on the leaders of the dharma hall and a warning not to break curfew again.' Ted forwarded it. He thinks it may be a good sign for our guys."

"But they were drunk and disorderly," Betsy said, with a snap.

"You don't know that! It's a *rumor.* And I know you love rumors," Lidia snapped back.

Clint rose from his seat. "Leave my wife alone! You know what? Why don't you go back where you came from?"

Franklin rose from *his* seat. "You know what, Hodges? You're a racist pig!"

Ed and Ann said nothing.

And, at last, Thila lost it. "Please to STOP! NO MORE!" she yelled into the mike.

29

THE EXTERIOR OF THE prison was, like the Victorian train station, imposing and magisterial, with added Namyanese architectural flourishes.

But as soon as the police van passed beneath the graceful, if crumbling, central arch into the prison yard, the place bared its teeth. *This is a prison*, it all but said—gimcrack, filthy, neglected concrete with wafer-thin captives in dirty wife-beaters and loincloths shuffling to nowhere in shackles, guarded by equally wafer-thin men in ill-fitting khaki uniforms, guns at the hip. Haynes cursed about not having a camera: what a photo-op this was. But of course they'd taken everything from him—wallet, phone, belt. And camera.

He was pushed into a ridiculously small cell where, when he stretched his legs, his bare feet touched a wall smeared with patches of damp; probably, he thought, dried-up old shit. It smelled that way. A sallow guard handed him a bucket and strips of newspaper and, later, a plate of chopped greens and rice and a cup of what seemed to be tea. At the top of the wall in his cell, a narrow, barred window provided what light there was.

It grew dark. Unable to sleep, Haynes hugged himself against the dank chill the walls gave off. He listened to the noise from up and down the rows of cells, understanding nothing. At least he had his own cell. At last, he fell asleep, head bowed.

In Namyan, the concept of *burn-out* doesn't exist. Asian languages have lots of words for death by overwork, like *karoshi* in Japanese, *gwarosa* in Korean, *Laolei siwang* in Mandarin. In Namyanese, the concept if not the phrase exists. Thila had become completely exhausted, played out, but she would keep on working. For her, there was an end in sight at least: the drenching months of rain which would come—soon!—would mark the end of the tourist season. The end of her income, too. But then Emile would arrive to take up a position training doctors in pediatric cardiology at the Royal Asia Hospital on a two-year visa. No matter what *a may* and the rest of Namyan said, no matter how she was treated, she would find a way to be with him. Because she had been changed in a fundamental way by all her interactions with Westerners and, of course, her trip to Europe. There were other ways of being in the world! But it would be hard. Very hard.

And now, although it was the last thing she wanted to do, given the colossal mess with the Lattimores and Mr. Haynes, the Head Office told her to go ahead with the farewell dinner. So she dragged herself to the room reserved for the dinner, where she found that the staff had set up a long table. Thila ordered two small tables instead. With nearly half the original group gone and a sort of war among the rest, this, she thought, would be best.

As she was about to leave to go rest or try to in her room for a short time, something with a pincer crawled by the wall, followed by another. And another. Scorpions!

"*Ka medam la!*" she said loudly, clapping briskly.

"Yes, Madame!"

She frowned at the waiter who came running in. "Just now I saw two *kina yeme ouk*! Unacceptable! Get the manager!" she commanded.

It was too late to fumigate outside, the assistant manager, who looked like a rich playboy, told her, bowing repeatedly, so he'd send in a team to search and destroy in the room right away and spray it thoroughly.

She went upstairs, but there was no time to rest. Instead, she took possibly her thirtieth call about the Americans in jail, and by the time that long call was finished, it was time to get ready for the last hurrah.

What, she wondered, would Mr. Ed Boren have recommended to eradicate venomous scorpions?

At dinner, everyone complimented Thila on her resplendent aquamarine *logni*.

As she sat down at the head of one of the two tables, she wondered if she'd made a mistake in choosing this seat, as the other table might take offence, though even she could not be in two places at once. After she escorted them to the airport at four that morning, she reminded herself, her job with them would be over and she would never have to see them again. Her spirits lifted and she turned to her seatmates at what she thought of as the "difficult" table—the Borens, Hodgeses, and Mrs. Hills—with a determined smile.

Mrs. Hills, who was dressed in a once—long ago—lovely pearl-gray *cheongsam*, looked well. The Borens remained faithful to their khaki; Betsy wore a colorful, flowing garment; and Clint had on his usual chinos and a wrinkled shirt.

Bottles of the Namyanese wine they had sampled at the vineyard (it seemed like ages ago now) crowded the tables: rosé, sauvignon blanc, and something called Thayaya red.

"Looks like half the year's harvest is here," Lars noted. As usual, he declined the grape, opting for a vodka tonic. Clint, of course, ordered a beer, while Thila had a mineral water, leaving Betsy and Ann as the only winebibbers among them.

While the waiter circled the tables, pouring, Catty pushed back her chair in the narrow space between the tables, trying to get comfortable, and in the process jostled Clint. He turned around, glaring.

"Sorry," she said.

"Hmph." He pointed at her Coke. "Don't you ever stop with this teetotal stuff?"

The next round, Thila thought wearily, had begun.

"No, I don't," Catty responded sharply.

"That can't be any fun," Betsy said. "Watching everybody else get to enjoy themselves."

"But *we* remember everything," Lidia said, raising her Sprite in a toast.

"If that's a good thing," Catty murmured.

"Ha!" Clint turned back to his table.

Nobody knew what he was on about, but it was clear this wasn't his first Dragan Special of the evening.

The first course arrived and Thila sighed with relief.

Clint frowned, poking at his plate. "What's this salad thing?"

"It's pickled leaves," Betsy said.

"Picked leaves?"

"*Pickled.* With dressing."

"Can't wait to get me to a Chick-fil-A again."

Betsy said, "Well, you love poke salad."

"That's different." Chewing bread, he said in a loud voice, "What exactly did they do to get thrown in the slammer? Anyways, Haynes prob'ly knows the drill, those people are used to being in the jailhouse." He reached for his beer.

Betsy leaned into him. "Clinton . . . Promise that'll be the last one."

Sitting across from Clint, Ed toyed with his food as he said, "*Those people are used to be in the jailhouse?* Did you actually say that? That's a racist thing to say." He wasn't feeling good. His breathing was getting raspy, his head was light. But he couldn't abide that old man's bullying any longer.

"He didn't mean it like that!" Betsy snapped, aggrieved.

Always ready to defend the old bugger, Ed thought. Like when he shoved that Lidia at the market. He should have said something to him then, even if he didn't like the woman. "Oh yes, he did." He began to cough noisily. "I'm not feeling too good," he wheezed.

"Ed, where's your inhaler? You need your inhaler." Ann tapped his arm.

"In the room." He wheezed. "I think I smell whiffs of pesticide in here."

"I'm sure they have to spray the grounds constantly, with all the bugs they have here," Ann said.

"Creepy-crawlies," Betsy clarified.

Ed stared at her. Creepy-crawlies? The sum total of her knowledge about entomology. He *really* didn't like either of these Hodgeses, he was glad he was never going to see them again after tonight. Why, he'd been forced to be with the old sourpusses at nearly every meal on the trip. The "Poisons": the Vonderpoops at least got that one right.

He kept staring at Betsy. She was wearing a hideous flowered sheet or something. What did they used to call it? A muumuu. With big swirls on it. The old bat. "I'm going upstairs and lie down," he told Ann.

"Want me to come with? No?" Ann leaned in and murmured, "Just say good-bye to everyone and thank Thila."

He pushed his chair back and took a step toward Thila, then turned back. "I'll let you do that."

As soon as he was out of the room, his breathing began to ease up. Probably some banned toxic product they used here with abandon that had seeped in through the windows. Maybe they'd even sprayed it inside; he wouldn't put it past them. He thought of the armies of insects, attracted by the crumbs and grease, and then the next wave that came to eat them. There were a quadrillion ants in the world, he'd read. Which was a million billion. Ten quintillion insects in total—the largest biomass of living creatures. Well, he'd gotten to see several hundred new ones in Namyan! Of course, there were also so many he hadn't gotten to see. He thought of the Namyanese mustard tarantula, that was one impressive killer. He'd really hoped to get it on his list. Too late now. His head ached.

Lars looked on as Ann got up and leaned over Thila, explaining Ed's abrupt departure. In the wake of his exit there was more wine, cocktails, beer for Clint, and water and sodas for Thila, Cattie, and Lidia. Their choice of entrees was Namyanese curry and rice or medallions of beef smothered in a mushroom sauce. They all chose the beef, except for Thila and Mrs. Hills.

After the main course had come and gone, Mrs. Hills tapped her (just-emptied) wine glass sharply. Then again, at which point it shattered, startling everyone.

"I think Carolyn would like to say something," Ted said loudly. By default, he'd been her occasional squire or practical nurse throughout the trip.

"Yes, thank you, Ted, I would." She put her napkin over the glass shards and worked her way up to a standing position, which for her was more of a U-shape.

"Speech!" Lars said, attempting joviality, though really he just wanted the meal to end so he could call the contact at the consulate and they could all finish packing and try to sleep for a few hours.

Forks were put down, chatter ended, and they awaited the inevitable, hopefully brief, words of thanks to Thila. Well deserved, of course.

"How my dear late wife would have loved this country!" Mrs. Hills began. (Clint's eyes popped. Franklin tittered.) "It was long our dream to come here but, as we all know, Namyan was a closed book for so long."

"Did she say *wife*?" Ann whispered loudly.

Betsy nodded grimly. "This *group*! Overrun with immorality!" she said.

"Perverts," Clint agreed, but weakly.

Lars didn't bother to waste his breath on any of them.

Mrs. Hills was warming up. "The great Golden Pavilion, the lake, the monks wandering along the roads with their bowls! And I have to say, even the misfortunes that befell us, our physical afflictions, and now even this *horrid prison incident*." She paused. "Well, Thila sorted it all out and she will see this crisis to a successful conclusion. Steady at the helm!"

She paused and it seemed that she had come to an end. Someone began to clap.

Mrs. Hills raised her voice, which made it quaver noticeably. "I know about overseeing groups of disparate souls, you see, as the former headmistress of the Overseas School in Hong Kong, with dear Louise at my side as Head Teacher. I can say with full confidence that Thila's job has been like *herding cats*!"

"More like old goats," Catty said.

Mrs. Hills smiled thinly as she fixed her faded eyes on Catty. "Where was I? Oh, enough. A round of very well-earned applause for our dear leader!"

They clapped vigorously for their T&K Adventure Tours leader, but oddly, Thila had turned away from them, with her phone pressed to her ear. They stopped. They waited.

"News about Haynes and the Lattimores," Ted guessed, looking at Lars.

Lars shrugged.

Thila ended the call but instead of turning around, she rocked slightly in place and let out a small cry. Mrs. Hills, who was still standing, rather as if she'd forgotten how to sit down, now plummeted to her seat and nearly fell out of it. And still Thila didn't turn to them. It must be very bad news.

* *

Lars's phone trilled and he left the table. It was a short conversation, mostly consisting on his end of exclamations. "Well, that's wonderful!" he ended and walked over to Thila, who was again in position, though ghostly pale. "That was the consulate and—"

Thila made a little head bow. "Please forgive . . . Mr. Vandavilla, will you take the charge for me? So sorry. I have received so sad news of family member."

Which was true enough: Emile was to have been her new family. But he had just told her that he couldn't come to Namyan after all. His elderly father had been diagnosed with terminal cancer; he must stay in Sweden.

As he talked, Thila had felt her future stretch before her, an endless round of dealing with old American tourists and old *a may*. Her heart stung with loss—not so much for Emile as for herself, which made her feel unworthy. She swallowed and, with an effort, remembering her job, asked, "But, Mr. Vandavilla, what is your news?"

"Yes. Well, first of all, we're very sorry to hear about your family member. I know I speak for all of us. If there's anything we can do?"

"Thank you. Not."

"Well. But good news on our end. Great news! They're getting sprung! Tomorrow or the day after. It's all set. Don't ask me how, that's out of my league, involved the exchange of the filthy lucre."

Everyone cheered. Even Clint, who then said he was going to bed.

"No," he added to his wife when she got up too. "You stay for the good-bye stuff. I'll be *okay*."

Slowly, Clint made his way from the room to the elevator down the marbled hall. His hips ached, his gut alternately sloshed around and squeezed with knife-edged pain. Betsy would be no help. She would fuss, chide, deny. But he knew he was dying.

30

BEHIND LIDIA, STANDING SO close she could smell his break-fast of vegetables and garlic, was a guard, and behind him a woman from the consulate. Haynes jumped up from his burlap mat.

Lidia winged it. "This place stinks even more than that *na-san*."

Haynes rushed to her, a matter of three steps. The guards pushed him back. Touching was apparently verboten, even now.

"You've come! I'm getting out now?"

"Well, soon. The consulate is wrapping up some loose ends, I guess."

She almost hadn't stayed in Gonyang. But at the very last minute, even as the others were getting on the bus to go to the airport for home, she and the night manager had rearranged her flight and she'd booked two rooms at the much cheaper Wehs Yo guesthouse for the next week.

"I've brought some clothes for you. The rest of your stuff is at the guesthouse where I've booked you a room. By the way, Thila couldn't come because she has some family problem."

"Weren't you supposed to be flying back?"

"Yes, well I—"

The guard's radio crackled and whistled. He listened, then gestured at her to leave.

The woman from the consulate who had come with Lidia said, "They're going to process him now, I think. We have to wait outside."

Lidia handed Haynes a note under the glowering eyes of the guard. "This is the address." She paused. "What I want to know is, how the fuck did you end up here, Haynes?"

"I'll tell you when I get out if you're still here? Long story."

After Haynes got blown off by Lidia at the hotel, he'd followed through on his resolution to get good and wasted. He'd brooded in the lobby for a while, until the Lattimores came by. They were going to check out what was said to be a famous old bar where the Brits hung out back in the day, so he joined them. He knew he should probably work on where to go next—the disarray of Malaysia or Indonesia, say—but he was in a rare mood for matching Sally drink for drink. And shit, that woman could drink.

The bar turned out to be long gone, so they decided to head down to the old British quarter. Maybe after that, he thought, he'd try talking to Lidia again before she left for the States.

In the pedicab, Sally said, "I should have got those coasters I saw at a lacquer place downtown the first day we were here. That's *all* I'm going to buy, Ken, I promise." She laughed.

Haynes thought she seemed mighty cheerful despite her condition, but then, she'd successfully wrestled her jade Buddha from the crafty boutique man. It was locked now in the room safe at the hotel.

They made good time to the old quarter, and went into a little shop crammed with lacquerware. Sally lingered by a group of vases.

"You said you weren't buying any more stuff, just coasters," Ken said evenly.

"This won't take up any room."

Ken and Haynes hung around while she bought a vase, coasters, and a plate. They walked on into the heart of the old quarter, which reminded Haynes of the scruffy Brooklyn where he'd come of age and been Americanized. A love-hate relationship. There, street kids worked for dealers. Here too, maybe. They stared at the foreigners, chewing their *yoongi.*

Haynes took a lot of pictures of a half-collapsed building with what looked like gargoyles hanging on the cornices of the roof. *Nas,* he thought. Probably everywhere when you really looked.

Turning a corner, they came upon a rarity in this part of the city, a bar-café that looked reasonably clean, if you didn't look too closely. Without a word, they sank into chairs in the patio—cooler than the street, with its bamboo shades—and ordered hair of the dog.

The beer wasn't as good as Dragan and it wasn't as cold; still, better than nothing. They ate spicy vegetables and rice. Street vendors approached, diffident, not used to tourists. *Soon,* Haynes thought, *they'll be aggressive and canny. And a Marriott will rise up, maybe right here, or maybe a Starbuck's. Overpriced gift shops.*

But then again, maybe not. Namyan might stay sunk into what it was used to being: bone-lean, its scarce resources funneled to the generals and their cronies and the world's drug dealers.

Sally was taken with the goods of one shy street vendor, but for once she was restrained in her purchases, buying only a couple of bangles. They lolled, drinking more beer and finishing their food. The heat of the day was now at its height.

Ken called for some of the local rum. A man darted in from the street.

"*Kaba,*" he said. "You want *kaba?*" He held up ten fingers. "*Takys.*"

The sole waiter, who'd been dozing in the back, came out and shouted at the man. He ran away.

"*Kaba?*" asked Sally. "That another word for betel nut?"

"Meth and caffeine pills," Ken said. "Big problem here."

"Ken, man, you have all the scoop, you're like the CIA, the DEA. When you were in the Golden Triangle? You must have seen some heavy shit go down."

Ken just smiled.

"*Were* you CIA?" Haynes added.

"Now, now," murmured Sally, her mouth curving in a smile.

"Ah, both of you."

"Do I look like a secret agent?" Sally asked gaily.

"And that would be why. Man, you two . . ."

"You know, I hate to say it, but I'm glad you're not going on that trip up there. You have no idea," Ken said, "how crazy that part of the world can be."

Haynes shrugged. Part of him wanted to punch Ken, partly for the hell of it. Know-it-all. So here he was, getting wasted. He knew it was his way of dealing with all the pent-up frustration and disappointment. He'd had his heart set on that trip. And then there was Lidia. He took a drink. "This rum is *stark*," he said.

Then he thought maybe he shouldn't blow the whole day getting juiced.

The waiter was back to nodding out on a chair. Haynes got up and put a hand on his arm and he scrambled up instantly.

"*Takys?*" Haynes said. He wanted, suddenly, to get away. Be by himself.

The waiter held up fingers. Ken pulled out his wallet. "I'll get this," he said.

The other two stood up, not very steadily. They walked into the high sun and building humidity. The rainy season was coming. Some garishly clothed women were passing by. Seeing the foreigners, they stopped and waved and laughed. "You come!" one said.

Sally laughed, a half-choked guffaw, and clutched her straw hat. "Are they trans, Ken?" She looked back at Haynes and added, "He would know."

"Sally, don't," Ken said.

"Party! Come!" said the one with English again. She or he or they were as dramatically made up as a RuPaul follower.

"Let's go for it," Haynes said, changing his mind on a dime because, well, this was material, he told himself. And luckily, he had a pair of glasses with a clever little camera on it that could film what went down. Something for the blog. He'd read about the gender-fluid *acaults* and *dakaws*—the spirit-wives and shamans who led possession ceremonies, who were seen to have the advantage of identifying with both male and females *nas*. Two for the price of one. Nope, he wasn't going to pass this up.

"I don't know . . ." Ken hedged.

"Come on, Ken, let's see how this compares to Thailand."

He-she-they encircled Ken's arm. "You like! Big party!"

Ken flushed.

The *acault* or *dakaw* laughed delightedly. "So! Here!" they said, pointing to a doorway across the street where more colorfully dressed people had gathered.

"Yeah, all right," Ken said.

31

"CATTY, EVERYTHING IS FINE. I'll be coming back in a few days. The guesthouse is cute."

Catty and Lars were stunned when Lidia told them she was going to stay in Namyan another week. A manager at the Golden Palace helped her change her ticket and even found her a much cheaper place to stay, which he assured her was safe and clean. "My cousin work there."

And Lidia picked up a burner phone, on which she was talking to Catty two days later.

"Well, how is Haynes after his ordeal?" Catty asked, after the usual preliminaries.

"Well. He's all right. A bit bummed out that he can't go up to the Golden Triangle and probably get himself shot at. Plus he had to shell out a big wad of moolah to get out of prison."

"Oh, Lord." Catty sighed. "Are you all right?"

"I am. I've been looking at street art everywhere and guess what, it's all the same. Except for that one guy I met at that pagoda. And I'm drawing again. It's just a few more days. Oh! And Lily called, she's getting in tonight for some job interviews. That will let you off the hook with the cats."

"Well, that's wonderful." Lily was Catty's godchild and they doted on each other. "Lars wants to talk to you. Bye."

"Lidia! You okay there? Not staying on at the Golden, I hear? We're quite jetlagged but glad to be back."

"Lars, would you tell Catty to stop *worrying* about me. I'm *fine*. And Haynes is too, or he's going to be."

"Well, tell him to stay out of trouble. You too, dear girl. Call us when you get to the city."

Lidia plopped onto her bed—more like a cot, really. She hadn't been 100 percent truthful with them, but they would only worry if they knew how she'd been going back and forth to the prison, how tired she was. Some unfathomable delay in their release. But tomorrow—finally—Haynes and the Lattimores were getting out. "Sprung," as Lars called it. She fell asleep immediately.

"I don't know when it turned crazy," Haynes told her.

Leaving the prison, even at the very end, had been a drawn-out process. There'd been a mountain of paperwork to sign, and then he'd had to go to the consulate. Basically, he and Ken and Sally were now personas non grata in Namyan. But he was at the guesthouse at last. He'd showered and was having a meal with Lidia on the patio.

"To be honest, I didn't want to go with them that day. I had a mean hangover and, well, I was feeling down. About you, too. But I wanted to go back to the old town, take some pictures and they were going too, so I went along. Then, we end up having drinks later in a café, a lot of drinks. And when we leave, this wild bunch of people insists on taking us to a party."

Lidia rolled her eyes.

"You would have gone!" he protested. "I mean, a bunch of trans spirit wives? Occults?"

"*Acaults.*"

"And I do remember *dakaws* means shamans. So we go in this place to this big room and I mean, it was a *party* going on. I picked up my daughter when she was like fifteen or sixteen from some rave. That's what it was like. But it's only late afternoon and everybody's high as shit on something. And they pass around a bottle and it's *obligatory* to take it." He shook his head. "I sneak out the camera. There's one of those *na* altars with all the weird shit on it and these people, half of them in drag, are bopping to these droning, whining sounds. You know, it reminded me of Black culture: party hard on Saturday, go to church on Sunday. Same thing, except here it's all together in one package—the Buddha, the *nas*, the booze, and the drugs. This one trans chick who spoke a little English was all over Ken, dancing around, showing her moves. His moves? I'm clicking away. Then, well, my head started getting *strange*. That bottle was spiked with something weird."

Lidia lit one of her remaining cigarillos and blew smoke fiercely. "Well, but why didn't you leave then?"

"Remember when you were walking around in your bare feet—bleeding—and talking crazy that first day and couldn't—no offense—function?"

"Vaguely. Ah, Haynes, it was that *crazy* drug?"

"Hell do I know. And yeah! I wanted to get out of there! But I couldn't. Couldn't find Ken or Sally. Lost the camera. Then I remembered I had the camera on the glasses and I should keep taking pictures, but the glasses kept slipping off. Suddenly, I felt like I couldn't breathe. I had to get some air. I'm pushing through the crowd, trying not to lose it and out the corner of my eye, I think I see, I *do* see, Colonel Ken. Under a table with that *acault*, whatever, and they're *going at it.*"

"*Colonel Ken?*"

"Colonel Ken. Then Sally's there too. She's under the table, whaling on them." He shook his head. "It all just went to hell. There's this loud scream and a crack, like furniture breaking. I turn around and Sally's on the ground, she's having a fit. And her feet keep smacking the altar thing. It *collapses*. The Buddha and the *nas* and all the stuff crashing down." He let out a deep sigh. "Next thing I know, those feet police are there, grabbing people. Sally. Ken—he's got lipstick smeared all over his face! Then they grab *me*. Damned if I didn't lose the camera glasses too. And you know the rest."

It was three days later. Lidia was on the patio of the guesthouse late in the day. She had her sketch pad, a cup of coffee and a fresh pack of cigarillos—she worried that she was heading for nicotine addiction again, but that didn't stop her from smoking them.

Haynes, who wouldn't admit that he was exhausted, took long naps every afternoon, including today.

Her phone rang. Catty again.

"We just took Lily out to lunch. She's fine and sends her love and the cats are fine. But she says once you're home, she'll never scoop poop again."

"Spoiled rotten. Let me talk to her."

"She's not here, she went on a job interview that sounds terrific. And I think she—well, I'll let her talk to you about that. How's Gonyang?"

"What? Oh, it's started to rain finally. Well, mist." Lidia sighed. "Well, there's no art scene, or if there is, I still can't find it. And it's so humid I expect to find mushrooms growing everywhere."

"And Haynes?"

"I don't want to talk about him now. When I get back . . ."

"Diversion's over?"

"You win, okay?"

"Well. I'm sorry, nevertheless."

"Oh, Catty. I'll call you when I'm back."

A bit later, Haynes came to the patio. They were eating all their meals at the guesthouse. The food was so-so, but cheap. They were both tired of going out.

"The Lattimores left," he told her, looking up from his phone.

"Finally. But together? That should be interesting."

"Makes me think how it was in Bed-Stuy. Probably still is. You know, the down-low. Remember, they didn't even have 'Don't ask, don't tell' when Colonel Ken was in the service. But," he added thoughtfully, "The Colonel? I wouldn't have pegged him for it. Had me fooled."

"But it explains a lot. Sally's compulsions. Her constant swipes at him."

"That's why there is di*vorce*."

"Maybe they like it this way. Can't bear to be together or apart."

There was no menu, they waited for whatever the cook put together. A couple walked in; this was their kind of place. In their late twenties, early thirties, German or Dutch, something like that. They dumped their packs, sprawled at a table, and immediately started touching each other. Fingers, arms, faces . . . Lidia looked away.

When she and Felipe had met at a party thrown by the art department in Ann Arbor and fell in love, they were indignant that Clara Montares, the head of the department, nicknamed them Los Pulpos. Octopi. But they always seemed to have their arms around each other. Needed to.

"Haynes?" she asked.

"Lidia?" He smiled at her.

"Oh, nothing."

The first night at the guesthouse, she'd let him sleep. The second night, they made love but it wasn't the same. They were both half-gone already. They didn't talk about it, they found reasons to be alone most of the time after that. But they still had dinner together each night, before going to their separate rooms.

Lidia had found a handful of boutiques in hotels that sold art. But it was expensive, and essentially the same as the street art except that it was expensively framed. Then she heard there were a few good comic book artists—but where to find them? She'd taken to sitting in the pocket park a few streets from the guesthouse, sketching and trying to meditate. The rains started at the end of the week, so then she hung out at the guesthouse.

They were both just marking time. Today after going out for a walk she'd come back to find Haynes in the courtyard, clamped to his phone. She had a bottle of mineral water while he tried to figure out a cheap flight to Papua, New Guinea by way of Australia. He was still on the phone when she left to lie down in her room. The bed was lumpy—how Betsy would have grumbled about the whole setup here. She finished the last chapter of her last paperback. Tomorrow she'd be flying home early in the morning. Haynes was heading out the next day.

Now as they sat having a last meal together, Haynes filled her in on how he'd managed to find a flight and what he'd read online about New Guinea's problematic past and present, its racist and classist upheavals. *He's as good as gone,* she thought. Some people lived for the road. Looking at his sturdy face, she wondered if she should feel guilty about their fling, but she felt nothing about it. She just wanted to go home.

Both their phones trilled, almost simultaneously.

"Mom! I got the job!"

"Oh, honey, wonderful." It took Lidia a moment to remember which job Lily was talking about—it was hard to keep up with her daughter—but yes, it turned out to be the teaching gig coveted among ceramicists (potters, in her day) that Lily had mentioned to her a few weeks earlier.

"I'll tell you all about it when you're back."

"Tell me now."

"Mom. That isn't why I called, really. It's about Dad." Her voice wobbled on *Dad.*

Everything in Lidia drooped—her blood pressure, her face, her voice, though Haynes didn't notice. He was occupied with his call. "You've seen him! How is he?"

"When I walked in, he said, 'Lidia! Where have you been?'" Lily began to cry and Lidia wanted to reach through the phone and hold her—hard, fiercely. "He thought I was you!"

"Oh honey. He does remember you. I know he does. But I—I have to go, Lily. We'll talk about it when I get back, very soon," she said. "A day and a half? I can't remember the time difference. Oh, I love you, Lily."

"Love you too."

Haynes had moved away. His conversation seemed to be intense. An argument, maybe?

He raised his voice. "Honey, it's all good." Pause. "Yes, I have money. Got the tickets dirt-cheap. You know me. No! It's not negotiable. Listen, I'll call you from Borneo. Soon as I get there. I gotta go." Pause. "Love you too."

He hung up and saw Lidia looking at him. "My daughter," he said. "Wants me to come home."

"Mine too," Lidia said. They knew so little about each other, really. She'd intended to tell him about Felipe, she told herself she would do it every time they met. How it was rarer and rarer that Felipe remembered who she was when she went to the memory care home. Or who he was. How even when he did recognize her, a few minutes later he was apt to ask her who she was. Sadder than that—and she was learning that there were infinitely lower depths of this particular sadness—Lily was right to suspect he didn't know her anymore. His beloved child.

After they'd been together a few years and decided, *Why not make it legal?* they'd talked about children. But nothing had happened. They'd talked about IVF. But they were both busy. Felipe had become the art director of a small, prestigious magazine about Latin American art. Of course he kept his teaching gig; the magazine didn't pay much. Lidia painted and taught three classes a week. They were happy, they didn't need much. Then, at thirty-nine, Lidia came down with what she thought was the flu. When she missed her period, she just knew, but went to the doctor to confirm she was pregnant before she told Felipe.

She would never forget the night she told him. She planned to break the news after they had dinner, some kind of pasta. But as he was forking his salad, she heard herself say, "I'm going to have a baby."

He put down his fork and looked at her—hard, almost, she thought, as if she had said something obscene. Then he jumped out of his chair and came to her. They cried.

The one thing Felipe had not forgotten, even now, was music. She'd read about the stages of Alzheimer's, how the part of the brain that stored music stayed intact. When she played him his favorite CDs, his face was transformed. He sang along with the melody, tapped out the rhythm. He no longer remembered the names of the musicians or the lyrics of the tunes. But he had the music.

As she sat with Haynes on the Wehs Yo patio with its huge pots of dusty ferns and backpackers and small waiter shuffling around, Lidia's thoughts shifted to the long routine of getting to Stonebridge Memory Care Center. She didn't have a car, so it was a subway and then a bus ride, an hour and ten minutes when the trains were on time, when traffic wasn't heavy on the parkway. Then back again. She tried to go twice a week, but often ended up going only once. She hated going there. The place was not bad. It was orderly and most of the staff were nice, if overworked and apt to cut a corner here or there. There was a courtyard with a little garden for warm days and a yellow, overheated common room with colorful fish prowling a tank for the rest of the time.

She roused herself and told Haynes that her daughter had just landed a good job. Oh, and a text had come earlier that day from a textbook publisher. A new commission. "Something about what differently abled kids can accomplish," she said.

"Is that good or bad?" he asked. "I thought you wanted to get back to *your* art."

Really, she didn't know. She had to earn a living. She could do her art on the side, just get more . . . disciplined and do it. "It's okay," she said.

He surprised her then. He reached over and ran his fingers down her cheek. "That night under the stars? When you thought the constellations were upside down?"

"The upside-down sky. Oh, yes, and then . . . Haynes. I wish we—"

"Me too."

32

SHE FINISHED WRESTLING WITH her suitcase. Everything seemed to mysteriously double in size on a trip back home. She checked again: ticket, passport, money, zipped in a pocket of her handbag. Then there was nothing left to do.

Haynes was still on the patio, working on his laptop. She was getting up at four thirty for the airport, so she'd say good-bye to him now, soon. But she didn't move. She sat by the window of the room and smoked one last cigarillo. There was a flowering tree right outside; its scent was vanilla, honey, and something that seemed to Lidia to be indefinably Asian. There were occasional sounds of people passing, the creak of a pedicab's pedals. An owl hooted, there was a burst of light laughter.

She looked again at the sketch she'd made for Haynes, of a grinning boy monk. She stubbed out her cigarillo.

She got out her sketchbook again for the last time in Namyan and drew a female figure on a dark street, half-turned near a streetlight, face stretched wide in what could be terror. Or maybe it was a smile.

33

One year later

Clint and Betsy Hodges

Clint dies in the hospital he's vowed never to return to. Betsy sits watching *Law & Order: Special Victims Unit* reruns and eating frozen dinners. Ann Boren, who's become an email friend, writes to ask if she'd like to join her and Ed on a trip to the Cayman Islands (a compromise: a lot of interesting bugs but also shopping and beaches for the "girls.") Betsy bestirs herself and says yes. With something to look forward to, she tackles neglected chores and starts going back to church. Sometimes, alone in her small brick house, she bursts into tears. She tells herself it is grief, not relief.

Tim and Tammy Steinman

With their granddaughter on the mend and their son fresh out of rehab, Tim and Tammy invite the whole family to a trip to the Badlands in South Dakota that summer. Though they haven't discussed it, neither has the desire to travel outside the confines of the good ol' USA, at least for a while. And there is still plenty of it they haven't seen. Plenty of buttons and badges to collect.

Ward and Trudy Wong
Trudy helps Barton with his rehab and joins a book club. Ward continues to go to his office three days a week and takes up tai chi again.

Barton Liu
Barton gets a job at a Verizon store and soon becomes assistant manager. After several months, he moves in with a fellow employee: Amy Ling, in her mid-forties, divorced, no children.

Ken and Sally Lattimore
Ken moves to a condo near a golf course. Lapsed but still a Catholic, Sally refuses to consider divorce.

Ed and Ann Boren
Ed has a mild heart attack, which triggers panic attacks in Ann. They call off the Cayman Islands trip (surprisingly, Betsy decides to go there on her own). Determined to resume his expeditions in the future, Ed reads up on the entomology of Surinam and northern Brazil.

Ted and Franklin Leibitz-Kai
Ted takes second place in the LBGTQ Firefighters Central California Marathon. Franklin gets an STD. They have an argument that gets physical but make up and plan a trip to Morocco.

Lars and Catty Vonderville
They go on a river cruise in Germany. For the first time ever, Catty blows off next month's Rad Book Club selection, *In Search of Lost Time*. She says she "cannot abide Marcel Proust." Lars, who dimly remembers struggling with Proust at Harvard, barks a laugh. "Free at last," he tells her.

Lidia DeCampos
Lily moves into her old room in her mother's apartment while looking for a place she can afford. Lidia moves her easel and art supplies to the corner of the living room that gets the most afternoon sun. She works on a series of drawings about Namyan and shows them in a group show at the local Y. She continues to visit Felipe once a week, sometimes with Lily.

Klaus Haynes
After his trip to New Guinea, which results in a blog feature, Klaus has a fall and breaks his hip. He moves in with his daughter and her family in Brooklyn while convalescing, and they work on discouraging him from planning another of what they call his "crazy-ass trips."

Mrs. Hills
Carolyn Hills dies in her sleep not long after returning from Namyan.

Thila
Emile sends Thila a ticket to Stockholm during the rainy season in Namyan, when tourism comes to a halt. After a short time, she realizes the relationship will not work. Back home some months later, she marries a second cousin, a widower with two children. She quits her job.

Afterword

THE FICTIONAL COUNTRY OF Namyan in this novel is modeled after Myanmar, or Burma, as it was known for many years. I owe a debt of gratitude to the warm, hospitable Burmese people (and the other ethnicities who live there) whom I met on a tour of this beautiful land. George Orwell's brilliant and prescient novel, *Burmese Days*, which lays out the decay, racism, and cynicism of the waning British imperialism in 1934 in Burma while also managing to be a funny book, was also a major influence on me in writing this book.

After being cut off from most of the rest of the world for some fifty years under military dictatorship, Myanmar's democracy movement, led by Aung San Suu Kyi, at last gained power in 2016. But as I write this, the military, immensely rich and powerful, has again brutally suppressed the will of its people, voiding recent elections and imposing a new reign of terror. The brave people of Myanmar, after having had a brief taste of freedom, are now fighting to regain their basic and inalienable rights.

About the Author

© Chris Loomis

LINDA DAHL IS THE AUTHOR of nine books of fiction, biographies of women in jazz, and a handbook for parents of young women with substance use disorder. She first worked as a journalist, writing about cultural topics in Latin America and the Caribbean and about jazz and Brazilian music, then as a professor of English as a Second Language before turning to writing full time. She is currently on the editorial board of *The Journal of Jazz Studies* and working on a screenplay and a new novel. She loves to swim and read Scandinavian noir in her spare time.

SELECTED TITLES FROM SHE WRITES PRESS

She Writes Press is an independent publishing company founded to serve women writers everywhere. Visit us at www.shewritespress.com.

Eliza Waite by Ashley Sweeney $16.95, 978-1-63152-058-7
When Eliza Waite chooses to leave a stagnant life in rural Washington State and join the masses traveling north to Alaska in 1898 during the tumultuous Klondike Gold Rush, she encounters challenges and successes in both business and love.

Toward that Which is Beautiful by Marian O'Shea Wernicke $16.95, 978-1-63152-759-3
In June of 1964 in a small town in the Altiplano of Peru, Sister Mary Katherine—a young American nun afraid of her love for an Irish priest with whom she has been working—slips away from her convent with no money and no destination. Over the next eight days, she encounters both friendly and dangerous characters and travels an interior journey of memory and desire that leads her, finally, to a startling destination.

Swearing off Stars by Danielle Wong $16.95, 978-1-63152-284-0
When Lia Cole travels from New York to Oxford University to study abroad in the 1920s, she quickly falls for another female student—sparking a love story that spans decades and continents.

Wild Boar in the Cane Field by Anniqua Rana $16.95, 978-1-63152-668-8
One day, a baby girl, Tara, is found, abandoned and covered in flies. She is raised by two mothers in a community rife with rituals and superstition. Poignant and compelling, her story contains the tragedy that often characterizes the lives of those who live in South Asia—and demonstrates the heroism we are all capable of even in the face of traumatic realities.

Lost in Oaxaca by Jessica Winters Mireles $16.95, 978-1-63152-880-4
Thirty-seven-year-old piano teacher Camille Childs is a lost soul who is seeking recognition through her star student—so when her student unexpectedly leaves California to return to her village in Oaxaca, Mexico, Camille follows her. There, Camille meets Alejandro, a Zapotec man who helps her navigate the unfamiliar culture of Oaxaca and teaches her to view the world in a different light.